the spirit stars

dedicated to all who helped me believe

The Story of Solia: The Spirit Stars (Vol.1)
Second Edition

Published in the US in the year 2025 by Solia Celestials

For questions regarding permissions use of materials, contact

Solia Celestials

amsmerekanicz@gmail.com

(603) 493-3093

ISBN 979-8-218-71479-6
BISAC
Young Adult Fiction
     Science Fiction
          General
          Time Travel
     Religious Fiction

Cover and content art illustrated by Asterope Smerekanicz
Layout and Design created by Asterope Smerekanicz

the spirit stars

FOREWORD

the spirit stars

After over 17 years of tedious work in worldbuilding, lore, and character development, the first novel of three is finally out for the world to read. At a young age, Asterope "Leaf" would often be found alone in her room acting out stories between her stuffed animals for hours and hours each day. They shared a language, experiences, and the thrill of adventure together for many years as the foundations came together to form what would later become a three-part series based on a universe completely different from our own.

In her first official novel release, "the spirit stars," Leaf highlights the importance of perspective through many characters experiencing the same story. The reader will often encounter scenes which seem to overlap and interlace with one another. Every character has their own thoughts and experiences, many of which won't be shared with all the characters in the story or even the reader themself. So, welcome this story as an invitation from Leaf to enter another world.

Remember, "the spirit stars" acts as a record created by the characters within the story. After all, it's their own lifes' tale to tell. This is what the creatures of Solia saw when it all began,

when "Thraesa" turned on once again...

TABLE OF CONTENTS

An account what happened that day,
according to the Soliean Protectors...

01. THE THREE STARS

Location: [Aviea Island Leaders' Center, Aliira, Aviea]
Perspective: Avie, Leader of Solia

A Soliean probe had not been released for eons due to the advancement of exploration ships and long-distance survey instruments, but this new probe was designed to head for the center point between the Three Stars, a location completely unknown and shrouded to the Soliean Core Systems. Our history was forgotten, perhaps this probe would be the beginning of our historical recovery. Our probe was launched just before Solia Noctia rose in the west, my live feed through the Leaders' tower showed the updates to the trajectory as it traveled closer to the centerpoint.

Despite the importance and unusual nature of the event, I hadn't attended the probe launch; Something didn't feel right about it. We had grown accustomed to sending scientists on missions to explore and survey in the moment, with their expertise to handle situations right then and there in the void, but then there was that one mission that never came back. It still felt too soon to send another crewed exploration mission, but also felt distasteful to replace it with a robot.

An alert came through the monitor, a massive object detected at the center. The automated navigation computer was already making some adjustments to its trajectory to avoid a possible collision. I sat up from the soft bed covers to enlarge the screen panel and get a better look; The probe continued functioning perfectly until it reached about one kilometer out from the center point. It was there that the systems started to break down. The instruments showed a massive energy anomaly just before the camera went offline. The spectrometer and other instruments went out less than five seconds later. The last picture taken by the camera looked like a green and teal iris in space, some kind of phenomena or storm, perhaps?

I quickly changed into my black cloak before exiting the top room of the Leaders' tower into the elevator, which gave a beautiful morning view of the Aliira Island Chain as the elevator descended. I exited Leaders' Center into the hot Aviean air and followed the rocky grey path to the Capital Mission Conference Center. The path travels right along the edge of Hiinhia Aviea's summit plateau, where below can be seen several lines of gold-silver skyscrapers gleaming at the base. Mission Authorities and Territorial Leaders would have already been notified to meet at the CMCC to discuss what events had transpired during the mission. Sure enough, I saw that several of the territory ships had already landed on the grey pad above me.

When I walked in, the others were just getting seated. Leaders of each major territory of Aviea were there: The leader of the Maurakjnaun Alliance Territories from the south-east, Qranyt, a rock-like Aviean Bear; the leader of Aquat to the south-west, Ket, a large black female cat; the leader of the Soliae Territory Alliance to the north-west, Selevenera, a black-brown cat with yellowish spots; as well as several others from smaller territories, such as Citrine Tourmaline and other other planets in the system.

"Seleo, Laersana! Early this morning we released a crewless Tel-K exploration probe to the system core to explore what has been causing anomalous energy signal disruption through the central sector." I said, introducing the subject. The leaders settled down at their seats and waited to hear what would come next. "Our probe detected an unusual object in the exact center before blinking out. We have the last picture the camera took." I pressed a button on the wall to make a projection. The green iris was quite bright against the background of space. It even almost outshined the other two stars, Solia Marazael and Solia Aqua.

"What—, is that, exactly?" Qranyt inquired.

"We aren't quite sure, Qranyt, although we do know that it is consuming a ton of kinetic energy from the surrounding matter. It ripped our probe apart like it was nothing." I replied, "Yet, it appears it might be some sort of rift. The technology creating this is ancient but we might have some information on how to bypass the deadly part."

"In that case, an expedition would be pointless," an Aquan ambassador cat from Zekj remarked. "Any ship we send there could be ripped apart too, as well as the crew."

"I think I've got something," Selevenera called out, "Thraesa Conversion Array, Section Avatai-Seliu-Mara in the Sanctuary's lower archive: high velocity approach, uncrewed objects and other unidentified threats converted into a 'digestible' form, plasma, as a defense system as well as a method of powering high energy systems."

"That was quick!" Qranyt laughed.

"It also says that the array takes time to recharge and can be overloaded; if we're quick enough, we could 'inject' a high amount of energy into the rift before entering. The oversupply could potentially charge it up enough for it to ignore the ship passing through."

"Great idea—we could use some kind of weapon system, perhaps a missile of some sort to give it all the energy it needs" Qranyt replied.

"It can't be nuclear, not that those work anymore. If it were, we might have our ship systems knocked out by an electromagnetic pulse" the leader of Tourmaline said.

"We could use a high-pressure deuterium missile. We have some of those left. As long as the armor of our ship is strong, we should be able to pass through without much of a problem" Selevenera responded.

Another crewed exploration mission to an unknown sector, after all these years. We still couldn't possibly be ready for that. Qranyt caught my concerned glance,

"We cannot have a repeat of *Kqaet-Avai*," he said.

"As leader of the Soliean Core Systems, I will send a ship to further explore this region per the vote of our leaders here today, but I cannot put your lives in danger for this mission in case it fails. I will go. Those who want to convince me they should go in my stead are welcome to try. We will bring three Hydrogen-Deuterium Short-Range Vacuum Missiles to give us temporary protection from the force of the rift."

"As leader of the Maurakjnaun Territories, I agree to this mission, despite questioning your decision to crew the ship," Qranyt responded.

"The Auqaut Territory agrees" Ket voted,

"The territory of Soliae-Nyt is on your side too!" the feline leader Selevenera announced. Several other leaders chimed in to agree before I made the final statement.

"Then it is decided. I will fly the ship, anyone who wishes to join will state their intention now." I declared.

"I propose to join you on this mission for your protection," replied Ket.

After a moment I continued, "Request is accepted, we will set out for the object of interest immediately. As adjacent senior territory leader I leave Qranyt in charge of Aliira in my temporary absence. Dismissed, and vaitren!" I told our leaders.

I walked down a separate hallway to the Conference Center Landing Pad with Ket and notified the Capital Hangar on the private line.

"Hey Avie, what can I do for you?" Terral, a short brown bear asked on the other side.

"Sel' Terral, I need a small starship, an explorer, loaded with three deut-type missiles, and operational with only two crew."

"Sure thing boss, I'll have it in five. You need a lift?"

"Nah, I've got Ket's transporter here, thanks though."

"Alright I'll have your ship on Pad 2. A Cyp-Dawn Tracer 6, Aviea built."

"Sounds good!" I said as I boarded Ket's transporter. The leaders' center was located atop the highest mountain on Aviea, so we had quite the drop to where the ships were stationed. The government operated district on Aviea Island was about the same size as the public ARSC starport located on a different island, but to keep emergency deployment and government operations un-congested they were kept separate.

We launched off the summit quickly and dropped towards the base of the mountain, where we could see our starship being raised up on Platform 2.

"Aviea Capital Hangar—this is Avie, Auqaut Official ID transport requesting permission to land."

"Avie, we have you on our scanners—proceed to LP5. Continue your descent—we'll have an escort team ready if you so desire. What is your destination?"

"LP2 for an official off-world mission."

"Sounds good, it is cleared and safe."

We landed softly on the platform and got out of the blocky dark grey transport to find a team of four security guards. We walked in the shadow of Hiinhia Aliira, where it was much cooler than the summit. The starport rapid transport was pre-aligned to bring us to Landing Platform 2 straight from where we landed, and the ship was ready for launch. It was a sort of long sleek starship that had three small missile tubes for defense and a very strong hull to deflect debris.

"Command Tower, this is Avie, we are ready for launch from Landing Platform 2, do you give us a green?"

"Of course they do, silly!" Ket mocked

"Yeah ok"

"Hey, it's Terral again, you are good to go, Avie. Fly safe!"

"Sure thing, Commander Terral; I'll be sure to bring you pictures." I sat down in the pilot's chair and prepared for atmospheric takeoff, opening vertical thrusters. "Alright, let's go!"

"Sure thing," Ket said, "just don't break anything"

"I'll try not to..." I replied as the ship jolted into the air. I sped up over the center of the city, flying past Akjo Ventrael then out over the Aviean Ocean towards the north. Our ship reached about 2.5 km/s as I passed through the outer influence of Aviea's gravity.

"Setting a course for the core," Ket announced, seated at the navigational panel "It won't take us long."

All leaders territory and higher district alike are required to have training on piloting government vehicles; It's not unusual to send a leader on official transport for meetings and even field surveys, but this was different. The last time we sent a leader on a deep-space mission was several long years ago and that mission changed everything about how we operated exploration objectives. Today's mission was far closer than her's, though, we thought we wouldn't have any trouble getting home.

"Great, let's talk public relations, then," I offered, making my way towards the back of the ship to get some fresh swordfruit juice from the on-board pantry.

"Official business on official business then? Oh how exciting... Aquat has all it needs to survive," Ket assured me.

"Oh yeah? What if we put you into kja production? Many of the territories are lacking in bread. Most of our bread comes from Ealtae, but they don't want to make more farms in the middle of the woods."

"You're so funny Avie, you know our soil can't grow your pop crops like that! No way! Make Citrine produce the bread, Auqaut already has trouble producing silicon for new computer parts; We already have our paws full" said Ket.

"Haha we're working on plans of getting you away from silicon production anyways, Auqaut would help far more supplying carbon and manganese supplying compounds, besides, Soliae is taking the top in silicon now that the new production center in Kjasqa opened."

"Now that sounds a lot more like a serious proposition!"

"Nah, official talk is no fun, we're on an official mission but I think we can spare some time for catching up during transit? How's your daughter?"

"Onyx? She's pretty busy lately scrapping our old defenses to make them 'improved,' I don't know how she does it but supposedly she knows her way around those turrets. By the way, we could use some support out there with the desert fiends, I don't know what's up with them and I don't like having to resort to shooting them but they've gotten more and more violent and destructive in the last few seasons. Something is happening out there..."

The ship came with some sensor arrays we deployed to collect whatever information we could off our approach to the core. The trip was several hours long, but the ship was built for interstellar transit at high speeds and had the drives for faster-than-light travel. After a few more snacks, chats, and beverages an alert went off in the ship navigation computer, informing us of our close approach to the point of interest.

"Well there you have it, we're here!" I declared, jumping back in the pilot chair.

"Great—let's be careful here."

Sure enough, there it was: a massive green and blue storm almost like a supernova, but staying steady around a central point. We held the ship back to avoid whatever fate the probe fell to.

"That's it," I said, pulling down a screen to display a feed from the ship's telescopes, "there's something at the center, I can't quite place it but I know it's something I've seen before, maybe in an old record at the Sanctuary."

"It's like two dark pyramids?" Ket continued, "End to end, pointing to what looks to be the poles of the three stars' orbits? Almost like this is what the three stars orbit around!"

"Well we didn't come here just to gawk at it, time to light it up!" I said.

"Are you sure about this, Avie? This seems risky, we could just fire a probe or a few from the ship survey bay to get what data we can and head back!"

"You're right, but let's hit it with one of the deut's first to give the probe a chance to get close, like Sele' suggested."

"Gotcha, hang on to something!"

"Setting coordinates, turning, FIRE!" The first of the three missiles was flung at the rift. It was instantly shredded, blowing out a huge EMP. "Magnetic shields up," I flipped a switch, "dropping probe and engine reversal—"

"Praying to the stars..." Ket whispered.

The probe feed showed up on the system display, appearing to get much closer to the object than the first probe that got destroyed. We even got some closer images before— gone.

"Avie, something's not right," Ket alerted, the ship creaked, "I think that first missile must have powered up the object enough to expand its influence... it's pulling us in!"

"Hang on Ket! I have a feeling we're making it out of this!"

"Wait what are you!?"

"Hang on! Prep tube two, three, FIRE!" The two remaining missiles shot into the core, shredded into oblivion like the first. The hull of the starship screamed and twisted as the object pulled it faster and faster to the core.

"Look! Something is opening!" Ket screeched,

"I was right, I have seen this before..."

~　　~　　~

I felt a strange tingling as I dissolved into the rift, quite surprised by what appeared before us on the other side. The ship was gone, leaving us in a new void where we could actually breathe from.

"No way," I said as I looked around at the long green filaments that filled the new space we were in.

"Avie, the legend of Thraesa was real! I sure hope you can read it, it may be our only way out!"

"Yes, it's not a legend, I believe the Soliean leaders at the highest security level got training on the operation of the *Control Point Thraesa* in case it was ever found again but I barely recall the texts on the matter. I think I might know how to read the lines but I don't have a place to reference from! I know how to read the strands relative to one another once I know where one will lead so it's going to be a risky move."

"You'll need to follow your heart or something? You have good instincts right?" Ket asked,

"We're still alive aren't we?" I swam to a filament and gently gave it a tug, as if I was playing a giant instrument. "This one feels like it's drawing me in...

We appeared in a vivid green field, tall slender blades of grass reaching up to a strange sky. This was not Aviea, and something was very, very wrong. Giant warships larger than any I'd ever seen appeared from the clouds above, dark clouds, black and a shade darker than black. Beyond all of it it felt like there was something watching, bigger and farther than even the ground we stood on.

"Ket, I feel like I pulled the wrong thread..."

"It's Ealtae, Avie." she pointed to the shadow of a ringed moon[1] looming above the horizon, she had to be right. "What happened here?"

We ran to the top of a nearby mound to get a better vantage, where we could see a silver flower temple as well as the wreckage of our exploration ship burning a distance away in the vast plains, it had followed us through Thraesa. Ealtae, the fourth planet orbiting Solia Noctia, but we would have known if a war was happening when we left? Ealtae seemed much different from how we left it, even the moon Ealtar was strange in color as if eons had passed since we last saw the place.

Battleships waged war around us, technology unfamiliar to us. We didn't recognize any of the ship designs or the weapons they used. Flashes of light, beams of different colors and shapes and intensities flashed this way and that, scorching the ground and the sky equal amounts. I motioned for us to get down as I saw a creature's shape coming our way.

A small green-furred bear holding two rusty knives. Not much against such alien and even divine forces which seemed to be at work in our presence. He walked towards us, looking injured and weak.

"Hide your face Avie! Someone is approaching!" Ket yelped, pulling a cloak over herself. The bear came over to us quickly.

"Please, help me. I am not strong enough to fight this war. I must

[1] Ealtae's only moon, Ealtar, is regarded as an anomaly in many regards, including the close proximity to the parent planet and the large set of rings encircling it.

leave this place, I am no use here."

"Leave how, where?" I asked, trying to hide my real voice. "What happened here?"

"You must have arrived from ze'Thraesa? The temple ahead holds a Thraesa stone." the small green bear told us. "I have been trained on how to use it, I'll take you back to your home as long as you promise to take me in."

Ket and I exchanged looks, how did he know any of this? The creatures of Ealtae are much more connected to ancient literature and perhaps they would know something about Thraesa that I didn't, but it still seemed a bit strange.

"We must get there quickly, I think it's our only chance to get out of here!" Ket said to me.

"I think you're right..."

I grabbed the small bear and placed him on the back of my cloak, we sprinted through the long grass field in the direction of the flower temple. These locations were built as spiritual sanctuaries of the followers of Kiraveal[1], those who thought they could communicate with the stars and celestial objects. Ealtae was filled with ancient scholars studying what most of civilization had cast aside as legend and tall-tale. Perhaps we owe a debt to their studies?

A stone sat on a short column in the main hall of the temple. The stone was jade, a cube with a rounded top. I held on to Ket,

"Grab the stone! Hold it firmly so it comes with us!" the bear said, "We need to make sure they cannot find the stone in the temple!" I did as he said, grabbed, and pressed on the top of the stone, throwing us back into the space within Thraesa.

"What is your name?" I asked the bear.

"Hiinhia, aatere. Hiinhia e'Ealtae. I am of the leader's blood, a close relative. The others were killed, leaving me the responsibility of the Ealtae Highlands."

"Right then, Hiinhia , which filament is the right one if we want to get back after the destruction of the probe sent in Thraesa?"

"That's where you're from...? You're from the beginning?"

I gave a cautious look before Ket replied.

---

[1]Kiraveal, also known as the Spirit Lamp, is the most widely worshipped icon on the world Ealtae. The first tribes of Ealtae who followed the Spirit Lamp are recognized as the creators of the Soletria language.

"That far back, yes."

"This is going to get complicated I think, Great Leader" he shook,

"How did you know?" Ket asked, pulling her hood off.

"We were expecting your arrival, it was foretold this is how the war begins." He held us and pulled off a strand of Thraesa.

We appeared in the same temple, perhaps thousands of years earlier, as Hiinhia seemed to believe. We were home, back in our time.

"There should be a large Soliean Transport at the nearby farm district, we should be able to get back to Aviea, unless of course you don't want to use Thraesa..." I told them

"I don't see why not, that would be the fastest!" Ket replied.

"You'll keep your promise and take me in, right?" Hiinhia gave a concerned glance, "I'd train hard, I want to help with what's to come, with what's to..."

Ket pawed at the little bear, "What's wrong Hiinhia?"

"I don't remember? Something about a war, something soon that would happen, it's all so fuzzy...?"

Hiinhia slumped over into Ket's black paws, unconscious.

"Quick, let's get him to the nearby village!" I said, gently lifting him up again.

"Avie, what was all of that about?"

"I don't know Ket, but we made it out, more than we can say about... her."

Object Classification: Thraesa

02. FILSA

[Viikja City Leader Center, Maurakjnaun the Emerald Territory, Aviea]
Qranyt

Even after Solia Noctia sank below the eastern horizon the chaos ensued. It was the first conflict we'd had in 103 years. The Emerald colony of West Fiilsa was destroyed by weather, and its inhabitants, upon returning to Viikja City, started a trade war. Neither territory had enough supplies, money, or food to share between the inhabitants due to a sudden climate change and the local decrease in volcanic activity. The West Fiilsa Territory needed repairs to be able to return to their lost colony. Viikja became a warzone, and the lack of food for everyone to share caused the citizens of both lands to go crazy. Any returning fishing boat was mobbed the moment it entered the Grand Harbor. I had to stay in the tall Viikja Leader Center tower, where I planned a way to stop the war.

There had been several whispers across the border in deep Fiilasan territory that the central governing body of the Fiilsa Territories was siphoning resources to ignite the conflict we were beginning to experience, and I had a plan to investigate it myself.

"Avie," I said over the message console in my office, "I have decided on our solution. I will require eight shuttles filled with tools, cloth, wood, and food in order to bring peace back to the territories. That should get things settled in the meantime while I conduct an internal investigation in central Fiilasan control."

"Why not open a case with the Sanctuary?"

"Nahh, they're too busy and I want to get this sorted by my own paws quickly as I can."

"Alright Qranyt, I'll send them over as soon as I can, but I need you to do me a favor in return. I have an apprentice for you, his name is Hiinhia. He needs a masterful trainer like you."

"Sounds good Avie, I'll be waiting to meet him when he arrives."

Moments later, the first three shuttles arrived and landed on the top of the Senate Building. Hiinhia came down from the first one. Contrary to his name, a Soletria term for "mountain," he was a small bear. He had dark green fur and some simple cloth robes. He looked like he would be a quick learner.

"Hiinhia."

"Laer' Qranyt Avinta. Thank you for inviting me to your territory. I will be a loyal student and assistant if you accept me into your guidance."

I stepped out to the deck overlook on the tower, motioning for him to join, and used our territory's traditional horn to call a meeting. The people of Viikja gathered in a huge, restless segregated crowd, eager to hear their leader's words.

"Stop the fighting to listen in, violence has scarred the land far too long, have we forgotten the era of peace we built together? We must return to the light! I know you're hungry, tired, and sick! Three supply ships have arrived from Aliira. They came to deliver shelter, food, tools, but no weapons. You do not need weapons, you need peace, let's get together again for the common need of healing, help each other out. Without peace, none of this mess will be resolved. Five more ships are going to arrive later, and then, my apprentice, Hiinhia, and I will go to Fiilsa and sort out repairs and negotiations there. Something is brewing within their land and I know I can get them back on our side!" One more shuttle landed and the other four flew over towards West Fiilsa. "Those who are from Fiilsa, the large sailing ship will take you to your home. Those who are from the Emerald Territory will help repair and start the re-establishment of crops and medicinals here." Another ship landed; this one was smaller and triangular, Avie's personal ship.

"I will be sure to keep your lands safe in your absence Qranyt, now go! You and I both know there's no time to waste!" Avie said as they stepped up to the overlook.

If I were to walk right into Fiilsa, we might start an even larger war. This meant we only had one option: to sneak into their land from the south.

I had a submarine ready below the Grand Harbor which was ready for our escape. I led Hiinhia back inside the Leader's Tower and into a small room filled with locked up weapons for the training of new apprentices.

"Well there you have it Hiinhia, pick your weapons—we don't have much time."

"Master Qranyt? What about these ones?" Hiinhia stretched up to point at a case with two small curved knives.

"You sure?"

"Why not?" he replied.

"Alright," I unlocked the case with my paw print and sheathed the knives. The straps fit great on his back, holding them in place so they wouldn't fall. "This way," I directed him.

"So you have a submarine?" Hiinhia asked as we walked in the elevator. I tapped the Cave 1 button, the lowest floor there was.

"Yep. Here on Aviea there's enough water to get almost anywhere by going through it. In case of secret operations, we tend to keep one here." The elevator stopped and doors slid to the sides, revealing the inside of a dimly lit cave. At the end of the cave, a small airlock opened, revealing the hallway to the submarine.

"Wow! This is great," Hiinhia said as we walked through. I pressed a few buttons by the door to close up the airlock behind us. "I've heard there are submarines on Ealtae, but I've never seen them..."

"Do they call the submarines?" I remarked, "I wouldn't call them submarines if they were under forests!"

"True. So what next Qranyt?"

"Well," I pulled a lever to release the ship from its dock, "press that button there, it will bring up a map of the ship." I set the autopilot to maneuver us out of the Akjurkjna-Maurakjnaun Channel that isolates the Maurakjnaun Island from the three surrounding territories. Hiinhia pulled the map up, a 3D display that stood in the center of the sub's control station. The sleek, flat white submarine looked like a flying creature swept-back with a long tail coming out the middle.

"Nice map Qranyt."

"Thanks, it wasn't cheap! Alright here we go," I approached the map to start showing him around. "Here we have the bridge, where we are now. This ramp goes to the door where we came in, but this one goes down to the lower deck, where there are three hallways. One goes to the right wing, where there's the Kitchen, Dining Room, and Bathrooms. The left wing has the Training Room, Forge Room, and Armory. The center one has the Bedrooms. Up near the head, up those stairs, there is the Weaponry Systems Room."

"Sounds good Qranyt, but how long do I have?"

"Oh plenty of time. This ship will take about 2.5 days to get about half of the way around the planet, to where our route to the Capital of Fiilsa is. We don't want to travel through their territory where they'd expect, or else their spies might find us. I suggest we get some training in tomorrow, it's already late."

"What's for dinner?" Hiinhia asked while he looked out the window to the water zipping by.

"I had some fish loaded up into our kitchen supply before leaving, I could cook up some spiced beadplant and fish."

"I have never had food from here yet, but I would love to try something new!" Hiinhia told me. I led him to the right wing of the ship and into the kitchen. "Wow this ship is fancy."

"Yep, I got it back when my territory was flourishing from how much food we were supplying to other territories. Unfortunately complications with the volcano altered the climate of the region, cutting our growth of plants, and we foresaw the time approaching when food would die off, but our efforts to reverse the process were unsuccessful." I got some beadplant "beads" and poured them into a pot.

"That's partly why we're on this mission." I continued, "Even though we've made great strides in bringing back the local farms and food production, trade between Maurakjnaun and Fiilsa has had some, unaccounted losses. Intelligence and surveys of ours in Fiilasan territories have suggested there may be a ploy at hand to cause civil unrest in Maurakjnaun and dismantle the territory from within."

"Sounds like they probably won't appreciate our arrival then!"

"We used to grow these beadplants all over the place, but now they grow better in Akjurkjna Territory, north-west of here. The plants want warmer weather, and the winds from Fiilsa were not helping with that." I poured in some water and began to boil them. I stuck a few small slabs of fish in the oven to cook. Hiinhia watched intently as I selected certain spice bottles from the cabinet and mixed in certain proportions of them.

"Brown pepper, red pepper, yellow pepper, salt, kja cream, all from Citrine Territory, even more north of here—right on the equator. Finest spices on the planet."

"Wow you sure have a collection there."

"Aviea can produce the best ingredients on her surface, just as long as you know where to grow them." The fish was ready within 15 minutes. I strained the bit of remaining water out of the beads and mixed them with the cream, which, poured on top of the fish, completed our meal. "Here we have it," I told him, pulling out two plates and scooping a cut of the fish on each.

"Great! It looks delicious," Hiinhia told me as he sat down at the table.

"Thanks, want any swordfruit juice?"

"Nah, we got that on Ealtae too. You have anything else good?"

"We got some deep red muolisc-ruct juice from Citrine Territory"

"Oh yes please!"

We soon finished our meals, and found that it was almost the middle of the night.

"Time to get some rest, Hiinhia. I'm sure it has been a long day for you." I told him as I left the kitchen for the bridge.

"Okay Qranyt," he replied "Good night."

"See you in the morning, we will get right into training." I informed him as he walked down the tail of the sub. I looked at our map of Aviea. We were just passing by Cornerstone Ridge on the south shore of West Fiilsa. I set up the automatic emergency alarm system before turning in to my desire to sleep.

~   ~   ~

When I got up, Hiinhia had already found something in the kitchen. When I rounded the corner where the hallways met, I could see him getting into stuff in the cabinets.

"Morning Qranyt."

"Hey Hiinhia, I see you were up early."

"I owe you for last night, here you go," he held out a bowl to me, "A recipe of my planet, Several call it 'fruit stew,' even though it's not really stew at all." I took it from him and headed for the table.

"So you were a cook on Ealtae?" I asked as he sat on the other side.

"No, actually. I was related to the leader of my territory. We had a great war and, well, I think they all died. I was left with the responsibility of leading my land through the war— but I couldn't, I was too weak."

"I'm sorry to hear that. I hope to train you to be the best so that you can fight with us."

"So what are we doing today?" he inquired as I stood to return my dish.

"Well, I could start your training."

"Is it safe to surface here?"

"No, not yet; in fact we should probably go lower. The Fiilasan Fort Tetral is nearby, and they have long-range scanners that would instantly detect us on the surface."

"Alright, so we go lower?"

"I've got some plans, and then we will train." I sprinted up to the bridge and set our course to run closer to the seafloor. The ship began to sink towards the bottom of the ocean as I led Hiinhia up to the top floor.

"What are we doing up here?" he asked me.

"I thought I ought to show you how all this works." Over on the console, I put my paw on a black lever. "This controls the shield density, you push it up to increase power directed to the shields, but that will slow the ship down. This trigger controls the forward streamline micro-torpedoes, of which there are 128, four loaded at a time. These buttons launch the top four cruise missiles to the selected target or location on this screen. Hopefully we will need none of those."

"Sounds good."

"And now, on to the training room."

Hiinhia

Qranyt led me back down the ramp, but this time, he took a right towards the left wing of the submarine. There was the training room. Several wooden dummies were lined up on the side of the ship. Qranyt began to explain the different tactics I would learn.

"I will let you choose your own discipline. You could sneak around the woods and quietly approach targets, injuring them by throwing knives; you could fight off enemies as a tank, blocking with one sword while attacking with the other; or you could find high places, dropping down on any unsuspecting enemies, learn the art of a dash attack and insanely fast

strikes."

"Wow! I like the sound of the third one!" I replied.

"Okay, let me show you the simplest moves first." Out of a small wooden case he grabbed two short curved knives similar to mine, stepped back from the first dummy, and held the knives to his waist. "First, you must relax. This allows your body to strike faster. When you are tense, your muscles must spend the extra time relaxing before you strike, which you can eliminate by loosening up. Then," he held the left blade out in front of him, as if blocking another blade, "prepare to block or hit the strike of your enemy off course. Bring your right blade across, as if preparing to strike at your enemy's stomach. Leap forward, deflect, and slash. If you flip the blade after slashing, you may be able to hit again."

"What about stabbing?"

"You would do that like this." He stepped back once more, but this time he held the left knife point-forward, ran, and swung around the dummy's neck, then stabbing its shoulders with both blades at once. He continued to show me various strikes, training so long we didn't even notice we skipped lunch. Dinner was just around the corner.

"Where are we now Qranyt?" I asked on our way to the bridge.

"Somewhere between Fort Tetral and Silver Bay; only about 1.75 days remain." Qranyt prepared some grilled vegetable sandwiches for supper, and he agreed to bring the submarine closer to the surface, where there were tiny creatures that glowed in the light of the moons Sleepy-2c and Reid, which were surprisingly close to each other that night. This made the tides very large, Qranyt told me, probably flooding some of the Upright Kja farms in Emerald Territory. We sank the ship again before going to bed, as we didn't want to risk being found by scanners.

Midday the next day was when things got much more interesting. We started training for combat in the morning, but right after our salads for lunch, our proximity alarm began to go off: a small Fiilasan Patrol Ship detected nearby.

"Have they seen us?" I inquired.

"It appears they haven't, or at least haven't changed their trajectory since our scanners first caught a glimpse. I'm altering our course and attempting to jam any signal they could catch when scanning back for us." Qranyt pulled a lever, revealing a split in the floor.

"What's that?"

"Hiinhia, there is one thing I didn't show you: a separate pod for cases like this. I'll prep the mini-sub in case we need to evacuate or even sneak on board their ship."

"About that," I glanced back at the scanner, "I think they saw us Qranyt!"

The Fiilasan patrol ship had turned our way, probably soon to report our location back to the mainland if they hadn't already.

"You take control of the ship!" he grabbed a small blue pistol-type thing. "I deactivated the autopilot so you could fly it around. Just keep it out of trouble. I'm going on their ship." Qranyt sank into the seat of the pod through the opening in the floor. The floor closed up, and I felt the thrust as he detached from the main sub. I searched around, looking at what things I had to work with. There! A blast door lever to prevent flooding in case of the loss of a compartment! I pulled it back and listened as the doors slammed shut throughout the ship. I also noticed a similar lever to the one upstairs, a shield controller and even a cloaker. I pushed both of them as far as they could go. I watched the map as the patrol boat approached the ship.

Qranyt

I detached from the sub quickly. If they noticed me, an ambush would be difficult. I then turned on the high-density cloaker and scanning jammer to try to keep invisible as I approached the patrol ship. That ship was a surface-subsurface craft, larger than ours with limited underwater capability. I would be able to get to their ship easily using my EVA gear and deep-sea tech. I took the auto-pickup remote and propeller board before leaving my sub pod on autopilot. It would end up in a position following the main craft half a kilometer back. After climbing carefully through the airlock chamber, my propeller board aimed for the ship in the distance and zipped me up to a position at the stern. Fortunately the scanners were not effective enough to notice me sneaking around outside. Spotting a streamlined antenna rig on the top, I dug a chisel out of the suit and began to smash it in. There! No communications! I was able to find the airlock quickly, and having once been an electrical engineer, was able to break right on in.

My electric tranquilizer gun was at the ready, I would much prefer not killing the crew. I ran to the back to hide and remove my underwater suit, and moments later, two guards ran back to the airlock to check what was up, and I took both down from behind a beam. Three more Fiilasan Soldiers came after me, I ducked behind a few crates labeled "Rubidium".

"Where is he?" one remarked.

"There!" another said after turning around.

I shot the three down and continued to the bridge; the autopilot was on, chasing my ship as well as firing at it. There was the autopilot switch! Locked? Wait—I went to the back in search of something to assist me, locating some mines that would explode under pressure. Nah, that's too far for today I think... A fire extinguisher would do the trick maybe? I slammed the bottom of the tank on the ship's controls until it seemed to stop the autopilot.

"Magnificent!" I exclaimed before exiting the bridge.

Back in the ship's main hold I dressed back up in my suit and shoved the crew into an escape craft which would launch from the ship to the surface, that way they couldn't regain control of the main craft. My board slipped right out the door with me and we zipped off to where my pod could come back to catch me when I called it with my remote band. Behind me the Fiilasan ship sat dead in the water, the escape craft cruising into the distance on an auto-evac program. A job well done! I really hoped they didn't transmit any messages regarding our incursion.

Hiinhia

I felt the pod dock on the bottom and rock the sub right before the floor opened and Qranyt came back up, "How's my ship Hiinhia?"

"We received only 2% hull damage, the ship is fine." I pulled down the shield and cloaker and turned the ship's autopilot back on course.

"Off on our way then, good job Hiinhia, we are almost there."

Qranyt

The next night we were ready to surface. I brought the ship up to the ocean's glowing waves and grounded it on the tip of the South Fiilasan Peninsula, where Mt. Lutane loomed overhead to the north.

"Here we are Hiinhia! We will need to get this ship out of here before anypassing patrols see it." I opened up the airlock door to reveal the barren rocky landscape of the Fiilasan Lowlands.

"This looks great."

"Get some supplies, there are packs in the bridge for us to carry. Then choose what you want to use from the armory."

"Yes Laersana," Hiinhia said as he walked off and began packing the bags. I went to the armory, where several plasma rifles rested in cases on the wall, and my swords were on the other side. I got an orange, low power rifle, my trusty noctium sword, a crossbow with high-tension rope darts, and an old dusty amulet for good luck. Hiinhia came in and took two silver-noctium knives and some stronger armor. I just grabbed my cloak.

"Off we go then," Hiinhia said, tossing me the pack. We got out of the ship via airlock, and I opened up the side hatch, which revealed two land speeders.

"These should help accelerate things." I swung the pack over my shoulder and pulled the speeders out and directed the ship to return to Emerald City using the remote, as we wouldn't be needing it anymore. "We best get going, perhaps we'll find a cave somewhere nearby." The ship shot its retro thrusters to get it back into the water. "Bye submarine."

"I got the tents and fuel for our camps," Hiinhia told me.

"Good, but we won't be resting till—" I looked at my wrist computer, "96.22.3. We have a very long way to go, I hope you catch on quick because these speeders are tough to handle!" We hopped on our speeders and I got my heavy armor out of my pack.

"Oh come on man. Why don't I get those?"

"These would slow you down, Hiinhia!" and I sped off. Fortunately these things have a map, or else it would have been difficult for him to catch up; this model has two thick wheels with strong suspension, perfect for the ice, snow and rocks that cover the Fiilasan mountain terrain. I led him up a bit of the side of Mt. Lutane, but not the whole way. My plan was to head northwest a bit before traveling north toward the Southern Pass.

"Why is it so cold here!?" Hiinhia yelled from his speeder.

"Air is constantly coming in from the poles here. When it collides with the hot air from Citrine and Soliae, great storms build up, dropping ice and snow all over the mountains here."

"Speaking of mountains, what are those ones coming up?"

"Terrat, Karel, and 01136."

"How original!"

Our speeders were going quite fast, perhaps 250 kph, but we still would take a while to get to the center of Fiilsa.

"There's a cave up ahead, Hiinhia. Let's set up camp here for now and get some rest before we complete the final stretch." The packs we brought had some supplies for a quick fire and emergency food supply, so we built a little fire in the cave and ate some bread and syrup.

"Nice spot, Qranyt,"

"Is that so? You like the ice cave?"

"Yea, very scenic."

"Get some rest Hiinhia, we've got work to do in the morning!"

We got packed up quick just as the glow of Noctia started to show on the western horizon, the direction our cave faced. Our speeders took us on a trail set out past the mountains tagged 5154 and 6528 before reaching the Southern Pass. The Southern Pass is a wide valley that is an almost direct route from South Fiilsa to Central Fiilsa, where we were going. It's a risky move, being the most exposed valley for someone trying to sneak in, but it would be far less treacherous than trying to round the jagged peaks on either side of the capital district.

"Up ahead Qranyt! Security Encampments!"

"Yeah, I see them—prepare for an attack, but let's try not to kill anyone!" I went off to the left and began firing my speeder's stun cannons, but that wasn't quite good enough. I searched my bag for grenades, which I used to take out some of their turrets. A few officers started towards a small fighter, but I knocked its engines out with another grenade. I spotted another small ship just a few dozen meters away, maybe we could take it for ourselves!

"Hiinhia! Here!"

"What!"

"This ship here, come on!" We got in the fighter ship at the same time, and we closed the hatch before any other guards could get to us, "Put your pack behind the seat!" I tried to squirm into a more comfortable position as Hiinhia squeezed in.

"Sweet! We have ourselves an express ticket!" Within less than a quarter-day, we reached the Xenaa Split, a giant crack in the glacier of the Fiilsa Highland Plains, which I flew to the right of. There to the left was Mt. Xenaa, and a good while later, Mt. Xelae on the left and Mt. Neufa to the right. Just ahead, Fiilsa's Capital City.

"Welcome to the Fiilsa Capital Valley,"

"Looks cold," Hiinhia shuddered, "though I guess there's that warm light in the middle!"

"Time to bring your skills to the ultimate test Hiinhia." We looked at the center from the ledge we parked on. There, in the center of the city, was the fortress temple. These temples are traditional Soliean architecture, a larger version of the Ealtaen flower temple. At the base, a large polygon has radiating ramps leading down from the raised foundation. At the center of the foundation, a large wall rises up and splits, like the petals in the lily flowers of Ealtae. Within the center of these large spires, there lies a single tower, which reaches into the clouds like a giant spear. The extra energy from the fusion reactor is released at the point, which causes the clouds to glow an eerie bright orange.

"What do we do?"

"Get onto one of the closer petals." The outermost layer reaches out far from the center, so a simple rope gun would allow us to swing to the next one over. I pulled out my crossbow and fired a dart, which whizzed through the air and punched through the metal easily. "See you later" I said, dropping the crossbow at his feet and swinging on the rope.

Hiinhia

Qranyt dropped down far, but he swung back up and landed mid-way down on the next petal over. My turn. I grabbed the bolt crossbow and loaded the next rope, winded up the charge assist and lined up the shot.

PFFEWW!

The dart skimmed the side of the petal and fell to the cliffs below; no good! I charged up the next with a little more punch and aimed a bit farther down the petal, hoping it would hit and hold because we only had a few left.

CHIINCH! The next one stuck, I gave it a tug-test before trusting my full weight on it and swinging. Success! —but I missed the petal at the far point of the swing! I let go, grabbed onto my knives and hit them into the soft metal just before I dropped out of range, phew!

"Nice quick thinking!" Qranyt said, reaching down to pull me up. I put the knives back on my back.

"Guess I'm not as heavy as you Qranyt, I think that swing slowed me down too much! Thanks for the lift, now what?"

"Sliding down to the outside top floor." He dropped onto his back and slid down the icy metal and landed on the roof access deck. I followed him, almost sliding off the side once more.

"What exactly are we doing here? What will being here even help with? Qranyt, what is the point to this?"

Qranyt led me to a thick door in the side of the upper hallway and plugged a device into the access panel on the door lock. After a brief moment the door vibrated and popped open.

"Keep quiet," he said, "just follow my lead and it will all go to plan."

Inside the building was much warmer, the hall was made of bright metal and dark marble that beautifully matched the soft yellow light.

"We are calling a meeting, here," he led me into an office room and pressed an emergency meeting alert. "Take a seat," he instructed after he sat at the head of the large table in the office. I sat on the other end, and waited to see what would happen next. Moments later, several cats and bears came in, as well as several guards.

"ARREST THEM!" one of the bears said.

"SIT DOWN!" Qranyt demanded, "NOW!" he pulled a deuterium grenade from his belt and set it on the table; a weapon banned by most governments for over 500 years. Several of the important looking members sat down at their chairs.

Qranyt continued, "Thank you. I, Qranyt, am here today to discuss the release of the West Fiilsa colony, currently owned, by trade consolidation, the Maurakjnaun Territory." The officials shuffled in their seats, exchanging puzzled looks with one another. "See, I have come to notice that our little trade agreement with Fiilsa has been running some unaccounted-for losses and I think you may have something to say about it. I know you want West Fiilsa to be decolonized, but maybe you should have come to me about it instead of inciting riots in both our territories!"

"Qranyt, Qranyt," one of the bears from Fiilsa began, "I'm so glad you've come to visit though I must say I would have preferred something a little less... reckless? I'm inclined to accept your decolonization proposal, however I can assure you I have nothing to say when it comes to your little trade circle loss—"

"I'm afraid I do," A cat across from the Fiilasan bear interrupted, "it's true, supplies have been cut short and redirected to Central Fiilsa as part of a plan to cause a steady rise in unrest in both West Fiilsa and Maurakjnaun. I'd say we didn't take much from them but my own guilt proves that I know how much the creatures there have suffered."

"Thank you," Qranyt accepted, "I hope your fellows learn to be more direct and honest about their objectives. And yeah, I would have liked to do something a little less, this, but I guess it's a little taste of your own medicine. You don't want war, Fiilsa, your civilians deserve security and safety with no costs cut to pointless bickering. Next time if you want something, just ask."

The room was still. A message was coming in from the screens, and Qranyt pressed the receive button on the table.

"Hello, this is Avie calling from Maurakjnaun's Viikja City. I insist that you listen to Qranyt's plans."

"Okay, then it is done," the cat in charge in the room said, "West Fiilsa is ours. Qranyt, you and your apprentice will be given transportation back to your home. Let this day be, from now on, Separation Day, on the 98th day of the Soliean Year!"

"Heard and accounted for—" a familiar voice said from around the corner of a doorway. A dark cat with light speckled markings peeked around, smiling deviously— Selevenera Zorae. "We'll be handling them from here, Qranyt. The Sanctuary has more questions for the current Territory Leadership of Filsa."

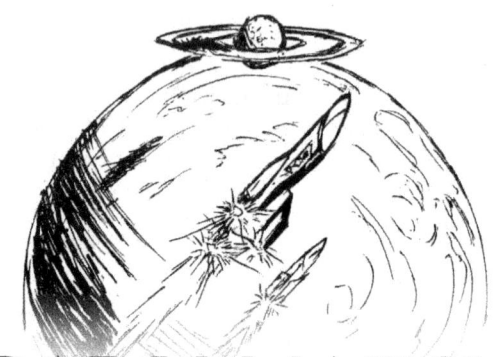

03. DARK MARSHES

[Approach to Viikja Spaceport, Maurakjnaun, Aviea]

Qranyt

I read over the reports from a system patrol this morning as I returned home from my trip to Filsa: Nothing, as usual. The Emerald Territory landing pad sparkled bright in the light of Noctia as I landed softly just before sunset.

"Thanks for the ride," I told the Fiilasan guards as I walked out of the transporter, "come on Hiinhia, it is safe now." We walked away from the pad to find Avie waiting by the Subterranean Rail Station entrance. "Thank you, Avie, for watching over repair efforts in my beloved land."

"No problem, my friend, " they assured me, "just don't get in any trouble with those Fiilasans again!"

"I'll try not to, but you know me."

Avie waved their goodbyes and took off in their shuttle; Hiinhia and I descended into the rail tunnels. The tunnels were dimly lit at this time of day in order to prevent those who entered the tunnels from being blinded. We descended to the private leader's transport, a small white pod that looked like the front of some starships. Once inside, we reached the Maurakjnaun Senate Building and Leader's Tower within two minutes. The elevator brought us up to the top of the tower swiftly, where we could observe the arrival of the first trade ship.

The sailboat came into the harbor, surrounded by the anxious citizens waiting for what the ship brought from the Filasan Territories. We support our new allies with sugar and beryl and get minerals from the mountain extraction sites in central Fiilsa in return.

"What now, Laer Qranyt?" Hiinhia asked.

"I've looked at a wide system patrol of Noctia Space but I haven't looked at the planet-based scanning network; Why not check the planetary scanner reports?" I suggested, "They are over here at this computer. You can check them out if you want while I take a look at our trade standings."

"Sounds good, we can see all that though?"

"Territory leaders get streamed access to planetary scans, even from other planets. The more eyes on the scans the better to pick out anything that looks unusual!" Qranyt replied.

Hiinhia

Qranyt walked off to look at the trade reports while I sat to look at what the scanners on each planet detected in the past hours. First I checked out Aviea; there were several arrivals and departures every second, making this planet the most lively of the six planets in the Noctia system. Yikjtae's scanners were all in orbit, and completely silent. This planet was dead, no action at all for the whole past half-day. On Noctae, a few large cruisers were being tested in orbit, but that was about it.

Ealtae was a bit different from the others; the automated scan reports said that there was nothing, but I spotted a small octagonal prismic object that had been disregarded as some sort of scan glitch. It had sharp angles and seemed to disrupt the scan data.

"Laer[1] Qranyt?," I yelled, "c'mere, I think I found something!"

"I'm right here, what is it?"

"Not sure... the scan ignored this octagonal looking anomaly, but it looks like more than just a glitch." I responded as Qranyt pulled a more detailed image from the records. He zoomed in as far as he could, and that was when we saw a bit more. Rather than just one octagon, there were two smaller ones as well, perhaps farther away. On the closer one, several small red lights appeared running down the side of the prism.

"Alert Aliira Capital and Noctae Command, get a live view on those objects! I'll need Command's permission before checking it out."

"Aliira Secure Band this is Hiinhia at Viikja, Maurakjnaun."

[1] Laer, short for "laersana," is a Soletria term for leaders of Soliean Territories.

"Hiinhia this is Avie receiving you."

"We've got something detected on the scanners in Ealtae orbit, looks like an unfamiliar fleet of ships. Qranyt is requesting a live feed of the location and permission to investigate further on his own ship and perhaps even hail the ships himself."

"Permission granted, tell Q' to keep me updated and not hesitate to call the Noctael Fleet for backup."

"He will deploy Immediately, Laersana. Qranyt what ship shall I prepare for you?"

"A Maurakjnaun-built Horizon Destroyer, we don't know what to expect out there."

"Viikja Rapid Deployment Hangar, this is Qranyt's apprentice, Hiinhia."

"What can we do for you Hiinhia?"

"Qranyt is requesting a crewed Maurakjnaun Horizon Destroyer flown to the Leader's Tower."

"Sounds good—we'll have it in five."

"Hold down the territory while I'm gone please," Qranyt requested as he entered the elevator.

"Sure thing," I connected over to Avie: "Avie, I got your live feed connection, I'm sending you the coordinates of what we're seeing."

"That looks new. You have permission to organize an assault fleet if you need to, I'll tell Noctae Command that you have control over the fleet when we get more information. That picture certainly looks suspicious."

"Thank you, Laersana."

"No problem. Tell you what, get a starship and head for Noctae. I will notify them of your arrival."

"Will do, I'm getting a notification from Qranyt myself—I'll patch you through. Qranyt! You hear me?"

"Loud and clear Hiinhia. I see you got Avie on too?" Qranyt replied.

"Hello I'm here, yes, what is your situation?"

"I've got a ship prepared and we're lifting off from Aviea, should be a quick jump to Ealtae Space and I'll let you know what I see. Keep us up on your monitors, the ship code is VK8E4[1] MAKE-2216."

"Q I got your ship tracking on the secure band," Avie replied, *"Stay*

safe out there!"

I grabbed the portable communicator and called the hanger once more to hop on the next scheduled fast transit to Noctia, as they already had a ship about to leave. The Viikja Spaceport was bustling with creatures celebrating the newly opened borders into Fiilsa and decline in tension between the territories. Up ahead, a MK6S0 Maurakjnaun Secant, a fast transport capable of seating a couple hundred passengers in comfort.

"Hiinhia, yes, right through here—" an attendant cat with a black spot on her face directed me through the thick hull door of the Secant into a second floor private cabin. "Press there if you need anything, we will be departing shortly."

Sure enough, it didn't take long to feel the tilt and jolt of the ship as it launched high into Aviea's atmosphere. I opened the window port of my cabin and watched as the blue-green world and its two moons fell into the dark.

"Qranyt in—I have located the anomaly. There are three unidentified ships in Ealtae orbit. They are motionless, as if awaiting the approach of a Soliean ship. I'm keeping my distance until backup arrives. Attempting to gather any possible information on the ships' sub-systems and manifest."

"Hiinhia, continue to Noctae like I said. Organize an assault fleet and get it over to Ealtae ASAP." Avie ordered.

"You want me to stay on Noctae?"

"Until otherwise told, stay on Noctae, yes." Qranyt replied.

Qranyt

I decided it would be best to completely avoid getting closer to the three ships, but I did hail them so see if they would pick up on our channel.

"Unidentified fleet," I said over the comm, "you have entered Ealtae Space. I peacefully request that you divert and proceed towards the planet Noctae for identification. If you refuse to comply, the Soliean Fleet will take a defensive position around the planet Ealtae to protect its inhabitants. If you continue to refuse identification, you will be forced to leave the system."

---

[1]Ship manufacturers throughout the entirety of the Saertian Rift abide by a specific serial format, first are two letters, a number, another letter and a final number representing if the ship is part of a series. Zero means the ship is either the only model in the series or the smallest, with increasing digits representing larger ships of the same line.

The following four letters and four numbers are an individual ship's code, which when combined with the model information makes for a transponder code unique to each vessel.

The ships remained motionless, and I received no response.

After broadening the communication band I continued, "Unidentified fleet, Ealtae is under protected space and we will not hesitate to fire upon your ships if you do not comply. It is standard protocol for new arrivals from out of system to register at Qorkjesa Orbital, Noctae Space, before proceeding to other worlds. I would need need your customs passage identification information to confirm you have gone through the proper inspection process."

I gave them more time to respond this time, still nothing.

"If you do not respond within the hour, a fleet of Soliean Battlecruisers will take a defensive position. Do not test us. You have little time."

Hiinhia

Most of the passengers on this Secant were of Noctael Navy profession, as Noctae is mostly used for military operation due to its less hospitable nature when compared to Aviea and Ealtae. The planet is covered in black rock and sand, dotted with seas of water. It makes a great location to operate missions like this out of.

"Hiinhia, we have connected with Laer Avie and Qranyt," a dark cat with green eyes led me from the ship to a sealed glass tube over the surface of Noctae. She was dressed in dark plated armor with silver gilding at the edges, it didn't look that comfortable.

The rocks outside looked sharp and uninviting, though quite beautiful in their own way, however: when looking at the stones in the dark they had a prismatic sheen to them, like a rainbow in the night.

"I've never been on Noctae before," I said to the guard, "it's... a strange sort of stunning."

"You're lucky you probably won't be here full-time," she laughed, "it gets unsettling after a while."

As we continued down the satellite passages towards a giant center orb we could hear a bunch of chatter over the local intercoms:

"NO9T4 approach strikjta A6 — Scrambling 8 NO9T2 destination Eal-space 2 80 ascension to degree 282.2"

"That sounds like your fleet, Hiinhia,"

"You could understand any of that?"

"It takes practice for sure," she motioned me to a large set of monitors and booted up the blue-lit screens. Sure enough, Noctael Command was already organizing a set of ten ships to set out for Qranyt's location. "Make yourself at home, Hiinhia, we got teas and snacks, just don't spill anything on the computers!"

I grabbed a tea and a fruit bowl before pulling up a map of the building, labeled the CFCD, Central Fleet Command Dome. The dome itself was massive, surrounded by multiple rings of smaller domes and towers, connected by twelve sealed walkways like the ones we took to get here. This place had everything for the full-time residents; there were pools and libraries, bedrooms, kitchens, and of course huge sections for greenhouses to grow all their food. Suddenly, my comm device woke up.

"Hiinhia! I suspect you are safe on Noctae?" Qranyt asked.

"Yes Qranyt, I have a whole setup just to check on all the fleet information, we have two guardian ships and eight destroyers headed your way!"

"Good, I'd get another wave at least ready in orbit just in case more ships appear. I just interrupted a possible signal for help from one of the ships, they may be calling in more of their fleet."

"Will do, be safe out there!"

Qranyt

The ten ships sent by Hiinhia soon arrived, immediately arranging themselves in a position between Ealtae and the three unidentified ships. I set up a secure transmission to the fleet.

"Soliean Fleet, I'm going to approach the ships and jump in a small boarding craft. Hold positions."

"Yes Laer Qranyt, we are holding position and preparing all turrets for defending the planet."

I left the bridge to the ship crew, taking my emergency transponder to help pull me out just in case. It fit neatly up against the sword across my back. I also took some explosive charges, just in case of on-board complications. The ship came with four boarding craft in the mid-section, built to punch through a weak point in a ship's hull and seal so whoever's inside can board the ship with ease.

The unidentified ships looked like a long octagonal tube with several blocky additions and sections cut out. The sides of it were covered in missile turrets, ones that looked like they could cause enough damage to take out the fleet in minutes.

"Hiinhia,"

"You need that fleet?"

"If this comes to a full-on skirmish, I may need a few more ships. Send them over."

"Immediately."

I removed what gear I had in the way and dressed in a void-suit to give me more time in case of a loss of pressure. The inside of a pod was just big enough to fit three crew, but nobody was coming with me on this excursion. I placed my gear on board and climbed in, sealing the hatch behind me.

"SELECT TARGET TO INITIATE AUTO DEPLOY," the pod computer lit up in front of me as the pod jolted into launch position. I selected the center unidentified ship and let the pod computers do the rest.

The craft shot out the side of the ship like popping a fermented swordfruit juice open, hurtling me towards the strange craft.

"WEAK POINT IDENTIFIED—" the pod thrusters redirected me towards what looked like a hangar door in the ship ahead, perfect! "BRACE FOR HULL BREACH, 3... 2... 1..." The craft slammed into the hull, the sharp end ripping a hole through the door. The sound of foam fizzing could be heard as the pod sealed itself to the open hole to prevent air loss, then the hatch opened once more. This was my kind of method, up close and personal to see with my own eyes what's going on.

Inside, I stepped down on the streaked red cement looking material and pulled my gear from the pod; the ship looked as quiet on the inside as it did on the outside, but as soon as I got my gear equipped and readied, I heard the sound of a door slamming shut and the echo throughout the large empty hangar. A few dozen seconds passed before some red lights down the length of the hangar blinked on.

I reached back and drew my greatsword, ready for anything. The black noctium metal glowed a dark burgundy in the light, as if soaked in blood. I walked toward what seemed to be the direction of the bridge, and the solid metal doors that blocked the exit slid open when I tapped them.

Ahead, there were several creatures that were about my height. They were all wearing silvery-grey armor and held long red spears. Their brown heads were greatly elongated out in front of them, and they made no attempt to stop my passage down the hallway. Once I passed the last two of these creatures, they turned and followed me, holding the spears on both of my sides. We walked down a very long stretch of walkway before coming across another large door. The creature to my right walked around in front of me and typed a code into the keypad, opening the door.

I was then forced through the door, this must be the bridge. Computers lined the sides of the large space, as well as on a platform above me. Ahead, there was a large reinforced glass wall, through which Ealtae and the Soliean Fleet were clearly visible. I was led to the front of the bridge, where another one of the creatures sat in a large chair. I was then put in front of the creature and several more guards came over, surrounding me.

"What is your name, bear?"

I remained silent.

"Did you have trouble understanding me, bear? What is your name!"

"Why is your fleet here?" I inquired.

"You are not in a position to be issuing orders, bear, you are in a position to die if you don't comply with our requests. Your name doesn't matter. We will descend upon the planet Ealtae, and you will call off your fleet or be destroyed."

"Under the authority of the Noctia System you are required to register for system access at Qorkjesa Orbital in Noctae Space."

"Your rules don't matter to me, I'm under orders too; Guards, take him away!"

I pressed the panic button on my transponder, signaling the fleet to begin the attack. Only a moment passed before the first shots began to hit the ship.

"What was that about who is in the position to give orders?"

"Shields up! Activate security protocols! Call in the rest of the fleet! And you, you are going down with our ship," the suspected leader barked.

Doors around the bridge started slamming shut. I threw the guards off me and took a mad dash out of the room, leaving one of my explosive packs behind just before the door closed. Here my daring escape attempt began, running down the hall swiftly with no idea of the ship layout, but the creatures quickly surrounded me, approaching from secret doors in the hallway.

"He went that way!" I yelped before body slamming a couple guards and pushing past back into the hangar. I backed to the rear of the hangar and drew my sword, "Hiinhia!"

"Qranyt? What can I do for you?"

"I'm—trapped on—the main ship. I don't think they would be keen on letting someone come dock and pick me up! I will need to figure out another way!"

"Got it. I will have the ships focus on destroying the bridge and engines."

"Good bear!" I slashed down one of the brown monsters with my sword just as I noticed several others pouring a sticky black tar over my pod. I looked around the back wall I was pressed against and found a small blast door. I stuck an explosive right in the middle and stepped to the side. BANG! The door buckled inward and blew some of the metal across the hangar. I swiftly jumped through the hole in the door and ducked behind the remaining metal as the tar and creatures went up in flame. Moments after the chaos ended I found a hall to continue down, leading up some stairs. There in the middle of the ship I found a turret, which extended out the top of the ship, giving it a wide field of fire.

"This is going to be a risky maneuver..." I said to myself before climbing into the turret cockpit and dropping the rest of the explosive packs down. "Here goes!" The turret blast door slammed shut and the ship's section beneath me buckled, launching the turret towards the planet Ealtae.

"WooooOOO!" I called into the transponder, the turret whirled about spinning at a nauseating pace, yet I still tried to use the turret motor to slow the rotation. The attempts fell short, so I instead tried to use the turret's remaining power to hit some of the enemy ships. It seemed they had requested for backup as well, as several more of their ships came into the crossfire. It soon became apparent that the wreck was quickly falling towards Ealtae, so I braced for the atmospheric re-entry, but just then, a Noctae scout ship swooped under the turret.

"Hey Qranyt wanna catch a ride?"

"Hiinhia!"

"Good to see you, Q'!" The top of the starship opened up and closed around my broken turret. The wreck crashed to the floor.

"Gotcha Qranyt!"

Upon releasing the blast door and jumping out I felt the ship shake as it was assaulted by enemy ships.

"Thanks Hiinhia, but it's not over yet."

"I know, let's fight these intruders until they back down."

"To the destroyer then! Let's go!"

"Yes Qranyt!" Bursts of shot hit our ship, knocking it to the side.

"Wait—Hiinhia," I said.

"Yeah?" We stopped in the hall for a moment.

"This ship has shield cluster missiles right?"

"It does, we could help the other ships loading them up with protection!"

"Load them up— quickly. Call to me when they're loaded."

"I'm on it!" Hiinhia replied. A few moments later I heard back, "I'm at the bridge and ready to launch!"

"Alright, fire tubes 1-4 in order"

"Gotcha!"

"NOW!"

I turned the ship swiftly towards the Soliean Fleet and watched as Hiinhia launched each tube. The missiles shattered into tiny missiles and bombarded our flagships.

"Hiinhia, come up here!" I said, "Activation in 3—2—1." Each of the tiny missiles released a shield, acting like a pillow around the ships.

"Hey Qranyt," Hiinhia entered the bridge, "we've got incoming, looks like a big one too."

"Yeah, I see it. This one will knock us down." I rotated the ship towards Ealtae.

"And you're helping it?"

"Yes, look!" I pointed out the window to a group of the enemy ships that was descending towards Ealtae's surface.

"Alright, this will be bumpy..."

"You think? Hold on!" I said just as the missile collided into the tail end of the starship. The ship spun out of control and the thrusters launched in retrograde to slow our orbit. "Get your gear on! We're gonna make a jump!"

"You're insane, Qranyt!"

"Don't you worry, I have done this before!"

"WHAT?"

The ship glowed an orange-red as we entered the atmosphere. We got on our parachute packs and got ready for the drop.

"Alright Hiinhia! Out the hatch!" I popped open the airlock and shoved him out. After quickly grabbing some gear, I joined him, diving straight down to try to catch up.

"Ealtae looks so cool from up here!" Hiinhia yelled to me over the rushing air. We watched as five enemy ships entered a hover position over the ground.

"Try to turn using your body and glide towards the ships!" I directed, swiftly positioning my arms to avoid being set off-course. Suddenly, I heard a faint voice from my belt.

"Qranyt, I see you have taken a leap?" Avie said.

"Yes I sure have!"

"You continue on your current path, take out the ships. Have Hiinhia evacuate the civilians to a safe point just by the volcano to the north." I looked in the distance to see a large volcano.

"Copy that!" I replied, turning to Hiinhia. "You heard him! Evacuate the locals to that volcano. I will take down the ships with my remaining charges."

"Catch you on the ground Q!"

I steered off to the right and pulled my cord right at the last moment, gliding onto the top of the nearest red-grey spaceship. The turrets had already begun firing at the ground, targeting the houses and forests, as well as fields of crops. It didn't make any sense to me, why were they pulling a pointless act of cruelty on a planet they likely never visited?

Hiinhia

Thanks to Qranyt's distracting landing, I almost forgot to pull my cord. Once I was on the ground, I quickly detached my flight gear and ran for the burning village. Several cats were running all over, and it was my task to organize as many as I could and get them to safety.

"GO, GO, GO," I yelled out, "GET TO THE VOLCANO!" In the distance I could see a wing of Ealtae ships descending towards the mountain. "Alright you guys! Don't worry about your belongings, let's go! There are ships waiting at the volcano! I will hold these creatures off as you run!" I led them in the direction of the massive mountain and readied my knives for the first wave of creatures.

The first swung a red spear at me, the tip crackling with some kind of electricity. I was little and couldn't attack with my weight, but I managed to jump onto the creature's spear and stab at its chest. Another creature shot a red bolt of electricity at me, but I was too quick and ducked behind the one I'd just stabbed. A local large cat jumped from out of nowhere and clawed at the creature that shot at me. All while behind us, I heard the ships falling to the ground and exploding into a pile of debris.

"GET DOWN!" I yelled to the cat in warning as a shockwave burst from the crashing ship.

"GRRR" the cat growled, "I'll cover you so you can help the others stuck in the village!"

Qranyt

"WAHHH" I yelled as the ship on which I stood upon the roof slammed into the ground and began to flip on its side. On board they had what seemed to be a jetpack, which I had grabbed just after destroying the ship thrusters. The pack blasted me out of the crash zone towards a nearby settlement.

"Qranyt! I need you on Sleepy2c! Something new is happening there, we can handle the ships in orbit around Ealtae."

"There's still creatures here they're attacking on the surface! Besides, Aviea's moon? That moon is barely part of Solia!"

"Exactly. We need to bring them back to Solia, plus we would need their help in case we are going to have a war with these new creatures. Finish your operation on Ealtae, I'll send ground backup and emergency supplies to help the civilians. I am sending a ship to your location now!"

"Okay, if you think it will work, then I'm in." As I waited for the ship, I ran about the forest edge, where several of the creatures were attempting to start a fire. "YAAAAAAARR," I screamed, charging at them with my sword and shock rifle at the ready.

"Qranyt! Qranyt! We're holding off on Sleepy2c! Twenty more cruisers just spotted sailing towards Ealtae! We need you to stay there until this fight is over!"

"Looks like you have your war then Avie, I'll take them out with Hiinhia this time— and get those people on the volcano to safety!"

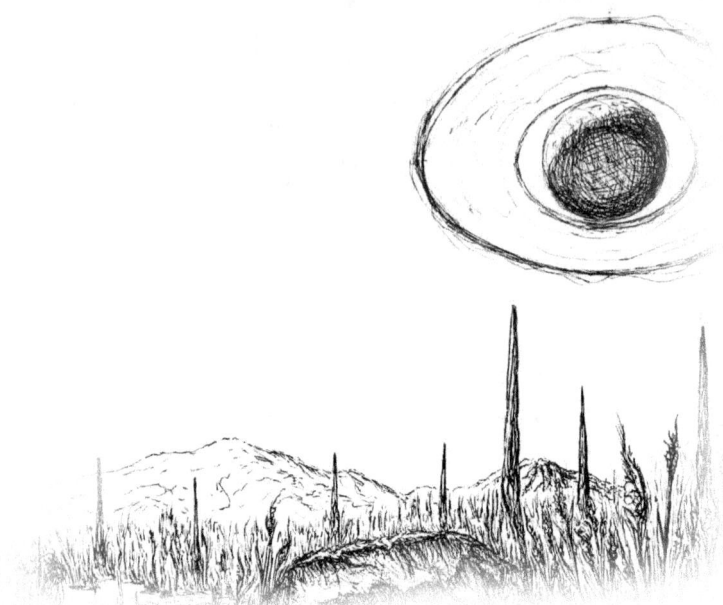

04. REBELLION

[Midland Plains, Faelk-kja District, Ealtae]

Qranyt

I led Hiinhia back towards the village as the new enemy ships descended; this wasn't just a skirmish anymore, but a full planetary assault. I could only imagine the their reason for attacking out here was to set up a base for further attacks. Up ahead, I saw the leader from the first ship I brought down led the dozen others that survived the crash to destroy what was left of the village's homes.

"Come around on the other side Hiinhia! We'll close them in!" Hiinhia ran off to my left and snuck behind the clay buildings that had stood on Ealtae for generations. I charged at the invaders, but something was distracting me as I hit the first spear out of the way; I heard something over the chaos, small but my ears picked it up and focused in. Was there someone still in the flaming buildings? I thought as I continued dodging attacks. I saw Hiinhia come up to the invaders on the other side and jump from the roof onto one of the creature's shoulders as I slashed down the last few of the group, leaving only the one who seemed to be in charge.

"Qranyt! Someone is stuck in one of these houses!" Hiinhia yelled over the sound of more invaders landing.

"Yes, I do too, hold on a second," I then turned to their leader, "Who are you?!" The brown lump made a dissatisfied grunt. I dropped down on top of him, threatening to stab him.

"You haven't seen all of the Dark Marsh!" I didn't notice as he cut the jetpack off my back. Once he got it free, he quickly activated the engines, slipping out from right underneath me and singing some of my fur.

"Great." I told myself with much disappointment.

"Qranyt! In here!" Hiinhia cried out. I ran inside the nearby house to see who he had found.

"There," he pointed.

"Go outside and guard the village for a minute Hiinhia, I'll see what I can do."

"Wait—" Hiinhia paused at the door.

"Yes?"

"What did you find out from that thing before he escaped?"

"I think he said he's the Dark Marsh? And that there's more coming..."

Hiinhia nodded an okay and ran outside. I looked back to the heap in the corner of the room; there was a small cat cowering next to a large dead snake. The dark brown and white kitten observed my every movement as I studied the snake. It appeared to have been hit by one of the "Marsh's" spears. I reached out to the kitten, but it just backed itself into the corner even more.

"ecHCHCHHH!" the poor thing hissed,

"It's okay little one, you're safe with me. I'm one of the Soliean Leaders." I reached out again, and this time the kitten climbed up my arm and held tight.

"Okay little thing," I said as I stood up, "we need to get you out of here." I saw Hiinhia off in the distance when I came out of the dark room.

"What is your name?" I asked the kitten.

"EH-nhree" it said softly.

"Ehnri?" I said back, "you're gonna make a fine warrior someday Ehnri, I'll be sure of it."

Hiinhia

The fight was constant. More and more of these Marsh things were coming out of the ships; We managed to crash a few of their ships but they just kept coming. I turned back to the small village house for a moment long enough to see Qranyt come out with a small cat, but had to turn back to the fight as more of the creatures threw their red sparking spears at me.

One advantage I have in a fight is that I am small and light, making me quite agile and able to avoid said red flaming spears, but it makes it hard to fight back. I found it easy to jump back from the hogs long enough to run back towards Qranyt.

"What's our move now Qranyt?" I asked.

A dark Noctael Transport dropped into the field nearby, opening its doors to reveal a collection of Noctael foot-soldiers to confront the "Marsh."

"Well who knows Hiinhia? Keep fighting these guys?"

"Ha sure but I'm really running low on energy right now! And look, the ground fleet is arriving!"

"No breaks till daybreaks."

"The sun hasn't even set y—"

"Wait, I heard something," Qranyt interrupted.

"Yeah that was my stomach growling."

"Helloooo? You guys alright down there?"

"Avie?!" I said with surprise,

"Great, you got good news or bad news?" Qranyt growled.

"Good I think— the Zekj fleet is on its way, as well as what is left of our Noctae Fleet. You guys are almost done on Ealtae so hang in there."

"You think that we can handle it?" I asked,

"Ha!"

"Oh, and we have a survivor here too, a black and white kitten."

"I'll ask around the survivors I picked up from the volcano— what was his name?"

"Ehnri is what he said his name was, do you want to pick him up?" Qranyt suggested.

"Does he need medical assistance?"

"I don't think so. I guess we'll bring him to the medical outpost near the mines to check him out." Qranyt told him.

"Well good luck. Your fleets will be landing in but a few minutes."

Qranyt

"Well you heard him," Hiinhia said, "we're free to go!"

"Let's just be careful getting to the infirmary, the Marsh are still around." I looked down to see Ehnri the kitten sleeping in my arms.

"He's gonna need some rest too," I heard Hiinhia say.

"Alright, it's not that far off, let's go." I called as Solia Noctia began to set.

~   ~   ~

Hiinhia, Ehnri and I arrived at the Ealtaen Mining Facility shortly after the blue-white star had gone below the horizon. The mining on Ealtae is limited, and the only things mined here are crystalline minerals and metals. There are very few locations set aside for mining purposes, Ealtae being strictly a natural and peace-driven world.

"Looks like the Marsh barely touched this place," Hiinhia said.

"Yeah, hey you mind staying with Ehnri in there for a bit?"

"Sure, you gonna look around or something?" Hiinhia questioned, taking Ehnri from my arms.

"Yeah... take this backup communicator. I'll be back soon."

"Oka— bring a light with you!" Hiinhia stopped me before I rounded the corner of the medical outpost.

"Good point," I agreed, noticing it was already pretty dark. We stepped inside the building, where I was able to quickly locate the stash of mining tools, including a light.

"Do you really need all your gear?" Hiinhia inquired as he laid Ehnri down on one of the beds.

"Just in case, and there should be food in one of the coolers in the corner there," I gestured to the opposite wall of the room.

"Thanks, and be careful out there."

"As always," I left the infirmary, entering the cool, dark Ealtaen night.

Something about Ealtae makes you feel strange at night; no, not creeped out or anything, instead calm, rested; It is the "Planet of Peace" after all. I turned to the sky to see the last of the Marsh Cruiser, confronted by the Zekj fleet. Off to the east I saw Solia Aqua rising, partially eclipsed by Ealtar, Ealtae's moon. Even though it was bright enough for me to still see, I twisted the light orb to turn it on.

I then turned my gaze to the mine, a large conical crater in the middle of the fields. The night air had cooled me down enough to have a bit of jogging energy, so I sprinted down the side of the crater, then leapt off the deep mine entrance and landed in the center of the giant cone. Around me were the dark tunnels that marked the entrance to the deep unknown.

Kneeling to the ground, I sensed what had led me here. I wasn't into anything like, spiritual or anything. Quite honestly I felt that the stories the creatures of Ealtae told were just stories for the young ones to keep their imagination going but something was different now that I was actually there, as the sounds and violence of the day was almost eaten by the world around and plunged back into a serene silence.

Something wanted me to take a very specific tunnel; I held the light orb far out in front of me as I continued. The darkness took everything around me away for several blurred minutes, maybe even an hour, it even started to reach in and fizzle the light of the orb.

Then, I saw them: the crystals of life. By law of Ealtae, it is forbidden for these green luminescent minerals to be mined by any of the producers on this world, as the crystals are considered sacred by many due to strange phenomena involving them. They must have stopped mining here once they discovered the natural crystal tubes beneath them! I eased farther down the tube, slowing my pace to avoid damaging any of the crystal shards.

It felt like it had been hours, the crystals began to change to a deep blue color, and normally I would have turned back a long while ago to make sure Hiinhia was safe and not thinking I'd gotten lost but something drew me further into the crystals...

The tunnel ended abruptly to a hole on the wall of a large, round gleaming cavity, where each shard seemed to be 20 plus meters in length. In the center of the cavity was a slanted blue crystal, which rose from the floor of the space to the exact center. I could see the top of the crystal flattened out where there was some kind of cube, but when I tried to look closer, things— broke down...

a chill went up my spine when I felt a fiery hot hand on my left shoulder.

~   ~   ~

"Qra-nyyt!! Qrannnyyt!!!"

"What?" I responded to the voice, seeing only a blur of green against the bright light.

"It seems you didn't make it far out the door, did you?"

"Hiinhia?"

Vision started to return to me, and I saw the little apprentice of mine getting right in my face.

"What is it, Hiinhia?"

"You were gonna go check something out, remember?"

"Oh, yeah that's right, I remember the stuff I saw down there now."

"Well, I found you right outside the door, your light wasn't even on yet."

"Oh, I guess I just passed out then," I chuckled, sitting up to look around the infirmary. "The war is over, but you're right, I need some food before I can go anywhere without passing out!"

"What, did you have a dream or something?"

"Yeah, I guess I did, I mean there were crystals and stuff. That's about it."

"Huh. Okay."

"Pbbhurr" said the little cat on the sheets of the bed I was in.

"Ehnri?!"

"Hi Qranyt!" Ehnri greeted me.

"Hi! Are you ready to go do some exploring with us?"

"Of course I am! And train to be a strong fighter like you be right?"

"We'll need to find a way to leave the planet first," Hiinhia interjected.

"I got that for you guys! C'mon outside!" I looked to my side to see the communicator.

"Thanks Avie!" Ehnri said.

"You're welcome Ehnri!"

05. RESTLESS MOON

[Midland Plains, Faelk-kja District, Ealtae]

"Aaarrrrrrrr" is the sound I made when I got up out of the hospital bed. Ehnri's fur stood on end for a few seconds as he took the sound in.

"Alright, let's get out of here Qranyt," Hiinhia said.

I quickly wrapped my gear back around me. Ehnri climbed up on my arm before I got a chance to step away from the bed.

"So you're a Siaka[1] cat aren't you?" I asked Ehnri as we walked out the exit.

"Yes, I am. Woah— that ship looks cool Grandpa Bear!" Ehnri told me excitedly. Hiinhia made a soft laugh when he heard my new name.

"I can call you that, right?" Ehnri asked.

"Sure thing, " I replied, rubbing his head a bit. Avie had sent us a small Noctael vessel to take off in, a ship that resembles a flying wing.

"Alright! Let's get loaded up Hiinhia" I declared.

"Right on, *Grandpa Bear*!" Hiinhia laughed.

We didn't bring much with us but our weapons and utility bags, so after a short time we were all loaded up in the ship and ready to fly back to

---

[1] A small feline subspecies native to Ealtae's Midland Plains regions, easily recognized by their soft cream-colored fur which darkens to brown on their ears, feet, tail and nose. They have lived on Ealtae for thousands of years, and likely will continue for thousands to come.

Aviea.

"Alrighty Avie, you got orders for us?"

"Hey Qranyt and friends, I sure do have orders for you! Remember that mission I had you on before the war started?"

"Sleepy2c conflicts, right?"

"Yep, you're still on, but I think you should bring Ehnri with you. Maybe you can teach him a few more things about helping people out, plus who knows? Maybe Ehnri has more than the eye can see!"

"That I do Leader Avie!" Ehnri purred.

"Where do you want me?" Hiinhia asked.

"You can drop Qranyt and Ehnri off at Sleepy2c's center. Qranyt will find the bear named Sleepy, the leader named after the moon. He and his son, Setai, are working together to end the struggle between the villages there. That moon could be a useful outpost for ships around Aviea too, so try to do well."

"You've got it Avie, but I have one question for you— completely unrelated."

"No Qranyt, Akjaeir has not returned yet."

"Oooohhh why's that Avie?" Hiinhia mocked, and we heard a click as Avie disconnected the line on their side.

"Nice job Hiinhia!"

"Who's Akjaeir, Grandpa Bear?"

"She's the second leader of Solia, and she left to investigate the stars Bevelan, Veldessan Tule, and Solia Gaeskja a while back. Some say the mission was fake, and she was secretly going even farther into space in a ship of her own design, the *Kqaet-Avai.*"

"Oh? Is she nice like Avie is?"

"Ha! Even *nicer!*" I started the engines on the ship and flew up into the night sky.

"Look guys it's daytime again!" Ehnri purred.

"Yeah sure Ehnri, but I need a rest," Hiinhia sighed.

"Only got fifteen minutes to do that, Aviea isn't that far away," I reminded him.

"Yeah that's when I get to drop you two off and go to my vacation home!"

Our ship passed out of Ealtae's shadow the rest of the way and revealed all three of our stars.

"Wow!" Ehnri exclaimed, "They look even brighter up here!"

"Yeah okay Ehnri don't go blind on us," I remarked, turning the polarization density up on the window to try to make it easier to see.

"I've never left Ealtae before, we going to Aviea?"

"Well, sort of. Aviea has two moons, Sleepy2c and Reid. We need to go to Sleepy2c." I turned the ship's autopilot on and brought Ehnri back to the navigation console.

"How do you get used to the low gravity?" Ehnri asked as he floated away. I reached my paw out for him to climb back on.

"Just don't let go of things I guess, here, look at this," I turned the map screen on to show a projection of our location. "This is Ealtae, where you were born. We are now passing over where Noctae's orbit is, although Noctae is in a different place in its orbit right now. Next, we will pass by Yikjtae's orbit, and then we will arrive at Sleepy2c!"

"Woah!"

"Alright Ehnri, give me a moment," I said, heading off to a private communication room on the side of the ship.

"Avie, come in?"

"Qranyt, I hear you. What is it?"

"I've been thinking, why did they put so much effort into invading Ealtae? It was almost like they were trying to set up a base or something, it just haunts me a bit. All that for what?"

"I've been thinking the same thing, Qranyt, something's been bothering me about how they did it all on one front, almost like they were trying to hold our attention."

"You think it was all a diversion?"

"Maybe, can't be too sure. We're increasing patrols and scans in case any of them stop by again."

"There's something else,"

"Yea?"

"I had this dream, or, I'm certain it was real... nevermind."

"Okay Qranyt, I don't know what I could say about your dreams but you know what they say about Ealtae..."

"Catch you later, Avie."

I stepped back out just as we began to slow down for our intercept with Sleepy2c.

"Why is the moon named Sleepy2c? That's kinda funny!" Ehnri asked as he drifted back to the floor of the ship.

"Sleepy2c is named not after the phenomenal ability to rest there, it is instead named after the spirit that protected its people in the ancient times, Sleprah. Sleprah was said to have been at their side when they had lost their home, so Sleprah used what energy she had left to build a new moon to orbit Aviea. The moon was to be named Sleprah the second, so that is what Sleepy2c stands for, as 2c is short for 'daecaser,' which means second."

"Wow Grandpa Bear, how do you know so much?"

"Oh you tend to learn a lot when you travel around the universe!" I told him.

Hiinhia brought the ship into hover over the surface of the dry moon, and I took Ehnri to the drop hatch, grabbing a couple of the ship's stun rifles before we dropped down to the sand.

"Cya later guys!" Hiinhia shouted as I dropped down the rope to the sandy desert ground. I covered Ehnri as Hiinhia flew off with his own personal dust storm.

"Phew!" I remarked.

"Now what Grandpa Bear?"

"Time to go to the city! It seems to be off to the northeast." I held Ehnri in my arms as I ran towards the city in the desert.

"So—pssssf!!—much sand!" Ehnri said, sneezing, "Isn't there any water around here?"

"Not with this kind of heat, the only natural water is high up in the atmosphere or below the surface. In the city there should be more though, they have developed ways to slow the evaporation of water there."

"It's sooo hot here too!"

"Tell me about it!" I responded as I stopped to lean on one of the sandy clay buildings in the city. Once I had a moment to rest, Together we climbed onto the roof of the building, trying to keep low and out of sight. Ehnri crawled off me and stretched out in the warmth.

"Alright Ehnri, It seems as though the rebels have Sleepy surrounded, I wonder where Setai is?"

"There!" Ehnri exclaimed, nosing towards a taller building.

On the side of the building I could make out a tan, sandy bear that looked a bit shorter than the Forest Bears like me. He seemed to be carrying a thin, curved sword, as well as a strange dagger-looking thing, which he hid in his clothes. He turned towards us, revealing his beady black eyes. He waved us to come closer when he spotted us on the roof, so we dropped down to the ground again.

"Alright Ehnri. Stay at this corner alright?" I whispered

"Okay Grandpa Bear!"

Setai signaled the start of our attack, making sure we jumped out at the same time. I drew the heavy sword from my back and charged into place next to the young bear. The rebels drew their swords too, and we could see that they were roughly made and weaker against our better funded ones.

"Alright Setai! Chase them off with me!"

"Glad you could come Qranyt!" Setai replied. We both slashed at the rebels, trying to force them out of the city.

"Here, take this!" I dropped one of the stun rifles to Setai, "Always better to hit them with this when we can!"

One by one, we sent the fighters back out of the city center, stunning anyone who came back our direction, but then we saw where they went: an entire army of rebellious bears lay at the city outskirts. Setai and I ran back to Sleepy and Ehnri.

"Thank you, Laersana, for joining us in this fight," the elderly bear said. "My son, you are brave to fight for us."

"Thank you, father."

"Sleepy, what is it that these rebels want from you?" Sleepy nodded to Setai, who pulled the dagger-looking thing out. Now that I was closer, I could see that it was in fact not a dagger, but some kind of artifact, perhaps as old as the moon itself.

"This," Sleepy pointed, "is what they are after. These rebels believe this artifact is the cause of their suffering, their starvation, their loss, but this artifact is the Matrix of Sleprah, thought to be the creator of this world. They're just a bunch of the neighboring tribes that are scared and confused,

Qranyt, they're our people and we have no food here for them. That's all they really want."

"What do you have here Sleepy? What can you trade with the territories of Aviea?"

"Who would even accept us?" Sleepy asked, putting his head into his arms. "What have we ever done to help Aviea?"

"That I do not know, but I do know that I can help you, Sleepy. The Emerald Territory has lots of food they can give up. Once, long ago, we had no food either. I know what it's like to be hungry." I put my arm around his back to comfort him.

"Thank you, Qranyt, but I am no leader— I can't end this mess. Setai,"

"Dad?"

"Speak to the people, my son."

I turned back to see an arrow embedded in Sleepy's heart, and he fell to the ground. Setai rushed to his side, trying to figure out what to do.

"No, my son," he whispered, "You are now this world. Unite us once more to join Solia, my great Sleepy," his dark eyes closed tight.

"Setai, you now take his place, you are their leader." I gave him a hug, bringing him back on his feet. "Speak to your people, Sleepy."

Sleepy

I walked slowly beside Qranyt, who held the little kitten Ehnri in his arms. Bows and swords were raised as I approached the crowd of rebel fighters. I held the Matrix high before starting my speech.

"Bears of Sleprah-Daecaser," many of the crowd booed at the first line, "This Matrix of Sleprah is not the cause of your suffering. It has no such power as that! In fact, there is no cause to your suffering anymore! You have no need to suffer any longer!" The loyal bears of the village came out from their homes to see what the buzz was about.

"There will not be any suffering here! Qranyt here is our new ally, and he has agreed to sending us his territory's surplus food. We here will repair what has been broken, that is our moon's unity, our pride! We will pay Qranyt back with the respect he deserves." Bears in the crowd began to put their weapons down.

"Wait—" Qranyt started, pulling out a long-range transponder and turning the volume to max. "This is Laersana Qranyt, calling in to Viikja Distributions Center."

"Qranyt, this is Aega, distribution management, I hear you."

"Load any of the supplies left over from the repair efforts and any extra produce from the new greenhouses into a ship destined for Sulentuun, Sleprah-Daecaser."

"Understood, we will begin immediately."

The crowd muttered and murmured about to each other in interest as Qranyt motioned me to continue.

"You need not starve, my people! You will instead grow! We will grow! To the stars we will travel! Just like Qranyt's Emerald Territory we will shine! We will trade across the Soliean Stars, because we are now a part of the Soliean Stars!" The bears cheered, louder than ever before, they cheered for what they saw would come out of this change.

"My father said he of was no importance anymore, but he was wrong. He may have helped start the suffering, but he helped end it by letting me call to join Solia! We are now one! Throw your spears, swords, and bows to the ground and build! Build a new Sleepy2c by my side! We live with those who believe in the power of the Stars!"

~   ~   ~

Qranyt

"Good speech, Sleepy, and congratulations."

"You really got them all to calm down!" Ehnri exclaimed.

"Thank you again for your help, Qranyt, I plead you, is there anything at all I can do in return?"

"Perhaps," I stepped aside, motioning for us to head back to the center Sulentuun districts. "Mostly I'm just curious about this item, you said it's the Matrix of Sleprah? What is it?"

"All I know is what my father told me, but I can bring you to the place it was kept for thousands of years before we found it."

The crowd shuffled and cheered rushing towards the small city starport where the Maurakjnaun ship began to descend.

"That would be great, Sleepy, I think there's something bigger going on with these things."

"There's more of them?" He asked, leading me through the city outskirts to a narrow canyon passage.

"I don't know yet, but I saw something like that in a dream, it was a cube with patterns in its sides, glowing blue from inside."

"Oooh you had a vision Qranyt!" Ehnri said, listening intently to our every word.

"Here," Sleepy pulled out a light orb and directed me into a cave within the canyon walls. The frame of the opening had several strange runes and pictograms etched in the stone.

"Is that Sleprah?" Ehnri asked as the light of the orb fell on a larger mural within the cave.

"Yes, this cave shows our ancient history, it's said that the dream spirit Sleprah sacrificed herself to make this world, her body became the moon and her soul," Sleepy removed the object from his belt, "They say that the Matrix of Sleprah is the solidified crystal of her soul."

"You said earlier," I started, "that the matrix doesn't have the power to cause suffering. Did you mean it does other things?"

"I don't know," Sleepy said, "but my father said he thought it showed him things, he never really said what things though."

Ehnri interjected, "If it is really Sleprah's soul, I bet it could do all kinds of things! She's probably still in there and can hear us right now!!"

I gently brushed the mural with my right paw, wondering how this all connected.

"It's... weird—" I began, but then trailed off into my own thoughts.

06. A DARK CAT

[Sulentuun Starport, Sulentuun District, Sleprah-Daecaser]

Setai's speech rattled the people of the village, both Ehnri and I were amazed to see how the crowd reacted to the words they had not expected to hear. Now that the Maurakjnaun supply ships had come in, the people were joyous and eager to start working together again.

"Qranyt! Are you done on Sleepy2c?"

"You sure waste no time!," I laughed, "and just about, yeah, I'll be there in a bit."

"You gotta go?" Setai asked.

"It seems so, but you should come to Aviea with me once I have dealt with Avie's next task."

"Alright, sounds good. I will stay here and help my people in the meantime."

"Of course, Ehnri?"

"Yes Grandpa Bear?"

"Why don't you stay here with Setai? Perhaps you can learn more about his world while you wait for me!"

"Hey, Qranyt, it's Hiinhia, I've got the ship landing right outside the village to bring you back to Avie. They say there is a problem in Auqaut Territory that you need to help with."

"I see you Hiinhia, I'll be with you momentarily. Setai, take care, release your father and start your moon's new age."

"Thank you Qranyt, I certainly will."

"Have fun Ehnri!"

I boarded the ship Hiinhia brought to get me and got right up to the comms in the bridge. Perhaps I should let Avie know of the Matrix of Sleprah?

"Take us away, Hiinhia!"

"You got it, Q!"

This time I typed up a message to send to Avie through the secure band:

Sleprah Mission Report: Local tribes grew restless, blaming some object Sleepy called the Matrix of Sleprah for the creatures turning on each other, when really all they needed was a better and more sustainable supply of food. Maurakjnaun will help get them back on their feet. This object interests me, though. They found it in an underground cave in some canyon with imagery of their moon's creation story. Sleepy says the moon itself is the body of Sleprah and the Matrix is the soul. This is far from my area of expertise, but during my dime on Ealtae I had what seemed to be a dream but also seemed so real, that I went through a long system of tunnels and found a cave with a strange cube. It had similar patterns to that of the Matrix of Sleprah so I can't help but wonder if they're connected. Then the strangest thing happened, someone placed their burning hot hand on my shoulder from behind. After what you said about Thraesa being re-discovered, I'm starting to believe there's something larger at work here.

The drop to Aviea and Aliira Center was quick, considering Sleepy2c's close orbit around the planet. Hiinhia and I saw Avie run to the Aliira Leaders' Hangar as we landed inside the mountain base. We quickly exited the ship to see what issues they had for us.

"Avie!" Hiinhia started.

"We have a similar problem in Auqaut, based on the report you sent on your way here Qranyt. Ket is in danger due to the secret station set up on the outskirts of the territory's capital. The base is set up to investigate the presence of a strange artifact. The people of the territory think the artifact is responsible for the increase in wild creatures' violence they have had in the territory lately. It's almost like the wild creatures are being driven to madness and attacking the city and each other!" We walked out of the hangar and started down the long hallway to the Territory Negotiations Center.

"Strange, it seems that there may be a connection between the artifacts. Perhaps they are driving everyone mad!" I responded.

As we entered the Negotiations Center I noticed a large muscular dark cat was already in the room.

"Onyx, " Avie said, "this is Qranyt." The cat came towards me carefully.

"You're the leader of Maurakjnaun, right?" she asked me.

"Yes, I am, and I'm guessing you are Ket's daughter?"

"Sure am. You ready to come get things sorted?"

"Yeah, but I'm just wondering, Avie, what are we supposed to fight off all these animals with?"

"That's where I come in," Onyx said, "I've been working on our territory's automated stun-defenses for a while now. I don't want to kill them, they're just animals and something's got them going crazy. Usually when they wake up from the stun blasts they just walk right back into the badlands they came from."

"And what else?"

"You seem to be picking up on some of the unusual happenings of late and their patterns," Avie replied, "see what you can learn about this artifact they're researching, maybe we can put a stop to whatever's happening."

"Great. Well we aren't accomplishing anything here. C'mon Onyx, let's see what we can do."

We carefully stepped out of the doorway to the landing pad with the small shuttle.

"Whew, that looks tight" Onyx remarked.

"Quick Escape shuttle model," I explained, "meant to carry creatures out of here for quick escapes or missions. This one seems to have been built on Zekj"

"Well you certainly know your spacecrafts Qranyt! I only know weapons," Onyx told me as we climbed into the small, blocky shuttle. Onyx directed her paw to a large plasma burst rifle in the corner. "This one here is my prized weapon of choice. Built it a while back. The original version was made of junk from our recycling center. I can switch it between kill and stun mode at will."

"Impressive!" I told her.

"You think so?"

Onyx flew the ship off the pad, turning to the south-west.

"I see a few possible upgrades you could make..." I said as I examined the piece.

"Yeah? Unfortunately I don't have the parts or the Noctia to get the parts."

"Let me take a look at what I can do."

"Go for it, all yours, just don't break anything."

"Got it—" I reached back to the plasma rifle to take a good look at its components.

"Well Onyx, you've got the basic idea," I reached to my belt to grab some spare parts I carry all the time.

"What's that mean?"

"Your accelerator magnets are a bit out of line, and the containment field a bit underpowered." I made a few adjustments with my multiwrench.

"Yeah, you have any xenon? The cells are almost at equilibrium to the air," Onyx said.

"This ship should have a bit," I reached out for the xenon tank in the opposite corner. "This should get it all charged up. I also adjusted the transformer output to be a bit higher. Should last about two hours by the looks of it."

"Alright, well we're here now," Onyx announced as she brought the shuttle down in the middle of the Auqaut Seppa Detanyt, or the Auqaut Grey Desert.

"Best take this," I lifted a hefty black blade from a dusty case and gave it to Onyx. "For when your power runs out."

"Right, of course!" Onyx agreed, slinging both weapons over her brown nanofiber armor. Auqaut cats are much larger and bulkier than the cats of most other territories, making claymore-type swords more effective weapons to use. Onyx stretching out would be about as long as one and a half of me! I also grabbed my sword and plasma burst pistol.

"Alright, let's get these turrets into position," I directed.

"Right away!"

After several minutes of shifting the legs around in the ground the turrets were anchored in the soft sand, ready to help us defend the capital. Just over the ridge was an expanse of dark badlands for hundreds of kilometers.

"Turrets locked!" I announced.

"How many hours until sunset Qranyt?"

"Six I'd say, why do you ask?"

"That means we have four hours to use that!" Onyx gestured to a giant cannon on a rotating mount. Around the cannon were several giant round dishes that were capturing the light from Solia Noctia. "I rigged that thing up as a giant star-powered stun laser!"

"A sunbeam laser? Wow, that's a surprise! Yeah we can use it for a bit, but once the star reaches a certain altitude the angle will be too low for the light to be captured in the dishes."

"Look there Qranyt!" Off to the northwest a dark cloud was moving toward the city.

"Alright Onyx, we've got company!"

"I'm ready!"

Onyx and I ran to the city as fast as we could. I could already tell the sunbeam laser would take a bit of time to activate, so I got right to work and positioned Onyx outside.

Onyx

Qranyt had me positioned on the edge of the sunbeam base behind a short wall. I watched as the turrets we had set up earlier went to work on the swarms of beasts from the north.

"Should take about ten minutes, Onyx!" I heard Qranyt shout from the inside. I rested my rifle on the wall and started firing at the swarm in the air. The electric bolts hit the swarm and took out a bunch of the creatures. A stampede of animals trampled out one of the three turrets.

"They took down a turret and are advancing on us! Hurry up in there Qranyt!"

"Yeah, you have some sort of access chip? It says it needs the code from an access chip."

"Yeah, uh, alright I got it," I replied as I dug a small memory chip out of a slot in my armor. After observing the position of the attackers, I grabbed the plasma rifle and leapt into the laser control room. Qranyt was typing away on a large console when I landed inside.

"You got it? It plugs in right here I think," Qranyt gestured to a small slot in the wall. The moment I inserted the chip the entire room rotated around.

"Whew! Alright sir now what?"

"The laser controls are on the upper level, you can take out the swarms while I check out the artifact's location."

"Alright, sure"

"And," Qranyt paused before walking out the door, "do lock the doors to the laser building, don't want any intruders to find you."

"Will do, good luck Qranyt!" I let Qranyt out the door before heading upstairs and putting the laser base on lockdown. In the laser assault room there were hundreds of controls. I opened the polarized window and turned the laser turret to the swarms of creatures just as the last of the turrets we set up earlier was shredded. I immediately zoomed in on the swarms and opened the lens apertures, focusing over 30 square kilometers of light from Solia Noctia on the swarm.

"Ha!" I laughed as the swarm began to diminish. Even as I cooked the crazy out of the creatures, more filled in. This was going to be a long fight.

Qranyt

It didn't take long for me to find the research station where the artifact was located. The facility was surrounded by tall fences and cement walls, each locked up by fancy security protocols. The doors were locked up by strong keypads that, despite their strength, were easily overcome by my electronic skills.

As soon as I broke through the cement wall's door, I could sense something was off. A grim mist flowed around the base, where in the center lay an instrument-filled crater. In the crater anyone could clearly see the artifact, wired up to dozens of terminals and screens. I slid down the side of the crater and reached out to the artifact, but to no good result. I felt a great wave of pressure hit my body and fling it back outside of the crater. Slowly coming back to my senses and looking back to the object, I noticed that words were appearing on one of the screens.

Hello Qranyt.

"What!?" I said aloud, was someone sending a message, or was this the object? The object was a flattened round shape, a disk but with no sharp edges. It was black in color with silver details circling its surface in different directions. I approached again, only to feel a sharp pain in my skull as if the inside of my brain was trembling. The screens flashed and read a new message:

Hello Qranyt. I can't let you touch the disc.

"Fine," I took a seat, "what's this all about!?"

Not you. Not yet.

"This is the disc, talking to me?"

I'm influencing the text on the screen you see before you. I am not the disc, I am sentient. You are not allowed to touch the disc.

"Are you causing the creatures here to go crazy?"

...

"The creatures outside grow restless, violent, they're hurting others and themselves."

It's their fault.

"What does that mean?"

The creatures of your territory Auqaut found this vessel, attached all these wires and computers and devices! They're warping the function of the disc and it's making the creatures' brains change!

"Okay, I got it, you want me to disconnect you and they'll go back to normal?"

No. You will not touch the disc!

Another burst of energy rushed through my skull and kicked my body back,

"Okay, then Ket? Maybe Onyx?"

It's too late for that, Qranyt.

The dark cat Ket came out from a corner I hadn't noticed earlier, bearing a menacing plasma rifle and training it on my position.

"Okay, so you did something to Ket, but what, made her a slave? What about Onyx? If you let Onyx free you will Ket be free?"

Onyx. She could be strong enough to free me. I will try to hold off the effects of the Key of Auqaut long enough for you to bring her to me.

Onyx

The power of the sunbeam was dying down as the star reached the low position over the horizon where its light was minimal. Unfortunately, the fight looked far from over. Animals were pounding on the walls, beasts of all types and sizes. I heard the door below explode open, and the creatures sped upstairs to take me down. Suddenly, the unthinkable happened. The creatures slinked back out of the laser control room and started back north.

"Onyx! Come quick! We need you!" I heard Qranyt yell from below. I quickly got to my senses and went to see what was up.

"Yeah Qranyt, what is it?"

"I found the artifact, this way," he grabbed my shoulder and sprinted towards the city.

"Are the creatures done attacking now?"

"Not quite yet Onyx, I found your mother too, she was possessed by the artifact just as those animals were."

"The artifact, what is it?"

"It," Qranyt skidded to a halt and dropped me in a heap, "I think it is the Key of Auqaut, some kind of weapon as well as database for knowledge, maybe?"

"Okay?" I responded, puzzled, as we entered the stronghold. "Anything else?"

"It wouldn't let me touch it, but it said the creatures would stop attacking if you were strong enough to free it?"

"The artifact talks?"

"No," he pointed, "It writes to that screen."

"I see, mom!"

"Oh my Onyx! You're here!" Ket ran to me and purred, "Qranyt, the key won't control her too will it?"

"I'm afraid that is up to Onyx, not us. Onyx, you must take the key. It might try to control you, but you must believe in yourself. Use all of the strength that you have and take hold of the key!"

"Your territory's key!" my mother announced.

"My territory?" I asked with surprise, an instant before the key wrapped the mist around and pulled me in.

I could barely hear Qranyt's instructions, "Block out the key's power Onyx!"

"You can do it!" my mother cried.

The key was strong, whatever it is, and it knows how to put up a fight. I felt as the key built dark walls in my mind, as if it were trying to block my emotions and thoughts, to redirect the very currents in my neurons. I felt my body collapse as my mind was transported to a new place.

"What is this?" I said aloud, not expecting a response.

"*Onyx,*" a soft voice began, I opened my eyes to see a vast dark desert and a grey, empty sky. "*You are the correct keeper of the Key of Auqaut. Time itself brought you here, but only those strong enough can ESCAPE!*"

In a flash, the ground broke open, taller, thicker, darker walls of unknowable substance and origin shot into space all around me.

"*Now RUN! Onyx!*"

Was this some sort of maze in my mind? Did the key find its way in my mind or did I find a way into it? Either way, I didn't have much time to think, as a fast moving dark liquid began to fall from over the walls, quickly approaching and filling the space in between. I needed to find a way out!

Good thing about being a large feline? You can run quick; I shot down the alley between the towering walls as the new wall of dark sludge fell down from above, but which way to go? At the fork I bounded off the wall and took a left turn. Up ahead was a dead end, but a hole cut out just a bit off the ground. I shot through the hole into a new alley, this one had three different directions to choose from, so I turned right. Was that the right way to choose? Did it matter? I could run quickly, but I was losing energy and the wall of dark liquid was always just behind... I needed to think up a new strategy as I ran. Then I thought, if this is in my mind, maybe I can control the rules of this maze just as the key can? Maybe I can fight back?

THUD! I tripped on a short wall in the middle of the path, sending me flat on the ground, the sludge barreling down on me like a tidal wave.

"No, no no no!" I said, scrambling back to my feet. I turned, faced with another wave of sludge, I was surrounded. "Come on, Onyx! Focus!"

It was too late! The dark liquid crashed down on top of me, swirling me out of control until I'd lost all sense of direction. I gathered up all the energy in my body that was left, and in one final push,

"*NO!*" I screeched, the sludge blasted back away from me as I fell back to the ground, now was my chance!

I gathered my senses and ran to the nearest wall, UP, I thought, and barreled up the side like it was a part of the ground itself. I was taking control. Atop the wall, I watched as the sludge crashed back down, but then it started to climb the walls!

"Not so fast!" I shouted down at the maze floor, "door?" I said, concentrating on the thought of an opening before me. Sure enough, a bright circle of light beamed towards me.

I felt my mind clear up again as I opened my eyes. My vision was fuzzy but sure enough I could see Ket and Qranyt before me. Suddenly I felt my grasp over the key, the mist cleared, and I could now see the dark disk, with a silver metal design over it. The Key of Auqaut.

"Onyx! Onyx!" they both yelped,

"What happened?" Ket said as she held my side, while Qranyt held my head.

I looked up from the key to see them both looking astonished. Dark stones began to rise in the air. With no warning, the stones shot outward, shattering the cement wall and the fence. Qranyt leaned down to the wreckage and grabbed something out of the cement.

"You got the key!" Ket exclaimed.

"Whew. Took all of my energy though," I growled with exhaustion.

"What I said earlier, about it being your territory, you must lead the territory of Auqaut now Onyx,"

"Mother?"

"No, Onyx, go with Qranyt, lead this territory with all you have. Learn the universe, work with Avie and Akjaeir. I will help you by rebuilding while you help us all from afar."

Qranyt

"Onyx, did you learn anything new about the key?" I asked as we headed back to the transport we arrived in.

"It built some kind of maze in my head, I only came back to my senses after I fought it out of my head and regained control."

"Then there were those rocks floating around you! Did you do that?"

"I really don't know, it's all slipping away like a dream almost. I'll need to lay down in the back of the transport, I'm sorry."

"It's all good Onyx, I'll get us back to the Leaders' Center."

I stepped up to the controls on the shuttle and sealed the hatch before sending in a voice report to Avie.

"Avie, our mission is complete here, all is back to normal. Onyx and I are departing Auqaut for the Aliira Leaders' Center Tower. I'll give you a full report when I arrive."

Just below the base of the Leaders' Tower is a small private landing zone, big enough to land our shuttle. Avie met us as we touched down.

"Grrrrrfffph" I heard Onyx sigh in the back.

"Come on up with us, Onyx, there's some beds in the guest area!"

Avie led us up through the tower base to the central elevator. Leaders' Center was mostly white in color, on both inside and outside. That way it would reflect most of the light of Solia Noctia to keep cool. Up inside the central lobby of the Leaders' Center was a large circle of comfy sofas around a circular glass table. Despite the nearby guest bedrooms, Onyx went straight for the sofas and collapsed on one, laying across almost the whole thing.

"This way, Qranyt." Avie directed me to a smaller room, the mission records room. "What happened out there, Qranyt?" they continued, closing the door to the lobby.

"It's another similar object, it seems. It looks different than the last though, a dark disk with silver details on its surface."

"Was it causing the strange behavior in the animals?"

"It seems like it was, though possibly not directly. The disc itself seemed to be able to display messages on the screens it was hooked up to, and it claimed the instruments were the reason for the animals' behavior."

"It talked to you?"

"Yeah, it makes me wonder if there's some sort of AI in it or creature, like Sleepy claimed was in the Matrix of Sleprah."

"This is most unusual, I'll get to looking for any other strange phenomena in the three systems."

"The only thing that makes sense is that it seemed to control a strong magnetic field. I think that would make the animals run crazy out of fear and confusion, and even cause the pain I felt in my head when I approached. After Onyx grabbed the key and pulled it from the instruments, a bunch of dark rocks lifted into the air in a circle and shot into the cement walls. Wait—" I reached into one of my pockets, "here's one of them!"

Avie took the stone from my paw, placing it into some sort of spectrometer instrument.

"It's a mix of magnetite, nickel, and solid iron." Avie said after a brief moment, "Certainly would respond to a magnetic field, but that must have been a very complex field for it to have controlled that many rocks like that in the way that you've described."

"You think all this has anything to do with the reappearance of ze'Thraesa?"

They paused for a moment in thought, "Almost certainly."

"What do we do now, Avie?"

"I'm organizing a new task force, Qranyt. I'll need you in charge when I can't be around to lead the group, but we're going to need to learn more about these keys."

"Who's going to be a part of this task force, Avie?"

"Us, and hopefully anyone who's ever touched one of those objects. Plus Hiinhia and Ehnri too if they're willing. I think that's the best way to track down exactly what these things are."

"I have a feeling it won't be long before we find the next key or matrix, Avie..."

"That's where you come in, the *Soliean Protectors.*"

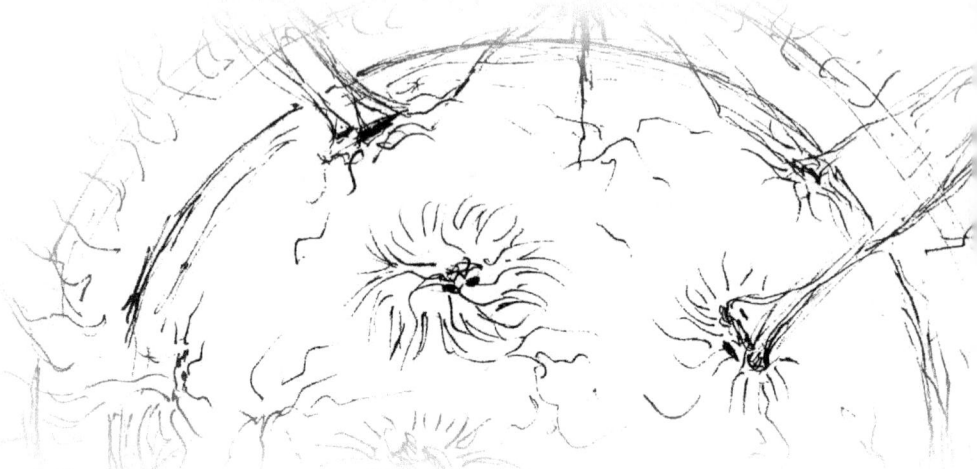

07. PROTECTORS

It's been a few days since the fight in Auqaut, a few days of peace and quiet we've been quite happy to have. All of us have been united for one specific reason, this peace will not last forever.

"We are gathered today, Qranyt, Sleepy, Onyx, Ehnri, and Hiinhia, as the new group of Soliean Protectors, to discuss the past. Today we will share what information we have gained throughout the years, starting with me. This will mark the official start of our investigation. Listen carefully to the past of the Three Stars, as told through my aged eyes."

We were new and inexperienced, Akjaeir and I. We dreamed together of a world that was not governed by war and violence, no need for strict borders and regulations. We left our world, an old world, removed from history by the thousands of years that had passed. In our search for peace we found the planet Aviea, a beautiful world of such diversity and and spiritual wealth. On Aviea we were able to extend our time to live by millions of years, not to become rich and powerful gods, no, but instead, as we believed, to become the most benevolent beings in all of creation. We simply wanted to see it all and protect those who had less than us. The being that experiences all is the most intelligent, the most powerful. That being's weapon is not forged of metal and death, its weapon is forged of stars, life, and creation. This weapon's power is derived from the number of lives it saves, the magnitude of beauty found by the one who wields such a weapon. Through this belief we built Solia. First there was one star, then two, and finally all three stars worked together to create technology we could not imagine centuries earlier. Together we became the Leaders of Solia. We showed the universe hope, creation, and life, but we knew that this would not always be sustained, so we decided to initiate a program to travel to the most unknown regions of space, to seek a manner in which we could keep everyone safe for all eternity, a method to protect the entire universe.

Who even knows if the story we think is true really was. What we recall may have all been a lie we told to each other to hide what really happened. That's when Akjaeir set out to find answers. The sieqtae tribes of Ealtae convinced her that what she sought was a place called Kiraveal, the planet of pure light, where they believe all life was created. That was her mission, on a starship she designed herself she flew across the entire universe searching for this world of light. Kqaet-Avai, her ship, disappeared those thirty ovitrae years ago, perhaps never to return. Then of course we discovered Thraesa, a piece of technology so old that we forgot it even existed. At this point, who can even say if who built it or if it was there before we even existed. Either way, once Thraesa was discovered, Solia was changed permanently. Thraesa showed us a future of war and pain, the future we sought to avoid was soon to unfold upon us. We need to find a way to stop it from starting.

Onyx

Our territory's history was simple on the surface, but deep within we always detected a strange presence buried far beneath the ground, the artifact known as the key. Many of us felt as if something was calling us to it, as if the key wanted to be found by us. We searched and searched, until it was finally excavated and held by our government. We studied it, tried to crack it open, find out its secrets but nothing gave. It seemed like the more we tried to break in, the more it looked for ways to fight back until finally all of nature itself came down on us and we stopped probing it for information. Now the key is in my paws alone, and I don't know what to do with it.

Ehnri

I always remember Ealtae's peace, the bright green forests, the soft blue streams, the tall, shining spires of the ancient temples. I do in fact remember the legends of powerful stones, Thraesa, and the times of old. I was born in a small village, where I lived for several years. My parents would tell me of the mysterious outer worlds, shrouded in darkness. I used to think, perhaps there was more to this universe. Sometimes I wished that the legends were real. Perhaps each planet was special in its own way, a little piece of history that could be learned, taught, and used to uncover deeper memories. When I was but a few years old, my parents gave me a stone. It is long lost now, but I thought that perhaps it would be my ancient "soul stone" as they were called in the books. Then the war came. Pond, a snake, was the closest family friend. As my house burned, my parents threw me out the window to Pond, who took care of me up until Qranyt rescued me. All I know of these mysterious items is that they sound like something my friend Safaeir would know about. She once told me she could talk to the planet itself, and hear the stars whisper in the night. Maybe she could hear the secrets of the keys too.

Setai, Sleepy of Sleprah-Daecaser

The moon Sleprah 2 is a world of dust and brick, some say it is nothing more. The truth is, we have our own stories. Perhaps there was no great god or goddess creature, but I know what my family told me and I know what I believe. I was told of our key since birth, an object of legend that would be used to defend, to build, and to change our world's landscape. I was told that the ancient spirit Sleprah sacrificed herself when our tribe was in need. Our ancestors were originally on a giant ship leaving the planet Aviea in a time of sorrow and destruction, our ship was headed for another world but broke down in high orbit around Aviea. Seeing us suffering and trapped on the vessel, our spirit Sleprah stepped in to save us, and in the process she ceased to be. Sleprah-Daecaser may look like a wasteland, but she gave it to us, and we make the most out of her sacrifice every day.

Qranyt

How did such a bear become the leader of the Emerald Territory, you wonder? It all began when I was but a wee little cub. My parents led our territory, a fertile farming territory powered by the furnace of life, literally. Mt. Emerald gave us fertile ash and silt to grow the sugar, kja grain, and swordfruit that we would trade with all other territories on the planet, as it was there that it grew best. Something was stirring in the core of the volcano, though. Many had tried to figure out what caused the sudden changes in climate, but to no success. Soon our territory was starved, shaken with fear of their losses increasing beyond the borders. And that they did. Soon the entire planet was beginning to starve. The heroes of the city drained out, they found a way into the volcano, and tried their best to find the source of the problem. Not a single being returned from the depths. Soon my parents decided that enough was enough, and they headed in themselves. My father was the only creature to ever escape the volcano's core, and he gave me the one thing that could save the planet: The Core

Emerald. After my father died, I worked as fast as I could to find a new path to the heart of the volcano, one nobody else had discovered. I used the Core Emerald to heal the centerpiece, and save the territory's crops.

In the wake of Mt. Emerald's disaster having shook the entire world, Avie invited me to lead a new team of creatures to defend the Soliean creatures against the unknowns of our planet. I believe that this Core Emerald may have some connection to the keys due to the effects it had on the volcano so long ago. Perhaps this was the core of the volcano calling out like the other keys.

Hiinhia

Our future is dark, so dark I can hardly remember what happened. I was left to lead one of Ealtae's Highland territories, yet I didn't know how to fight. I was a cowardly small bear, no use in the war efforts. What do I remember of the future? Avie and the Soliean Protectors traveled to the dark worlds and found a new enemy, one that escaped from Thraesa and began to destroy each world of Solia, one by one. Our team had new weapons, powerful ones that they used to fight the darkness. They were there, on Ealtae, you were there. Suddenly, another rift to Thraesa opened, and a ship came crashing through near the strange, mysterious, Pyramid of Life. After that I was discovered by the Avie of the past and Ket, they brought back here. I am afraid that is all I have to share.

08. POWER OF STONES

[Aviea Island Leaders' Center, Aliira, Aviea]

Qranyt

❝Well I hope all that information got your gears turning, it certainly did for me!" I laughed to the team.

"Yeah, so now what should we do, Avie?" Hiinhia looked up.

As I looked about the room, a small piece of paper caught my eye. I reached out and took a closer look.

Don't tell anyone about this note!

The next key must be found, it is in your home. Where do you think it could be? Try to get the team to go to your home; you'll thank me later. Don't tell them about the note though! They must not know! I will see you soon,

~A

Strange; Who would write this message, and why they would want to hide it? My thoughts were cut short by Avie.

"We should follow these keys—" Avie started, giving me a chance to reveal the existence of a key in my home territory. I decided to go along with the note's plan, hoping this was a "benefactor" and not a trap.

"Wait," I interrupted, "I feel something, perhaps another key."

"Where is it?" Ehnri piped in.

"I think, my home, Emerald Territo—."

"Can we go?" Ehnri interrupted excitedly.

"I don't see why not!" laughed Avie, "Okay team! Let's find us some more answers!"

"Yeah, we can get your trade sorted out too, Sleepy!"

"You're right, Ehnri, we'll get Sleepy all set up. Our farmers would be honored to take part in helping you!"

"Let's go!" Sleepy added.

The note I found was just plain weird, but what bothered me even more was the signature, the "A" at the end. Within minutes, Avie had the team on a shuttle to the Emerald Territory. I suspected they were the most likely culprit, but why act weird about it? If they'd mentioned it to the team themself we would have gone along all the same...

"Where do you think this key is?" Hiinhia asked on the shuttle.

"Hate to say it, but you might have been right, Qranyt," Avie said.

"Of course I was!" I replied; I could feel my eyes shift nervously.

"Wait, so is this right referring to the volcano by any chance?" Onyx inquired, "I'm not walking into a volcano..."

"I don't think that will be necessary, right Qranyt?" my apprentice looked up.

"You're right, Hiinhia, nobody wants to walk into a volcano, we're jumping into the volcano!"

"You're insane, Qranyt!" Onyx screeched.

"He's done it before..." Avie and Hiinhia stated, harmonized.

Sleepy quickly chimed in, "Really? That's pretty epic if you ask me!"

"Here's your chance guys, who wants to join the drop crew?" I asked.

"Soo not happening!" Onyx retreated.

"I can get trade negotiations started while you are busy, Onyx you can come along with me if you'd like."

"I won't miss out on a chance like this Qranyt! I'm joining the drop!" Sleepy announced.

Hiinhia also agreed, explaining he had already dropped from high altitudes before.

"Ehnri, you can come too if you are up for it, you'll just want to stay with me on the way down."

"Oh now you're just irresponsible!" Onyx scoffed.

"Okay!" Ehnri replied.

"Alright everyone let's get suited up; Onyx and I will position you over Mt. Emerald for the drop before flying into Viikja City." Avie announced, taking a quick look at the shuttle's positioning system.

"Okay Ehnri, Sleepy, Hiinhia— you all set?" I asked as I helped Ehnri get adjusted on my chest, Ehnri of course being too little for his own parachute pack.

"Eeeeerrr" Ehnri replied, squeezed by the straps holding him in place.

"Yeah sorry about that, Ehnri."

"I think we're good to go!" Sleepy declared.

Hiinhia soon followed, "Sure, I'm ready!"

"There goes West Akjurkjna and the Maurakjnaun Channel!" Onyx stared out the large window. Ehnri and Sleepy rushed beside her to look out on the west coast of Maurakjnaun running parallel to W. Akjurkjna Peninsula. The west coast of Maurakjnaun is covered in dense forest, where several dark and wild plants grow.

Soon the shuttle was gliding over the treetops and up the slope of Mt. Emerald, Siinhaunuu Maurakjnaun! The slope of the mountain exponentially increased, the shuttle pulling a great amount of acceleration as it sped into the air.

"Here goes!" I shouted, pulling the switch to open the side door. "You'll want to dive straight towards the caldera's edge! Pull the cord to the chute on my signal!"

"Cya later, Qranyt!" Avie said over the sound of air rushing by.

"So long!" I replied, falling backwards out of the door. As I tipped into diving position I saw Sleepy and Hiinhia jump to join me in the fall.

"Everything is so pretty up here!" Ehnri commented as loudly as he could muster up with his small lungs. I watched as the shuttle flew back below us and off to the city in the west. "Your territory is amazing Qranyt!"

"You haven't even seen the best of it yet Ehnri!" I told him. "OKAY EVERYONE!" My chute shot out of my pack the instant I pulled the cord. I heard the other two packs successfully burst open and fill with air as Hiinhia and Sleepy followed my lead. The four of us came to a slow descent over the caldera of Siinhaunuu Maurakjnaun, where we could see multiple vents spewing hot lava and steaming water.

"This looks safe!" Hiinhia laughed as we skidded across the edge to a halt.

"Alright team pack your chutes and let's get moving!"

Unfortunately the jagged summit of Mt. Emerald makes it difficult to land anything there, even someone with a parachute doesn't have much space to drop to. As soon as our bags were packed up, I led the three through the grey spires marking the summit.

"That was—so cool!!!" Sleepy said excitedly.

"This tunnel here should bring us where we want to go." I directed.

"I'm trusting you, Qranyt!" Hiinhia followed.

"How hot will it be down there?" asked Ehnri.

"It will get a bit toasty, but this tunnel has been blocked off for centuries."

"It'll be fine! Let's get going before it gets too dark!" Sleepy eagerly suggested, pulling a light orb from his belt.

~   ~   ~

The beginning of the tunnel was quite steep and required careful shifts in weight to keep from tumbling into the volcano's core. I kept in the front of the line, Sleepy behind me. Hiinhia and Ehnri were at the back, keeping close together. The smooth lava rock made keeping a grip difficult, even with all the climbing gear I hadn't had the first time around.

"You'll need to press your back to the wall behind you, your feet to the wall in front!" I said, "Don't want to slip and fall below, we want to take this slow!"

"These scars in the rock, are they the ones you made when you came through before?" Sleepy inquired.

"Yeah, I only had a few rough hooks and a rock pick."

We shuffled on for a bit, sinking a good hundred meters into the volcano through tube after tube before anything seemed to change.

"How much further? It's starting to get warm in here" Hiinhia pressed.

"There's a good sign! The hotter it gets the closer we are!" The tunnel slowly leveled out, giving us only a slight incline to walk down.

"I think I feel it too." Sleepy whispered, his voice echoing down the tunnel infinitely. He carefully removed his moon's key, which suddenly lit from deep within, the yellow core illuminating the tunnel far more than any of the light orbs. A surge of energy flowed through the tunnel as the key glowed.

"Let's run!" I directed, taking the first steps into my sprint. The walls shifted into narrow strips of smooth rock as I remembered from before, but this time a strange green glow shone through the cracks, up until the core.

We soon reached the core of the volcano, where I recognized the Core Emerald. Underneath the hexagonal stone console where the Core Emerald glowed nestled six panels of stone that, it seemed, could block an entrance of some kind.

"Woah" I could hear the others gasp as they entered the chamber.

"Alright let's see what we've got" I said, stepping forward to the Core.

"Qranyt," Sleepy called, tossing me a 3D scanner, "Got this!"

"Thanks, Sleepy, " I said as I caught the device. The Core Emerald seemed to be attracted to my presence, and quickly responded to my touch with a pulse of light.

"I think it likes you Qranyt!" Ehnri purred. I did a quick scan of the Core Emerald's geometry before tossing the scanner back to Sleepy.

I once again reached out to the Core, "Alright guys step back... here goes!"

I grabbed on to the Emerald, which began to illuminate patterns on the ceiling of the cavern. The six stone slabs shifted below the floor, revealing a tube for the center where I stood to slowly sink further into the ground. The others tried to get to me, but I gestured for them to stay back as the stone slabs moved back into place.

The tunnel then was overcome by darkness, leaving only the light of the Core Emerald. This part of the volcano I had never seen before, a tunnel of darkness that stretched several kilometers deep. Several minutes of darkness passed, so I held the Core Emerald tight and closed my eyes. Just as I did, I felt the console accelerate downward, not as if it were moving faster, but more as if time was passing much quicker than usual. The pad came to a halt, and I slowly opened my eyes. The walls were jagged, snug tight at the bottom against the pad. Only one way out from the shaft I'd descended down, and it was a narrow passage, almost too narrow for me to fit through.

I shuffled my gear around, moving my pack to the side and scrunching into the split left-side first. With my head turned to the left as well, I could see another green glow just ahead in an opening. Scrunch after scrunch, I moved through the tight space. I could see I was making progress, but it was slow. I removed a spare light orb from my pack and whipped it down the split into the open space. The room filled with a bright white light, where, sure enough, I could see a stone pedestal with something on top. That must be it! A few more determined scrunches and the split began to open back up.

The Key of Emerald, deep within Siinhaunuu Maurakjnaun. The Key itself was in the shape of the most pure shape of an emerald, covered by a complex design of iridescent pure noctium metal. On each side, three rhombus emblems of Early Emerald Territory were positioned on top of each other over the glowing crystal center, outlined with a detailed network of noctium embossings.

I carefully stepped to face the key, which shone stronger and stronger as I reached for it. When I touched the smooth glassy surface, the key instantly created three green loops of energy, like cracking electric fire that spun around both itself and my body. As if automatically, my left arm moved to control the motion of the energy, allowing it to flow in all directions in the chamber. I slowly took hold and removed the key from its resting place on the stone, backing up to the passage I came through. I held the key tight and looked to the tunnel wall. Now, how to get back out?

The edges of my vision swirled and swayed as I slumped to the floor.

Sleepy

Qranyt had been gone for hours, we began to wonder if he would ever come back this way, and decided it was likely his tunnel could have another exit.

"Hey Sleepy, you have some paper or something?" Hiinhia asked me.

"Yeah, somewhere around here, a pen too."

"Write him a note? Sure!" Ehnri agreed.

"Here we go..." I put the paper on the wall and began to write a brief message.

Hey Qranyt, hope you're as okay as we are and you got the key safely, buuut we were a bit concerned you might have found another exit. Anyways we are gonna look around a bit if you don't mind, so if you do find this note, follow our—

"What are we leaving behind for Qranyt to follow?" I asked the others.

"I don't know, you're the one with all the stuff!" Hiinhia replied.

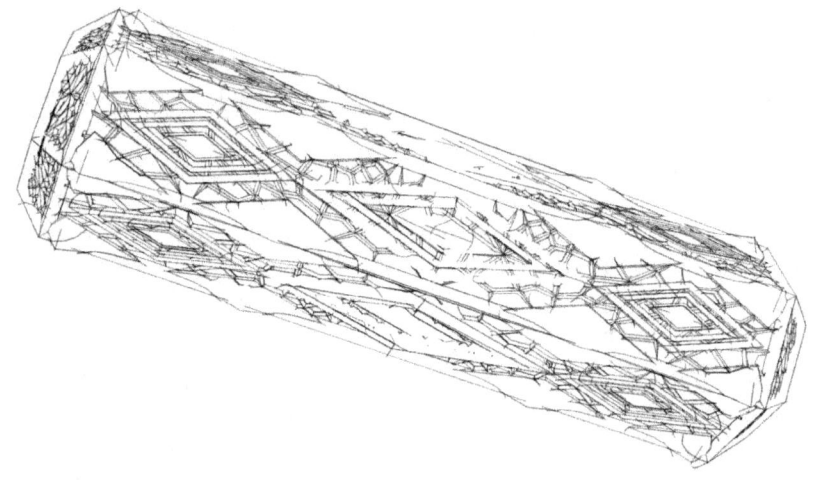

"How 'bout we use your key? Maybe you can use it to track Qranyt?"

"Nice idea Ehnri!" I complemented the fuzzy thing.

—follow my key using the special powers of the magical key-whatever. Cya Qranyt! -Sleepy and the others!

I stuck the paper to the cavern wall with a bit of glue, then held out the Key of Sleepy2c just as the room shook and the door to the depths opened once more. We watched intently as the console returned to its original position, but this time there was no sign of Qranyt!

"Told you he found another way!" Hiinhia retorted. I once again held out the key, feeling its energy pulse. The light inside the key began to shift to one side.

"He's at the same level as us?" I said out to the others.

"Just, over there..." Ehnri pointed with his nose. "Woah Sleepy your eyes are glowing yellow!"

"They are?" I put the key down to see Ehnri and Hiinhia staring at me.

"Not anymore" Hiinhia shrugged.

"Use the key again Sleepy!" Ehnri told me.

"Sure," I held it out in front of me once more, this time focusing even more energy than before.

"YOUR EYES!" Ehnri screeched!

"Okay, okay," I lowered the artifact once more, "no need to shout! Let's find Qranyt!"

Qranyt

In the fog of my mind I saw an industrial world, Tetratakj. Something, perhaps the key itself, was trying to get my attention on that world. Tetratakj is a planet of pure industry, a planet made entirely of metal and processed asteroid material. We use the world today as a nanotech production location, not much else.

The world faded away and I was left in the dark and silence for another moment.

"This is only a small amount of my power," a voice whispered, *"use it well, Qranyt, and perhaps I'll be your veriise..."*

Swirls of dark gave to a familiar room, just like the one I'd descended from. I pulled myself up and stepped back to the middle console for balance; Sleepy, Hiinhia, they were nowhere to be seen. I scanned the room, looking for evidence of the others, but there was no sign anyone had been to the chamber, ever...

I shook my head, attempting to gather my senses. *"Veriise? What does that mean?"* No matter, I needed to get back to the others before working it all out or they'd likely get lost.

No entrance tunnel in this room—not even the signs of a closed off door. This was not the room I started in. Carefully stepping from the center, I observed the key.

"Key of Emerald... do you have a way out of the volcano?" I asked the artifact. No response, perhaps as expected. I held the key out and shook it around a bit, then focused on it as if I wanted to pass all of my energy to its heart. The key shot the three bright green energy rings out once more, each one spinning around the key with an immense power. But what to do with them?

I focused on one of the rings, trying to control how it spun. Was it a weapon? I flicked my paw towards the wall and the ring skidded along the rocky surface. It didn't seem to leave any mark or anything, just made a sort of hissing sound and bounced off. I brought it back towards me, wondering what it would feel like to touch the ring itself. Upon making contact with the ring, the green glowing energy enveloped me in an orb of more glowing energy, then everything went dark and I felt weightless. The surprise made me blink, and when I opened my eyes I was surrounded by darkness filled with glowing green threads, almost like a web. Was this ze'Thraesa? Maybe the key had some sort of connection to it?

I of course only heard rumors of Thraesa, unlike Avie, Ket, and Hiinhia who had actually ventured inside, yet somehow it all became a memory to me. Thoughts flooded my head, blueprints, layouts, maps of every thread and every mechanic of Thraesa, it felt like I knew everything about Thraesa. Every tiny detail of how I could pull certain threads, how I could travel to other worlds, not only was it in my head now, it felt like it had been there all along. I searched for the thread that would bring me back to the chamber with the others. From the thousands of tiny green filaments, I reached out to the one that would bring me back to them. A strange glow erupted from the key before I could pull on the thread, causing me to bump into a different one!

There! I appeared, back in the chamber tunnels, but not with the others... I heard faint voices coming from the wall,

"Hello?" I called into the dark tunnel.

"Shhhh! What was that!" I heard a voice ask. I knocked on the wall a few times, waiting for a response.

"Was that Qranyt?" another voice asked. I held the key out in front of me, then bent the energy loops to form a ring.

"I'm coming! Stand back!" I shouted, trying to force even more energy into the key. The ring burst, creating a hole straight through the wall, seemingly made by Thraesa itself. I stepped through, greeted on the other side by the warm yellow glow of Sleepy's key.

"Qranyt!" Sleepy exclaimed, "I knew we would see you again!"

"Nice key!" Hiinhia shrugged.

Ehnri, of course, "Your eyes are glowing green Qranyt!"

"Some move you pulled there, jumping through the wall!" Setai remarked, reaching to give me a pat on the shoulder.

"Apparently this key has a connection to Thraesa, I'm not sure what else it can do other than moving me around through walls, but now it's like I know everything about the inside world of Thraesa, like the key told me how to travel there!"

"Well whatever it has connection to, we should get back to your city and Avie." Hiinhia reminded us.

"Cool!" Ehnri exclaimed with much excitement.

Avie

After Qranyt and the others had been dropped off at the volcano, Onyx and I flew off to the Capital of Maurakjnaun Territory, Viikja City.

"Alright Onyx, let's take this ship into the hangar, shall we?"

"This place looks amazing, Avie!"

"Well, tell that to Qranyt, it's his home!" I told her as I set the shuttle down in the cave-like hangar carved out in the side of the Maurakjnaun Channel's cliffs. "He has been taking great care of his territory since he first became Laersana here!"

"Wow! Aquat has no chance of becoming this amazing!" Onyx said with awe as she ran out of the ship to look in the water. "He has hangars right on the water! And," she ran to the stairway to the surface, "What could possibly be up here?!"

"Why don't you go find out later—the S.R.S. is right over this way."

"Aww come on," she sprinted over, "S.R.S.?"

"Yeah, the Subterranean Rail System, a network of fast levitating snake-like vehicles." We walked down the long ramp to the Rail Station, where a white Rail Transport waited for us.

"Aquat needs these too!"

A hatch opened in the side of the transport, revealing a large compartment with several rows of three seats each.

Then Onyx asked me, "Why's it so empty in here, Aev?"

"Everyone is off doing things; traveling, playing games, growing food, celebrating!"

"Wow! Really?"

In no time the worm craft pulled into the Leader's Center Building of Viikja City. As soon as the elevator reached the main floor, Onyx and I saw thousands of bears and cats roaming about, some were dancing to live music, others were fencing or playing different games. Some were just walking about talking. In the center of it all, a gleaming golden orrery of the entire Noctia star system.

"Maurakjnaun is amazing!" Onyx said as we came to the stony road in front of the Leader's Building.

"Alright Onyx, let's get to the point on why we are here, we need to help set up trade with Sleepy2c."

Ehnri

"This is so cool Qranyt! You can use Thraesa?" I asked, looking towards the big bear.

"I guess so! Alright everyone, hold on again, I found Avie!" Qranyt pulled one of the threads, landing us somewhere outside of the volcano.

"WAHH!!" Onyx shrieked in surprise.

"Just in time!" Avie remarked, "Sleepy and Qranyt you can get the trade sorted out! Ehnri and Hiinhia, what did you see in the tunnels?"

"He found the key of Emerald!" I said, "and Sleepy's eyes glowed yellow, and Qranyt's eyes glowed GREEN! Qranyt can walk through walls now!"

"there goes our privacy..." I heard Onyx mutter.

"So there was writing on the wall mentioning Tetratakj?" I overheard Avie ask Qranyt.

"Yeah, that was before I closed my eyes and ended up in the second chamber."

"Can we go to Tetratakj too?" I requested from the group.

"Looks like we'll need to learn more about these keys, it seems like they're powerful technology they might know about on Tetratakj!" Hiinhia said, "I've never been to Solia Aqua before either!"

"Of course! I want to go too!" Sleepy exclaimed.

"So be it then. Qranyt, get ready to teleport us all there!" Onyx said.

"Yeah, I'm drained." Qranyt uttered back. "I think that might be a little far for me on my first day..."

"Taking all your energy away, is it?" Sleepy asked, returned with a funny look from Qranyt.

"Well we should get right on our way then, we don't want to sit around here until night passes by," announced Avie.

We all clambered onto a Personal Maurakjnaun Shuttle, which we could use for quick passage to Noctae. Noctae was a super dark world, covered in smooth black rock and water. This planet is special though, as it is the planet of the giant starships. Noctae is the command planet for all of the Soliean Fleet! I'd never been there before, but Avie, Qranyt, and Hiinhia have.

"Maurakjnaun looks so teeny from up here!" I mewed, peering out from the shuttle window. "Do we get to land on Noctae?"

"Not this time," Avie said, "but I'm sure you will soon!" They pressed some buttons and said something into the message thing, a Dawn Starship? Dust classed?

Qranyt showed me how to play a game of scidyrocks while we flew to Noctae, and he won all three times! At the end of the third game we pulled up to a space station and I could see Noctae out the window but it was really dark against the spacey background.

Avie pointed through the top window to a narrow black and blue spaceship with really big strong engines and said something that I forgot.

"This way, Ehnri!" Avie motioned me towards the exit, "Our ship is ready!"

The inside of the station was busy with lots of creatures going this way and that, but our route to the other starship was quick, and soon we were boarding a big fancy Noctael Explorer craft!

Tetratakj, Avie explained, is really far away. The planet is a giant city that has tall towers, so from space it looks just like the sticky burrs I'd get stuck on me back at home. Because of this, the planet has a big atmosphere, you can only breathe on the main floor! Avie also explained how the planet is important for the creation of tiny electronics we use every day. Then of course, they told us to all go to bed, as it would take a lot of hours flying through the space between the stars for us to get there! Tetratakj doesn't even orbit Solia Noctia, it orbits a whole different star called Solia Aqua!

Hiinhia

The ship approached the planet Tetratakj straight on, giving us a good view of the spiked planet. Qranyt set the ship down in a large hangar, where the team got out to take a look around.

"The most important thing to remember here," Avie started, "Don't trip... ANYWHERE!"

"Certainly not a good place for people afraid of heights!" I commented, looking out the large hangar window all the way to the core of the planet.

"Yeah guys, no falling to oblivion!" Onyx laughed as we continued on to the main hallways.

"This should be the central factory tower, with the information on the entirety of the facility," Avie explained.

"What exactly are we looking for?" I asked the team.

"Maybe an older section in the factory with a database on past productions?" Qranyt suggested as he searched a map terminal.

"There," pointed Sleepy, "that room looks promising." The large narrow stretch on the map appeared to contain arrays of data chips put into storage.

"Well there we have a place to begin!" Ehnri exclaimed, "I can't wait to find out what these keys are!"

As we traveled to the lower levels of the main factory tower, I began to think back on my previous life. I thought I had remembered something from before the war, something about the keys being used to access a stronger tool, but all of my past memories were blurred together by then. All I had left of them was jumbled bits of history that still has yet to come. It made sense though, they must have been called keys for a reason...

The Factory Database was just as it looked on the map. The room was long and tall, but only a few meters wide.

"Here! I found a consooolleeee!" Ehnri shouted to the rest of the team.

"I just realized, where is everyone?" I asked Avie.

"Many of the older and outdated factories such as this one have yet to be repurposed. Tetratakj's trade with Kjitafor has been at a bare minimum, so the world is having a difficult time re-establishing its factories, plus, a lot of the factory efforts have been moved to the ring of Zekj." Avie replied as we went to find Ehnri.

"Great find Ehnri!" Sleepy exclaimed.

"It seems as if the database can only be downloaded with an older model datapad, something that you don't find very often lately." Qranyt reported, examining the console's circuitry.

"Thank goodness we have a not-so-often with us!" Sleepy stated excitedly, pulling a box-like device from some pocket of his sandy cloth armor.

"You're full of surprises, Sleepy!" Onyx laughed, "No clue what we would have done without you!"

After Qranyt got the datapad hooked up to the old console, we were able to recover parts of a file on the device file labeled "Keys and Matrixes," which we downloaded to Sleepy's datapad and read off a projection.

Keys and Matrices

*** Summary of the matri██ oratory ██ earch before closure. ***

One of the formative ████████ ████ actories of Tetratakj
██ s the research ████████████ of ██
ecame underst ██████ an█ atrice ███████ nanostructure
laboratories investig ████████ detail of any key
████████ wasn't many, ██ e results ███████ ible.
████████ structure of ████
comprehension, ████ ture it ██████████ change right

The engineering ██████████████ reate an exact copy of
████ e matrice ██████████ years of resear█
████ fabrication attempt ██████
████ identical form t█████
carried few of the propertie█
████████████████ riginal could break the

Devastate█ ████████████ o idea where to ████████
███████ such an ancient design, th████ ittle the
enginee██ ████ ould do. ████ ne promising lead
located on Ealtar, ████ keptics foun█ t an unsatis██████ to
a "research founded in science."

"Looks like the information's pretty degraded!" I commented. "You got any ideas on how to recover this, Sleepy?"

"Ah, let me have a look!" He jumped into action, "No!"

"Let me see," Qranyt said, "I might be able to get a bit more out of it."

"Ealtar... curious. I seem to have no recollection of the moon's significance." Avie noted. "It seems to say something about the moon of Ealtae, maybe we should head there next."

"Crap." Qranyt grunted,

"What is it?" Onyx slouched over to have a look.

"It's gone! The rest of the file got corrupted even more. It looks like the system was stuck trying to erase it and us pulling it from the archive might have helped."

Avie continued, "Thanks for trying, Qranyt, we might already have our next lead though."

"Well I guess we know where to head next, everyone! To Ealtar!" Ehnri proclaimed just as Solia Aqua rose through the window behind us, bringing a brilliant blue glow into the room.

"A short trip and we're back to Ealtae!" I shrugged at Qranyt.

"It was bound to happen sooner or later," he laughed.

09. MOON OF EALTAE

[Safaeir Ineala's House, River Forest, Ealtae]

Qranyt

We decided to visit Ealtae first to check out a source of information there that Ehnri had in mind, and it obviously wasn't much out of the way. Ehnri led the team to a village he used to visit when he was young, about 23 degrees to the east of his own village in Faelk-kja. On the way he explained how every so often he would fly in a shuttle from village to village helping others with his parents. One cat he remembered was especially into the history of Solia, her name, Safaeir.

"Here we are at Safaeir's house!" Ehnri exclaimed at the door of a mossy cabin embedded in a stony hill, "She knows almost all the legends of Solia!" Behind us I saw several more houses, as well as cats playing and splashing about, hunting for fish in the streams.

"Great!" I told Ehnri as I stepped forward to knock on the rustic wooden door. This village was quite different from the one Ehnri lived in. Instead of being in an open field, this was a river village, located deep in thick Ealtaen forest with narrow, gurgling streams and rivers. Out of the house came a blue-grey cat about the same size as Ehnri.

"Sel[1]—Heluu?" it meowed, glancing around at all the visitors. "Ehnri? Is that you?"

[1] In most tribes of Ealtae, Soletria is either the only spoken language or it is mixed with the common tongue. "Sel'" or "Seleo" is a common greeting ae'Soletria. Safaeir and other children of the sieqtae would be taught their ancestoral language from birth.

"Hey Safaeir! I'm a Soliean Protector now!" Ehnri announced.

"Avie?" Safaeir looked up, "Sel' Laersana!"

Safaeir led the team into the small wood and stone house and sat us at a table made of a giant stone slab.

"I've brought the rest of the Soliean Protectors too!" Ehnri explained as Safaeir prepared some tea, "Avie, Qranyt, Hiinhia, Sleepy, and Onyx!"

"You've been busy Ehnri! Why are you here?"

"Well, we've been searching for answers, " I started.

"Answers? To what?"

"The forgotten past, what lies beyond," Avie continued.

"Little Ehnri here led us to your home! He says you know of many forgotten legends!" Sleepy explained.

"Well, " Safaeir approached, "That was mostly my parents. I lost them in the fight against the aliens, " she whimpered softly.

"I did too, Pond took me out of the fight and kept me safe until Qranyt saved me." Ehnri told her at her side.

"I can still help you," Safaeir said as she placed the tea tray on the stone table. "This home is filled with old books recorded by my great ancestors of old. Many people off Ealtae would think they are crazy, but the cats of this village all have great respect for the forgotten past." Safaeir went to the back of the cabin, where, wrapped in cloth, were several small cat-books.

"Wow." Sleepy remarked as he examined the complex structure of the paw-made books.

"My parents were honored as sieqte, but did not have the gift." She looked back to the shelves, almost as if looking at some distant past beyond them, "Nobody has the gift of sieqte anymore, they're all just teachers of Kiravaen now."

"Here!" Hiinhia pointed, "this one says something about Ealtar!"

"Oooh you want to know about Ealtar?" Safaeir searched.

"We found information on Tetratakj that led us to believing something important may be on Ealtar." Onyx told her.

"Here, I've got more," Safaeir reached for more books on a shelf.

"This is great, Safaeir!" Avie remarked, "Thanks so much for your help!"

"Avie," I mumbled to the side.

"Yes?"

"If I may... Safaeir may be a valuable asset to our investigation, you should invite her to the team...?"

"That would be great!" Ehnri shouted, above the mumbling.

"Oh Ehnri!" I sighed.

"Safaeir?" Avie began.

"Yes, Avie?"

"Would you like to join the team?"

"Of course! I would love to!" Safaeir exclaimed, jumping to hug Avie— or, something to that effect. "I have great bow skills to help in fighting too!"

"Cool! A bow?!" Sleepy laughed.

"Well we best get going soon, Ealtar's gonna get eclipsed!" Hiinhia warned, collecting some books.

"Here, I found something," I began, having found a passage that seemed a rough translation of a story about Ealtar.

The silent moon hangs above;
she haunts, she hunts, she reminds
she says no more in words,
her body speaks all the same.
Release her from pain and silent vow.

Fallen before her sisters,
they took up her heart,
they fought for her honor,
no love in her final breath.
Release her from pain and silent vow.

Her soul's crystal fell to the deepest part of her heart.
"I'm sorry, sisters. I'm so sorry."

[Surface of Ealtar, Moon of Ealtae]

Sleepy

The only challenge of the trip from Ealtae to Ealtar was getting everyone into custom-made spacesuits, Ealtar didn't have an atmosphere. Safaeir fortunately fit into Ehnri's extra suit and we then could embark on our way into the unknown!

The surface of Ealtar looked much different from my home. Rather than the silky smooth dusty dunescape, Ealtar was a barren wasteland of rocky outcrops and rough bedrock. It seemed that Ealtar had minimal craters due to its proximity to its parent, Ealtae.

"Hey you with the keys! Maybe you can find the stuff we're looking for!" Hiinhia suggested through the suit comm system.

"Wait, you've already found keys!?" Safaeir yelped.

"Whoops, forgot to mention that, sorry!" I replied, maneuvering the suit's pockets to grab the key from within. I then watched as Qranyt showed Onyx how to use the keys to locate other artifacts. Safaeir, extremely intrigued by the keys, was analyzing Qranyt's every move.

"Here Safaeir, this one is my world's key," I said, holding the artifact out to the small cat.

"The patterns are so intricate! Where did you find it?" She asked as she examined its surface.

"It's pretty complicated, " I explained as we started on our way following the motion of the glow. "I didn't find this one, but one of my great ancestors did. The Key of Sleprah-Daecaser."

"You're a 2c Bear..." Safaeir said quizzically, "I remember a story about that world, left behind by my family!"

"Yes, I am. My name is Setai, but when my father died, I took his name in honor of our traditions."

"Something's different here," Qranyt said, "The keys aren't showing any signs of anything..."

"Well we've certainly found something," Avie started, "take a look here..."

"Wait, a triangle!" Hiinhia laughed, brushing loose silt off an engraving in the strangely smooth stone.

"Huh..." Onyx uttered.

"The Three Stars," Safaeir brushed a corner, "I think we may have arrived just in time."

"Oooh" I thought out loud, "Look! The eclipse is gonna happen!"

"But I see the other two stars rising on the other side of Ealtae!" Ehnri said.

"We're in time for them all to line up!" Safaeir exclaimed.

The ground shook as the triangle sunk into the ground, split into three parts, and revealed a dark staircase into the moon.

"Alright you guys, I've got firsts!" Qranyt proclaimed, jumping into the abyss.

"Quick! The door probably won't stay open for long!" Safaeir told us.

"She's right," Avie agreed, "Solia Noctia will be blocked soon"

The rest of us scurried down the dark stairs with our light orbs, continuing on our way after the door closed up and the only way out was forward.

"Well guys, the air here is safe." Avie informed us after looking at the data from their suit.

"Good to know" Onyx sighed as she wriggled out of her suit and compressed it into a vacuum pack.

"Safaeir, what else do you have about Ealtar?" Qranyt asked after helping her get the suit off.

"Well, I think there might be a bit more on what we thought would be under the surface, like here" she held the light orb over the leafy paper.

The way to one's heart has many paths,

every path is wrong,

she has no way to her heart anymore.

The quiet heart belongs to she who embraces her,

the way is dark.

"A maze?" I suggested.

"Seems so," Avie added.

"These poems are creepy..." Ehnri whined, "this isn't like your other stories Safaeir!!"

"Don't know about you guys, but I don't wanna fall through anything!" Hiinhia growled.

"Seems like we don't have a choice," I reminded Hiinhia.

"Who is this 'she' the poems keep talking about?" Onyx looked to Safaeir. "If it's a real person, it sounds like some seriously awful stuff happened to her..."

Safaeir looked to her paws, "It must be Diiviide, the silent spirit. Ealtar is what she became when she fell. She was a cosmic spirit who was betrayed by her own kind."

"Wow," Onyx shuddered, "usually children stories are less—brutal?"

"Well, here at the gate we must press forward!" Qranyt proclaimed.

"The gate?" Ehnri looked about, "Woah! That's big!" In the faint light of our illuminating orbs a giant archway could be seen, bearing words in Soliean.

Safaeir looked up, "It says 'Core of Ealtar!' 'ventreal e'ealtar!'"

"Well I guess that's the way to go," Avie directed through the archway. "Why don't we let Safaeir lead the way! This is her area anyways!"

"Ooohh!" Safaeir hooted.

"Just be careful!"

Safaeir

The stone floor of the passage was cold, and as we walked in, the light orbs faded to nothing. Even the keys were completely dark.

"Uhh, we need these," Onyx uttered.

"Oh well," Hiinhia whispered in reply.

"This challenge the book speaks of must involve keeping things dark, it's intentional." Qranyt surmised.

"I can't see a thing," I told the others, hoping they had some ideas.

"Don't worry I can see!" Sleepy remarked.

"You can?" I asked. There was a brief pause before he replied.

"No."

"I think that's the point," Qranyt continued, "we aren't supposed to see anything. The only way to get through these tunnels is by feeling around and by listening."

"The quiet heart belongs to she who embraces her," I whispered. I was certain this meant taking the story literally would help us get through.

"Right, so basically, everyone be quiet?" Onyx suggested.

"Yeah everyone shhhh!" Hiinhia said.

With that, the tunnels lost all life within moments. The only sound left was the sound of dripping and our breathing.

"Water..?" asked Ehnri, puzzled, *"that's strange."*

"Let's hope so!" whispered Onyx.

"Okay Safaeir lead the way!"

I was able to locate bends in the path in a few locations, but we soon reached a dead end in the path.

"Oh great," Hiinhia laughed, *"it is a maze."*

After a bit of back-tracking we found an alternate route, but something felt different ahead. Suddenly, as we walked down this branch, Hiinhia reached an edge of the tunnel.

"Woah-woah-woah!" Hiinhia exclaimed, with Qranyt jumping to catch him. *"That... is an edge!"*

"Oh no it's not!" Onyx growled, *"We're doomed now!"*

"Keep to the floor! No one falls off!" I told the others.

"Nice idea, Safaeir," Avie complemented, *"Now let's get a move on!"*

We each followed a route, calling out when we hit a dead end and helping each other back to a common spot. The maze was massive, at least it seemed to be in the dark.

"Dead," I heard Onyx call from up ahead, *"ughhh."*

"I'll try right at this fork, back this way Onyx!" I called into the dark.

"This place is really getting on my nerves!" She called back, *"if only we had a fire or something!"*

I reached the end of another path and called back, *"Dead!"* but I felt something under my paws, a carving? *"Wait, I feel something different on this one! It's an engraving in the floor! I think it says, autaah!"*

"Says what?" Sleepy called from farther back.

"AUTAAH! It means sound!!" my words echoed back from the far walls, followed by a faint green glow from far below the maze.

"Woaaahh," both Ehnri and I said, him having caught up to me at the edge.

Ahead I could just barely see a collection of pillars scattered about with a large platform at the end, before the green light died out.

"Oh great..." Onyx sighed, "this'll be fun." The light below faded, leaving us in total darkness again.

"Uh-oh!" I whined, "it looks like they're at least all the same height!"

"I hope you remembered where they all were, Safaeir!" Qranyt laughed.

"The first one was-" I jumped, "here! Phew!!"

"Right, and the second one?" Sleepy asked, his voice filled with regret.

"Uhuh-uhhh" I stuttered, "Wait... feel the ground, is there anything to throw?" I heard the others shuffling about, searching.

"Wait," I heard Sleepy's voice, "I have some crispy beans you can throw."

"Crispy beans?" Onyx asked judgingly.

"In case I wanted a snack!"

Sleepy carefully tossed the sack of beans in my direction, and with the help of my cat hearing I managed to catch it.

"I hope this works," I uttered before tossing a few beans into the abyss. I just barely heard one of the beans bounce off a stone pillar on its way down, which I carefully leapt to. "Alright, who's next?"

"Not me!" Onyx yelped.

"I guess I'll take my chances," Qranyt decided.

"I'll be right behind you Qranyt," Avie joined.

After Qranyt made his jump to the pillar behind me, we all became quiet once more so I could locate the next pillar. Qranyt used the sound of my jump to the next pillar to find the one I left, and it sounded like Avie found their way onto the first pillar pretty easily. Pillar-by-pillar we progressed until we all reached a large platform, it wasn't too difficult with our strategy once we got into the rhythm.

"How many crispy beans do you have left?" Sleepy asked me.

"About a dozen I'd say—hard to tell without, you know, seeing!" I replied.

"Okay guys, feels like there's another edge here!" Avie informed us.

"Well I guess we'll be needing those crispy bea-"

"Wait!" Qranyt interrupted me, "There's a beam, just hanging here; I can feel it..."

"Hanging? Oh gosh!" Ehnri started, "I think my little legs have had enough of jumping from object to object."

"I think that if I got on first I could analyze the pendulum motion of the beam to let all of us jump on at certain intervals," Qranyt suggested.

"Alright, I guess that's our best bet!" Hiinhia agreed, trying to keep optimistic. I heard Qranyt leapt onto the beam. The sound of chains clattering could be heard as the beam rocked back and forth.

"Okay, the pendulum has a two second period. It's making me a bit disoriented but I can hold on here and catch each of you! I'll tell you all when to jump—"

"You first Safaeir!" Sleepy said. I was able to clumsily navigate to the edge where the others stood.

"One, two, JUMP!" Qranyt shouted, "got you! Okay Safaeir, why don't you head to the next beam?"

"Are you sure?"

"I've analyzed this beam's motion. For you, if you jump about two meters forward off of each beam then you will make it."

"How do you know how far apart they are?" I asked Qranyt, who placed his paw on my front leg. I looked to where my leg would be if I could see, and there I saw a tiny speck of light. All around the room I could see tiny specks of light.

"Now go, Safaeir, take the key!" Avie declared.

"Me? Take the key?"

"We would have never gotten here without your help," Sleepy agreed.

"Alright! Here goes! I'm trusting you, Qranyt!"

"Good, now JUMP!"

Just as Qranyt said, I was able to bound across the beams with ease, and after a few jumps I skidded onto cool, grey stone.

Onyx

I in fact did not jump on last, like I had wanted to all the other times. Just after I jumped onto the third beam, Sleepy was ready to jump. Qranyt was in charge of telling us when to go.

"Ready, GO!" he shouted. I heard Sleepy shuffle a bit in his jump, but he slipped on his landing. I reached out into the darkness, feeling around quickly for a paw. Within a fraction of a second, I made contact.

"I got you Sleepy!" I exclaimed.

"Thanks Onyx." He replied. I felt myself slowly slipping off the beam. Qranyt grabbed onto me just before I would have dropped.

"Hiinhia and Ehnri, hold Onyx!" Qranyt ordered, dropping down. "Sleepy! Grab on!" Qranyt said as he stretched out beside me.

"No Qranyt. I'm only gonna make it harder for the others to get over."

"Shut—up we've got you!" I yelled at Sleepy.

"We're not going anywhere without you Sleepy!" Avie promised, still on the beam before ours.

"Here!" Qranyt said, grabbing a rope he had tied to his waist and tossing it to Avie.

"Safaeir! Remove the key! Maybe it could save him!" yelled Hiinhia, "REMOVE THE KEY!"

"Try to get the rope snagged on his pack!" Qranyt told Avie.

Safaeir

Just ahead was a pale altar with a blue triangular key. As I approached it I heard a struggle back from where I left.

"Sleepy! Grab on!" I thought I heard Qranyt say.

"No Qranyt. I'm only gonna make it harder for the others to get over."

"Shut up, we've got you!" Onyx yelped.

"Safaeir! Remove the key! —it could save—!" I heard Hiinhia yell, "REMOVE THE KEY!"

I ran up the now dimly lit stone stairs to face the altar. I lowered my head in a bow the moment I saw her statue behind the altar and whispered,

"I'm sorry, Diiviide. I'm so sorry."

The instant I grabbed the key, the whole moon shook. The key began to change its form, unfolding before my eyes into the shape of a bow. The ceiling began to crack, and air shot from deep below through the roof.

"I've got you Sleepy!" I heard Avie say.

The tunnel then closed up on the bottom, stone panels sliding into place underneath the beams. I felt as the bow pulled energy from deep inside, silently persuading me to draw back the string and release a phantom arrow on the ceiling.

"You want me to dry-fire?" I asked the bow, "alright, I guess."

I pulled back the string and released. I felt as a current flew from the front of the bow, blowing the stone roof to bits and several kilometers into the air.

"WHAT WAS THAT!" The others asked as they ran across the newly disarmed traps. Within seconds after I blew the roof into orbit, the walls started to crack. Water sprayed everywhere, as well as more air.

"Wait, is this moon terraforming itself?" Qranyt asked, astonished.

"This is insane!" Onyx exclaimed.

"What happened back there?" I asked.

"Sleepy almost met with oblivion! Thanks to the suit pack and a bit of rope, Avie was able to save him." Ehnri explained, "and I think thanks to you too!!"

"Wait, what's this?" I turned to see Hiinhia studying the altar I removed the key from. Qranyt stepped next to him to look too.

"Noctaikiilakj?" Qranyt observed the word written on the altar, "Why would anyone want to go there?"

"I don't know," Onyx started, "but someone's dragging us place to place and it almost seems a little... unsettling."

"Cool——bow—safaeir" Sleepy was still catching his breath from his fall, "how'd you do that!"

"I think I broke her silence, and now she doesn't have to be alone anymore..." I felt warm tears flowing from my eyes.

10. NOCTAIKIILAKJ

[Tomb of Diiviide, Ealtar]

Qranyt

"This, I will agree, is amazing," I told the team as we climbed out of the collapsing chambers to the surface of the moon.

"No need for these packs then?" Hiinhia asked, shaking the suit pack around a bit.

"We haven't suffocated yet, no!" Onyx laughed.

"We're gonna want them on Noctaikiilakj!" Avie reminded us, glancing at the new landscape.

"How is any of this even possible?" Sleepy inquired, looking at the green shoots rapidly coming out of the grey dust. "And that bow! You shot the whole roof off that place!" Safaeir collapsed to the ground, the key folding into a triangle. I ran over to her side to see what had happened.

"The key took all of your energy too, huh..." I observed at her side. Vines were growing to cover the ground rapidly, probably a sign it was about time to leave the moon. I gently lifted both her and the key and found a soft spot with blankets on the ship.

"We will go back to Ealtae first, perhaps to learn more about these devices." Avie suggested, climbing into the cockpit of the ship.

"Hold on..." I started as the ship exited the atmosphere, "Ealtar is in such a low orbit around Ealtae, neither the rings nor the atmosphere should be able to maintain a stable form around the moon."

"You're right!" Onyx agreed.

Sleepy joined Avie in the cockpit, "I believe there is more at stake here than we thought, Ealtar defies all that we know about planetary physics."

We landed on Ealtae in Safaeir's river territory once more, this time to learn more about how these keys work. Inside Safaeir's house we found more books on keys, but also something else; a matrix.

"What's this thing the books keep mentioning? These matrices?" asked Ehnri, who lay resting on the stone table.

"Not sure yet," Hiinhia replied.

"I will agree, they always appear beside each other," Sleepy said as he traced the words The Keys and the Matrix on the cover of a book.

"What about this?" Safaeir sleepily sighed.

"The matrix of a world," I read, "must be found with use of the keys. Usually each territory of a world has its own key that, when united, can be used to unlock the final matrix of the world. There is a matrix on every planet, but only a few moons have their own matrix, such as the moon Ealtar, which has no keys. So that's why they're called keys!"

"Wait!" Ehnri jumped, "Is this bow a matrix!?"

"It must be, the book says there's no keys." Onyx added.

"This is insane!" Safaeir laughed, "I can't believe this is all happening to me!"

"Everyone please calm down!" Sleepy chuckled, "Let's let Qranyt continue!"

"Thank you, Sleepy." I then continued, "It says here that, like a key, a matrix binds to one creature, who will then have the ability to wield its power using what strength the owner has. Unlike a key, some matrices have the ability to shape-shift, to bind to the owner's mind so they may change the very shape of their matrix."

"So Safaeir can tell her matrix when to turn into a bow?" Onyx asked.

"Here, I'll give it a go—" Safaeir stepped by the deep indigo colored matrix and closed her eyes, concentrating. Slowly, the matrix began to move. Tiny shards of insanely complicated technology slid into place, changing the triangular block into a bow.

"That's so cool!" Ehnri bounced.

"Here I found a bit about where the matrices and keys get their energy!" Sleepy exclaimed, holding out a dusty brown book.

"Well go on, read it!" Hiinhia provoked.

"It says that the keys and matrices gather their power from the wielder in the form of strength, like in Qranyt's book, but also in willpower and courage, but also the spir—"

"Doesn't happen to say anything on food now does it? I'm starving!"

"That might be the strength part. How about we go get a bite to eat then!" Avie suggested.

"Hunting fish in the stream?" Safaeir offered.

Avie agreed, "Sure, but I'll take whoever doesn't want to deal with fish."

Safaeir

"Wait—" I called to Sleepy, "here's the story I remember..." I handed him a worn old book only about as big as my head.

"Sleprahj's Sacrifice," he read the title, "thank you Safaeir! I'll read it later! But who wrote it?"

"I— don't remember. All my parents ever said about the book is they got it as a gift from an old friend."

Avie left for the woods with a part of the team, leaving the rest of us, Qranyt, Sleepy, and Hiinhia, to explore the streams.

"This stream here enters the tunnels. There are some long cave eels there." I explained as I led the way.

"I haven't gotten a share of tasty fish in forever!" Sleepy told us.

"We like to catch fish in my territory, we'll be sure to send some moonward!" Qranyt assured him.

"You know what we'll do with the fish we'll catch?" I taunted, "we'll steam half of them with fruit from the woods, and the other half we'll dry in strips with all kinds of spices so we can eat them later!"

"Alright cat, my stomach was rumbling before you went on a rant, now I'm just ten times more hungry!" Hiinhia retorted.

"Here's the cave entrance, the fish hang out in the pool at the bottom of the falls here." We got tied onto the already anchored ropes the tribe uses in the cavern entrance and started our climb down. "Our villages often use these caves for fishing, celebrating, and even sometimes a place to sleep on warm days, even though Ealtae is on average much cooler than the other Noctia planets."

"Wow this is a big cave!" Sleepy exclaimed as he splashed into the shallow edge of the pool. The rest of us came down beside him and turned to see the voluminous cavern glowing with bioluminescent plants. The caves were cold, and I watched as dozens of fish swam in circles inside the pool.

"Hey Safaeir!" Qranyt called, "why don't you try your bow again, this time try to, errr, feel more determined?"

"Sure Qranyt," I pulled out the matrix, "I'll try to 'feel more determined!'" I pulled back the bow, aiming for the center of the pool. "You should probably step back!" I warned the others. The invisible arrow hit the water with a loud clap, spraying fish, mist, and rock everywhere.

"Yeah maybe that wasn't such a good idea?!" Hiinhia laughed, rubbing the grit from his face.

"That was EPIC!" Sleepy jumped excitedly.

"You certainly look much better now than after your first attempt." Qranyt informed me, before looking around at the mess on the cavern floor. "You certainly took out all the fish."

I could feel something, different and small in the back of my mind.

"Quit standing around!" Qranyt scolded the others, "Get these fish together and let's go!"

I fell to the cave floor as a pain grew stronger in my skull, I'd felt similar things before, but never this strong; I knew what was coming next.

"Safaeir! What's happening!" the voices of the others fell away, *"saaff... saff, get her up let's get back to—"*

eal'aehj'zhi zhe vauqoh'stze zahu

It wasn't ae'Soletria, I didn't know what it meant but I felt—

eal'aehj'zhi zhe vauqoh'stze zahu

I heard it throughout my life, each time stronger than the last—

EAL'AEHJ'ZHI ZHE VAUQOH'STZE ZAHU! EAL'AEHJ'ZHI ZHE VAUQOH'STZE ZAHU! EAL'AEHJ'ZHI ZHE VAUQOH'STZE ZAHU! EAL'AEHJ'ZHI ZHE VAUQOH'STZE ZAHU!

...

"so it's you."

"?"

"as your veriise, I wish I could help you, but... this is her *design."*

"Diiviide?"

"Safaeir. I'll try to ease your pain, but those words? That's only the beginning. Oh sweet Safaeir, I'm sorry for what is to come."

Onyx

Avie, Ehnri and I decided to take the other route, where we would peacefully search the woods for fruit to cook with the fish.

"The kind of fruit we're looking for should be around here," Avie explained from far ahead of us. "Sunaructa, a tree," they pointed to a tree whose height showed great contrast against the extremely tall, thousand years old Ealtae Darkwood trees. There, amongst the branches, were soft, orange fruit. They looked as if someone took a bunch of orange balls and glued them all together. The less ripe fruit were green and yellow.

Avie tossed one to me, "Here!" I reached up with my paws, which punctured the silky surface. I managed to pluck one of the fruit's orbs off and bite into it.

"This is crazy good!" I told the others, plucking another orb off for Ehnri.

Avie pulled out a bag to stuff all the fruit in while I decided to take a look around the amazing landscape. Turning around, I saw an overhanging rock, where hexagonal stones seemed to stick together supporting more small trees and rocks. Soft vines flowed down from the trees and cliffs. There were plants of all kinds, and I recognized a few types of kja grain as well as ocaskj, a type of bean plant.

"Well you all, it seems as if we're done here!" Avie declared as they walked up behind me.

"Alrighty," I sighed, taking one last look at the deep green forest.

Sleepy

Back at the house we found Safaeir's bed, laying her down just as she started to stir.

"You gave us a scare back there, Safaeir!" I said.

"What happened?" Qranyt asked.

"Uhhh," the small cat shifted into the pillows.

"It's okay, Saf," Qranyt continued, "Hiinhia you keep watch over her and Sleepy and I will get started on cleaning the fish!"

Hiinhia nodded, pulling the blankets over her limp body. We got the wood fire oven started and went back outside, where Qranyt and I sat in a little stone fish-cleaning area with the tools to easily remove the nasty little bones.

"Do you think it was the matrix thing?" I wondered out loud.

"Maybe, but it didn't happen the first time."

"My father said the one I have is the Matrix of Sleprah... I wonder if it does cool things like that too? Or maybe it's just a key and he was wrong?"

"Unfortunately, these are all good questions for Safaeir!"

"She'll be okay, right?" I asked, placing half the first set of fish into the oven and hanging the others.

"Hey! Avie called in the distance, "Brought you some fruit!" Avie remarked as they placed a sack in the grasses just outside the doorway. "Did something happen?"

Qranyt explained, "Safaeir blacked out in the caves after using the bow again, we brought her back and the fish and she seems to be okay, just tired."

"Did she make an even bigger blast with it?" Onyx asked.

"No, actually, it was a much smaller blast just to hit the fish out of the water." He continued, "I don't know if it was the matrix or something else."

"Wait, I know!" Ehnri jumped in, "This happened sometimes when she was younger I remember!"

"What do you mean, Ehnri?" Qranyt pressed on as Avie took over the cooking.

"Sometimes she would pass out and be really tired when she woke up, then say she heard some girl chanting something in her head! She never could figure out what the girl was saying though..."

"Let's get the rest of this food together," Avie said, "I've got the first round ready then we'll pack the rest and get going. I'm sure Safaeir will explain it all to us when she wakes up."

Before long we had all satisfied our stomachs on fish and forest fruit and were just about ready for our trip to the moon of Noctae, Noctaikiilakj.

"Well we've got all the food packed," Avie said as they carried the last supplies up the ship's ramp into the cabin. I pulled the lever to close the main door behind them, and Qranyt turned to me with Safaeir in a bundle of blankets in his arms.

"Here, take this, Sleepy."

"Now that we've got ourselves settled," Avie started the main engines, "we'll be on our way to Noctae!"

"Let's see," Qranyt stepped to the map display, pressing buttons on the console to reveal a map of the planets orbiting Solia Noctia. "Ealtae is here at the three-quarter point, and Noctae is here at the two-quarter point. It will take about two hours to reach."

"Thank you Qranyt!"

"Well what's good for two hours?" Onyx asked as we passed out of the atmosphere.

"Well?" I said, trying to think of something. Safaeir wriggled in my arms as I took a seat, then opened her mouth wide with a yawn.

"heyyy, sleepy," she mewed, "have any food?"

"Yeah! I got some food! She's awake guys!!"

Safaeir excitedly ate some of the fish and berries we packed up, telling us just about the same as what Ehnri had to say.

"Could you write what the voice was saying?" asked Qranyt, pulling out some papers.

Safaeir shook her head, "I can't really write it, it's not like a thing you say or write but I can feel it, it's a language I've never experienced anywhere else..."

"But Ehnri said it was a girl's voice?"

"I'm sorry, I don't know how to explain. I hear her but I feel her, like listening to the heart of a tree or a stone— and; There was something different after. I think somehow it was Diiviide talking to me as if she heard or felt the voice too... she said she wants to protect me as my *veriise*."

Qranyt turned, focusing in on what she said, "Veriise? What does that word mean? I'm not familiar yet it keeps showing up."

"I don't remember," Safaeir continued, "I think it's because I have her matrix her soul is bound to me somehow?"

Onyx found a magnetic board game for us to play which we circled around for some time during the flight. I didn't really understand how to play, but somehow I beat Hiinhia and then everyone else beat me!

"Quudiikjii!" Qranyt shouted, "I did it, I'm in first place!" He stacked up six green pieces in a row just as I started to zone out.

It seemed like we still had a large distance to fly, so I pulled out the book Safaeir had given me and slumped against one of the walls. The pages were worn, some parts were difficult to read, and much of the story seemed familiar but didn't make much sense to me...

Soon enough a small dot orbiting a dark world appeared ahead: our destination, the moon Noctaikiilakj. Avie flew the ship into orbit around the small moon that looked like a black spiked ball with a thin ring around it. We set the ship down on the top of one of the immense black crystals that stretch from the core of the moon to the point at which the atmosphere is breathable.

"On this crystal we have a small base," Avie pointed out the window to the round white building. "In there, there should be some cables and equipment for the drop, as well as pressurized suits for entering lower levels of the moon's atmosphere. The building should be accessible with the code 2211483."

"Oooh, fun!" Onyx commented sarcastically.

"Yes, very much. Even more exciting, I have reasons to believe that the information we seek will be located near the core of Noctaikiilakj, just above the point at which the atmosphere turns to liquid, so in other words, don't remove your suits."

"Where you going?" Ehnri stepped in.

"I'm heading planetside, Noctae Command has something for me to check out."

"Oh so you're just gonna leave us?" Onyx laughed uncomfortably.

"Qranyt will take care of you all!"

After we gathered our basic supplies and books, we left Avie to the ship. Qranyt stepped forward to the base to type "2211483" into the keypad, successfully unlatching the clean-white base's thick door.

Inside we found several lockers, each containing various types and sizes of suits that were built to shape themselves around the wearer if

needed. Qranyt was kept busy helping the others get dressed up and attached to the rappelling gear, so I decided to give him a hand and look through the other bits of supplies. I decided to collect some extra lights, as well as a few pressurized canisters, communicators, and sensor instruments.

"Hey Qranyt, I've got some other things here, maybe each of us can take a few?" I suggested.

"Sure thing!"

We soon returned to the top of the giant black crystal outside of the base, where multiple hooks were set in the dark stone. After I passed out all the additional gear I found, Qranyt helped us link onto the hooks before setting us on our path to the core.

Qranyt

I decided it would be best if I descended ahead of the others, just to make sure it was safe for the rest. The cables we had hooked up were very long, thin, and sturdy enough to make sure we would make it to the bottom safely.

"Okay you guys!" I called through the suit. "Put your back legs against the crystal and push backwards, letting your line spin out of the coil each time." I watched as they tried to figure out the best way to perform the tasks I had them face.

Hiinhia slid down next to me, "Let's just hope none of them are afraid of heights..." he shuddered, glancing down the drop of about 1000 kilometers, it's a good thing we didn't need to go anywhere near that far.

As time passed, it became apparent that the air was thickening. Wind speeds and the force they gave greatly increased, making it difficult to keep in control while rappelling.

"Hey, Hiinhia!" I called out, bringing him down once more.

"Yes?"

"I'm leaving you in charge of the others—I'm gonna do some scouting ahead."

"Okay, sure."

"Keep contact over the comms though, hopefully they will still work." I turned to an upside-down position, which turned out to be pretty safe and secure. Pressing my stomach against the smooth crystal, I was able to accelerate down the side much faster than before.

Avie

As soon as I saw the team find their way inside the base I lifted off for Noctae. The small planet wasn't that far off, even though Noctaikiilakj orbits at a much farther distance than any other moons in the system. I decided that the Noctae Command probably wanted me to see what their messages were about, plus, the ship we had been using needed to refuel anyway.

I set my ship down in the small dark island's hangar of the large command facility, where several full resident dark cats and humans were busy training and analyzing data on the system's patrols.

"Hello Laer Avie Kiravaen, just this way," a human dressed in the Noctae Fleet Commander uniform led me.

"Thank you, aatere" I replied as they led me from the hangar to the Center Command, where they then directed me to an office.

"Great to see you Avie!" Admiral Ziltri greeted, she's a famous Noctael Guard in the station, "I am so very pleased you could join us!" the cat continued, closing the office door behind me.

"So am I, Ziltri! It has been much too many years!"

"Please, take a seat! " She instructed.

"So, old friend, what news have you got for me?"

"Well, unfortunately I couldn't explain earlier, as I was afraid to stir up any commotion about this curious transmission we have detected."

"A transmission? From where?"

"That's the disturbing thing... the transmission was aimed directly to Noctae, directly from," she pulled up a starmap on the office desk, "here." The grey cat placed her paw in a very strange location, a void in space. As far as we know, nothing should be there.

"That is," I paused, clearing my throat, "very curious? What is the transmission?"

"That is what we don't know. The transmission is not only encoded, but it hasn't technically reached us yet."

"A sub-light message?"

"Not quite, just much slower than our usual communication speed. The message is sent faster than the speed of light, but our sensors detect the signal traveling towards us in a way that we can tell exactly where and when it will arrive."

"Wait—do you know how fast it is traveling?" I stopped, a strange suspicion filling my heart.

"Let me see..." she began scanning through the information recorded on the signal, "ah here it is, somewhere around 3.64 parsecs per hour."

"That is... that's the speed our communications had over three decades ago..."

"Are you suggesting that that may be our lost leader?"

"Akjaeir..."

Hiinhia

I watched intently as Qranyt slipped into the mist far below, knowing that soon we would be down there too. With the wind speeds at our current height being so high, only Qranyt knows how bad it could be down there.

"Hey, you all hanging in up there?" I called.

"You're hilarious Hiinhia!" Safaeir laughed.

"I'm blowing all over Hiinhia!" Ehnri screeched.

"You know I am too!" I replied, "just make sure you don't blow out and slam back into the side here."

"You'd better hope I don't catch up to you or you'll find yourself beat!" Onyx warned.

"Wheeee!" Sleepy exclaimed, following Qranyt's tactics to catch up to me.

"Just be careful, guys!" I told them.

Qranyt

It didn't take long for me to hit the mist zone, where winds felt like they had reached over 200 kilometers per hour. Very slowly I lost visual of the other crystals protruding from the core, where I was then consumed by the darkness of the thick atmospheric gaseous and liquid vapor. The suit was fortunately strong enough to withstand the quickly multiplying air pressure and the rising temperature, allowing me to continue on my way. Far below I could see the end of our drop, where a flat sea of opaque gas, its temperature likely near the usual boiling temperatures of water on Aviea.

After a good hour or so I came across a large crack in the crystal's surface. Noticing an itraseletia symbol engraved in the dark stone, I paused to retrieve the key from my belt, focusing what energy I still had on locating the core of the moon's key. Sure enough, the light in the key shifted towards the crevasse.

Sleepy

Our team continued down the side of the giant crystal, struggling to keep from being blown out into the abyss.

"Wait here for a minute!" Hiinhia stopped us, searching around on his suit. "We are gonna need to link together, the wind is still increasing in speed and our combined weight would keep us more steady!" He reached out to Safaeir and Ehnri, linking them to Onyx and I. Hiinhia reached back for another clip, but in less than a split second, a gust of wind crashed into his light body, sending him streaking out of sight. I watched as his cable followed, quickly unraveling from his coil.

"Oh my gosh!!" Safaeir shrieked.

"We need to help him!" Onyx ordered. I saw in the other direction a giant cloud rushing towards us.

Grabbing the others, I quickly pressed against the side of the crystal, just avoiding the burst of air.

"We can't," I told them. "It would only risk our lives even more. As long as he's still connected, which it looks like he is, we will be able to get him from the top more easily."

"Well we can't just leave him out there!" Onyx shouted.

"I agree with Sleepy," Ehnri said, "even so, Hiinhia's really smart! He's probably on his way planning his own escape."

"Either way, we need to make contact with Qranyt, he'll want to know." Safaeir reminded us. "We can't just leave him either."

"You're right," I agreed, "we need to keep close together though. I've got Hiinhia's plan figured out. The only reason Qranyt made it as far as he did was because he is both heavy and skinny enough to keep safe from the wind. If we want to make it, we need to keep as close as we can."

"Sounds good enough," Onyx mumbled.

"Qranyt, can you hear me alright?" I called into the communicator relay of the suit.

"*I c—n so—t of y—ah,*" we heard as a response.

"Sounds like a no... " Onyx commented.

"We are having great difficulties up here Qranyt! The wind is outrageous. We've lost Hiinhia! He was blown straight away from us!"

"..."

"Qranyt?"

"Did his cabl— bre—k?"

"No, not that we can see."

"The— you ha—n't poss—bly lost —im." He assured us, *"Hiin—nhia is the strong—st little bear I know and there's no possib— wa— he wo—nt find his way ba—k."*

"Glad to hear it from you too Qranyt but the situation doesn't look so bright for him up here. We need to press on though, and I'm organizing a better suited descent formation to speed things up."

"Keep your path, ent— the large cra— in the crs—al's side."

"What was that, Qranyt?"

"pff—ffp—hf——ffff—fffff———"

"Oh, great." Onyx growled.

"I heard something about a crack in the crystal's side." Ehnri suggested, shifting about.

"Careful Ehnri, we don't need you to join Hiinhia." I warned, "We need to keep to the side of the crystal, to group up and flatten out."

Hiinhia

I felt the trouble coming quickly, too quickly for me to react. The gust of wind threw me out into the open, where I was soon pulled and stretched by the main force of the moon's air with little hope of return. I tried to lock my cable coil, but it was too late, spinning out of control until it would reach the end. I was already finding it hard to breathe from panic, but then my back struck another crystal, knocking the air right out of my lungs and driving me into darkness.

Avie

It took quite a while for me to process the new information I had acquired, that perhaps we had hope after all. Akjaeir and I had always seen the possibility of a new danger in Solia, a time that now seems to be on our doorstep since the re-discovery of Thraesa.

About 34 years ago, the creatures of Solia had a chance to vote for or against the exploration of the far regions of space by the Soliean Protectorate to search for what the creatures of Ealtae called Kiraveal. It was decided that one of the leaders of Solia would go, and the other would be left in stasis. Akjaeir decided she should be the one to go, leaving me with only partial control of Solia. On absence of one of the Leaders of Solia, the one remaining leader has limited power. The rest of the power is given to the Territorial Leaders of Aviea. This is supposed to only last for 35 years, as after this time, the missing leader is to be replaced by a vote of the creatures of Solia, a time that will be grave for all.

The reason I have been a leader for so long is not because I wish to be a sole ruler, but instead because Solia is a system of love and hope, a strength everyone shared with Akjaeir and I. Raising a new leader would not be easy for any of us.

Qranyt

As I waited in the dark crevasse of the immense crystal, I decided to do a bit of exploring to ease my thoughts on the possible loss of my beloved apprentice. As I felt the walls I detected a strange pulsating beeping noise. There on my leg was one of the sensors Sleepy had grabbed. I paused, noticing my cable was still attached to me, starting another whole chain of thoughts. What if he needs my help? I can't just leave him out in the wind to die! No no no! I couldn't let myself think those things! Not with a mission at stake. I held the sensor out in front of me, reading the dim screen.

ALERT!

ACTIVATION TERMINAL SIGNAL DETECTED!

REMOTE ACTIVATION ENABLED

#LOCKING CONNECTION

#CONNECTION SECURE

#REQUESTING ID

#ID RECEIVED "TempleDoorNoctaikiilakj.asuo"

Curious, I pondered that perhaps there is in fact some door to go through to whatever lies in the core. I once again reached for the coil, carefully unclipping it and trying not to think. Anchoring the coil to the ground for later use I noticed the texture of the floor: it was completely smooth. Carefully removing a small chisel Sleepy gave me at the base I worked out a few chunks from the wall and filled a sample container I had also linked on my suit earlier, still waiting on the arrival of the others.

Safaeir

I still couldn't get the sight of Hiinhia flying out into the open out of my head; Something I would never forget. Our remaining team turned to the depths, speeding down as fast as possible and tied to each other to avoid the same fate. Despite the others' assurances, I still couldn't help but feel great concern for poor little Hiinhia.

"We're almost there." Sleepy said as we continued to fall, slowed only by the buildup of drag from the heavy atmosphere. I sighed as I saw a dark split in the crystal, shallow at first, growing wider and wider as we approached the point Qranyt spoke of in his messages.

"Let's call Qranyt again!" Ehnri shouted.

"Qranyt, we're coming in!" Sleepy warned, pressing on the descent brakes for the coils. The crack quickly increased in width to the point of a few meters, where we could see a light orb inside.

"Yeah Sleepy, we can see that. It's all clear down here. Any visual on Hiinhia?"

"No, sadly no." Onyx told him.

"It's alright guys, I'm sure he'll get back."

The four of us touched down carefully at the entrance of the split cave in the crystal to see Qranyt in the distance.

"Good to see you Qranyt." I ran to him, hugging tightly, even with the complications of the suit.

"Good to see you too Safaeir." He helped us anchor our coils to the cave's floor to keep the thin but long cable from blowing out of our reach before explaining the situation. "It seems that this sensor you happened to give me proves its worth. I believe it can be used to open the door out of this crevasse."

"Seems so, but I'm gonna need to drop this suit if we're going any further." I told him.

"Perhaps on the other side the air conditions are just fine?" Sleepy suggested.

"Let's hope so, I'll have to agree with you on that one Safaeir." Qranyt remarked drearily. "This way."

Qranyt led us to a large triangular door. After pressing several of the buttons on the sensor, it soon seemed apparent that the door would not open remotely, despite the convincing message Qranyt showed us the screen displayed.

"Look!" Sleepy pointed to the door. "A paw print!"

"Perhaps the door needs identification from a certain being to open," I offered. Following my suggestion, each one of us stepped forward to place a paw into the door.

"Ehnri, you go forward too!" Sleepy encouraged. Ehnri stepped forward carefully, placing his paw in the center of the panel. The door shuddered, then pulled itself apart on his touch.

"Wow Ehnri, it seems you have the power!" I told him, pushing him through the now open door. A series of lights flickered on inside the room, and ahead another illuminated door. Once we had all entered the space between the doors, the one Ehnri had opened began to close behind us. Qranyt turned in alarm, throwing the sensor out the small aperture that was left in the door opening.

"Hopefully Hiinhia 'll find a way to open it up without Ehnri." Qranyt sighed.

We then heard a soft sizzling noise, followed by the door ahead opening.

"An airlock, I bet," Sleepy said.

"Yeah, seems like," Qranyt agreed, leading us out of the space into the brightly lit white room within. The large black door closed behind us, sealing us in for the next challenge.

Hiinhia

I woke in panic to find myself still in the air, the wind rushing past me. I fought the wind to grab ahold of the suit's coil. The coil has a built-in retract system, but with such fast winds, I needed to provide extra force on the cable for it to get me anywhere. I set the coil to lock every time the cable was wound up and started the long trip back. Making myself as small as possible against the wind I was able to pull on the line and allow the coil to wind up. Far below I saw great billowing clouds whipping around the core. I surmised that should be where the rest of the group is, making their way into the moon's mysterious center.

After some time I formulated a pattern. I would reach out ahead of me, ducking to reduce the surface area, then pull with both arms, then I would duck once more, then pull. Every few pulls I leaned back into the air to rest. At this point, there wasn't much I needed to do to keep afloat. I could see that the cable was almost straight, meaning that I was very

likely at elevation with the top of the crystals, just floating there. I quickly realized there was no chance of me making it to the others in time, but perhaps I could at least make it to the crystal top.

Ehnri

We were deep down in the moon Noctaikiilakj, navigating our way through what seemed to be an abandoned, or perhaps never used research base. Fortunately we didn't need our suits anymore, they were very bulky to handle and also pointless in the perfectly survivable building. The room was filled with shelves of hard drives, all of which Qranyt and Onyx kept themselves occupied with.

"We'll stay around here to download the information on these drives," Qranyt explained. "Ehnri, the rest is on you, you got us in here."

"What should I do?" I asked.

"Take the others to find what let you in. Maybe we can learn something more about Sleepy or Onyx's keys at this facility, and since we haven't figured out their abilities yet, we need some information."

"Sleepy?" I called to the tan bear across the room.

"Yes Ehnri?" he replied, turning from a shelf of some sort of containers.

"Maybe your key will be of use here to find the key that might be here? And maybe your matrix Safaeir!"

"Yeah!" She said, removing the triangular matrix from her back and standing on her back legs to hold it. "These Solia Protector uniforms are great for standing up like this!" She commented randomly.

"Let's see," Sleepy said as he pulled out his key. The light inside slowly shifted, moving to the middle tip of the key.

"Well I guess we know where to go!" I laughed.

"Good luck!" Qranyt wished to us.

~   ~   ~

We found another brightly lit hallway out of the main room where Qranyt and Onyx were, but this hall was behind a secret door! The three of us carefully walked down the hall until we reached another room. This one was shaped like a sphere, but in the center, the poles of the sphere made contact to a cylindrical glass case, where a dark red key in the shape of a sharp thin crystal rested .

Things started to blend together around here, memories intertwined in a complicated mix. All I can recall was my approach to the cylinder, which slid open upon contact with my paw. The instant I touched the key, a wave of deep red energy blasted from its center, throwing the others back just from astonishment. I felt as if my brain was being scrambled, the neurons re-organized. I suddenly felt every battle tactic and strategy being worked into my mind as if I had years of experience and training. That's not all though; I also became filled with knowledge of Noctaikiilakj itself, or that is, before I passed out.

Hiinhia

I knew that I wouldn't have much of a chance at getting back up to the group, something I had been prepared to accept for a while. At this point the wind felt like a constant barrage of knives into my skin, it was too much to handle. Now, I thought, was the time. I had already done so much in my time here that there wasn't much more for me to wish for. I reached for the coil, unclipping the link—no, not because I was accepting my death, because I knew what would happen if I died. The very universe would shatter, I thought, as the wind shot me into oblivion.

Sleprahj's Sacrifice, Author Unknown

Long ago, Simisaurehj was tasked with one final project. This project was his ultimate and final purpose in this cosmic order, and he wished not to disappoint. Almost all of his energy was spent perfecting his piece of the pillars, leaving just enough to transform himself into his final work of art. Aviea was his creation, as well as his tomb. He just hoped one day that his sister would come to visit before she too moved on.

When Sleprahj heard of Simisaurehj's transformation, she set out to search for his essence. She soon found the world Aviea, but his soul had yet grown so faint and her own energy diminished, she could not find the final resting place of his soul. For years she searched over the entirety of the planet, both her and Simisaurehj's power growing fainter and fainter. Along the way she amassed quite the following, too. Many of the creatures she helped through the years of her search repaid her by becoming acolytes of her spirit.

Finally she found the place of his spirit's rest; by this time, much to her sadness, tension had risen to quite a noticeable amount between those who followed Simisaurehj and the followers who had pledged themselves to follow her. After her parting words with the final essence of Simisaurehj, she decided it would be best to leave Aviea, with the hopes that her followers would simply forget she ever existed. Much to her shock, the followers felt otherwise.

The followers of Sleprahj constructed their own colony ship, one to escape the world and all traces of Simisaurehj and his devoted believers. Fate, however, worked in mysterious ways, and the colony ship left the believers stranded in Aviea's orbit. With no hope for escape or return, they simply prayed their goddess would save them for having shown their faith. Seeing there was no hope of them forgetting her, and that it was her meddling that led them to be in this situation, Sleprahj performed one final act of kindness for those who loved her.

The creatures of Sleprahj's world only grew more devoted to her after her sacrifice; When her soul fell to the desert dunes, they recovered the form it took and vowed to protect it for all eternity, just as she had protected them.

11. SAKJAICARATIS

[Noctaikiilakj, Moon of Noctae]

Hiinhia

As I flew through the air, I began to close my eyes, expecting the certain doom I had awaited. Just before the aperture of my vision met its final point, I saw a strange dark object getting larger and larger. Before my mind could comprehend, I slammed into the side of the object, blacking out yet again.

Safaeir

I watched as Ehnri fell back, hitting the grilled walkway with his new key on top of him. I rushed to his side to see what happened.

"Ehnri! Ehnri!" I shouted.

"I think he's out cold, let's take him back to Qranyt." Sleepy said, scooping the black and white cat into his arms. I walked alongside Sleepy as we backtracked down the long hall, wondering if Ehnri was alright.

"Hey you've returned!" Onyx congratulated us for our survival.

"Yep and Ehnri got knocked out by his own key," I told them.

"Oh?" Qranyt stood, "He did?"

We felt the crystal shake as one of the walls in the room shifted, revealing yet another long hallway.

"I guess I'll be taking Ehnri then if you want to carry our winnings?" Qranyt suggested to Sleepy.

"You hacked into the drives?" I asked.

"Unfortunately nothing on the Key of Aquat though..."

"Nice work nonetheless!" Sleepy complemented Qranyt, walking to hand the limp cat over to Qranyt. Qranyt handed him a large sack, and then he walked to a shelf where there were several capsules. After selecting a certain few of the containers, he carefully placed them in the sack. "Plant seeds," he said, "Plants that are centuries old."

"That is soo cool!" I told him. After a brief moment Qranyt led us to the door, where we looked down the hall and up the ramp inside. We sprinted, hoping we could make it to the end in time to save Hiinhia if he needed our help. Onyx ended up in the front, where we soon came across a round door. On her contact the door slid open, revealing a pod-like structure.

"This is a rocket elevator it looks," Qranyt explained, leading us into the pod's door. "The pod will shoot through the tube into the atmosphere then descend back onto the crystal, or at least, it should..."

"That's reassuring!" Onyx said.

"Well if anything goes wrong, I'm sure I can get us out of it with my key!" Qranyt winked and pulled the lever to seal the pod door, then announced. "Ready? Hold on tight!" We quickly pressed ourselves into stable positions, watching out the pod's thick glass walls to see the launch.

The instant Qranyt pressed the red button on the console, the pod exploded through the tube in the roof, accelerating towards the sky. The tunnel darkened as we continued, but just as it reached the pitch black, another hatch opened ahead of us, opening our path to the sky.

Our escape pod started to slow its upward motion, reaching the height of its trajectory. We each stood up, other than Ehnri, now that the scary part was over. I looked through the top windows just in time to see a bunch of tilted flaps spring out from the pod, which began to spin.

"Nice!" Qranyt said, "A simple slowing device!"

The pod started to spin as well while we descended towards the tall, dark crystal's summit, where we could see the base we started at. The pod fell to its target, deploying a chute only a few seconds before impact.

"Quick get out get out!" Qranyt ordered us, scooping Ehnri into his arms. Each of us jumped out of the pod door, running to the place where our lines were anchored.

"One line is still out!" Sleepy exclaimed. He reached out for the cable and pulled with all his might, with the help of Onyx to keep him from slipping over the edge. Once the line was pulled in far enough, Qranyt placed Ehnri on the ground and joined our efforts. Each of us had a piece of the cable and worked to pull it in, fighting the strong winds that worked against us.

"Wait," Sleepy called as I saw him reach for his belt and retrieve a telescope of some kind. He left us to hold onto the cable and pull it in as he looked through the scope to the end of the cable. "Guys," he said, "he's not there." Everyone fell silent as we dreaded the worst had really happened. The equipment was strong though, how could he have fallen off the cable?!

"Wait- there's something else though... coming straight for us!" We looked in the distance to see a dark ovular ship approaching us swiftly. Within moments the ship was over us. We could see the deep blue engine intakes, marking it clearly as a ship from Noctae. The transport ship descended to the surface of the giant crystal and landed, opening the ramp entryway. We quickly gathered our things and ran to the ship, where inside we saw Avie holding the now delicate looking Hiinhia in their arms.

"You saved him?!" Onyx screeched in amazement.

"SHHHHH! Gosh Onyx, you're gonna wake the little thing up!" Avie retorted.

"If he were awake and heard you say that, you would need to say goodbye to your face." Qranyt informed Avie as they came up the ramp behind me.

"What happened to Ehnri?" Avie asked as they walked to the back of the ship to rest Hiinhia in a bed.

"A little accident with his key." Qranyt placed Ehnri in another bed and handed the key to Avie.

"This one is curious. I wonder what it did to him." Avie placed their hand on the Soliean Itraset[1] of Ehnri's uniform to feel his heartbeat. "He seems to be alright, just a bit shaken like Hiinhia over here." Avie stepped back to the center of the craft and pulled themselves back into the cockpit above. I moved back as the ramp lifted into position, marking our departure. The ship had one large window that looped around the equator of the ship, making it easy to see what was going on outside.

"Leader Avie," a voice could be heard through the ship's intercom as

---

[1]The Itraset is a name for the symbol of the Three Stars, often a simple three points radiating like spokes from a centerpoint, the "up" point representing *Solia Noctia*, left representing *Solia Auqua*, and right representing *Solia Maurazeal*.

we lifted off the dark stone.

"Oh yeah and we've got communications with Admiral Ziltri at Noctae Command too"

"Hello crew! Alright, now onto business."

"Yeah?"

"We believe that the first easiest place to locate the exact origin of the transmission will be near Aviea, allowing for the first triangulation point through which the signal passes."

"And where near Aviea is this?" Avie asked the Admiral.

"And what signal is this?" Qranyt pressed, to which Avie just responded with a hand.

"I would say the moon Reid is our best bet."

"Woah, Reid!" I exclaimed, "Is that the world with the big temples and giant skyscraper rock towers?"

"Yeah that's the one, and haven't you had enough of giant rock towers?" Qranyt laughed.

"Thanks for the info Ziltri, and keep those ships flying!"

"Sure will Avie!"

And that was it- we were off on another adventure.

~   ~   ~

Sleepy

It didn't take us long to reach the moon Reid, or at least from my perspective. I went to the back of the ship, where I found a pile of cloth that seemed comfortable to take a nap on.

I awoke in a great surprise with Onyx's paw in my face, batting it out of the way and making for the door with the others. I was once again startled to find that both Hiinhia and Ehnri were awake and moving around, versus me who could barely stand (get it, because I'm a bear). The others didn't enjoy my joke.

"Well on that note, we should probably get going..." Avie led.

We filed out of the spacecraft, retrieving our gear on the way out. I was instantly entranced by the scenery. Qranyt explained that we had landed on the planet floor, and that everything above was the sky plains. I looked up to see a giant stone mountain, with steep cliffs on all sides. The pillar of stone rose high in the air, slicing the oncoming clouds in two. On the floor of Reid, the ground was covered in bright green grass plains with scattered boulders, perhaps dropped from the pillars.

"Wait guys," Hiinhia started, "We're on Reid? I think I remember something about Reid from my sleep."

"Strange..." Safaeir said as she examined a spiky round plant.

"Okay Avie, we're here, so what are we looking for?" Onyx meowed.

"Not exactly sure, I believe there is a Transmission Triangulation Station somewhere around here," Avie said. "Qranyt, your scanner should detect it."

"Well we should get moving then, I'll carry the food." I declared.

"Oh yes you will!" Onyx laughed sarcastically.

"I seem to have a signal," Qranyt told us. "The stone rise to the left appears to be the location the admiral wanted us to visit."

After gathering our things, we grouped together and set off for the Transmission Triangulation Base.

"What exactly is it we're after when we get to the base?" I asked Avie as we walked.

"Fleet Command detected a signal approaching Noctae, but they can't get an exact read on it. Ziltri expects that to recompile the signal, we will need to visit three different locations, one from each star to scan the transmission to compile it and find the exact location from which it came."

"Sounds nice, but why would Hiinhia have a dream about Reid when he clearly wasn't around for us to tell him?" Onyx reminded us.

"Maybe he overheard our conversations while he was asleep?" Safaeir suggested.

"I'm right here, you know!" Hiinhia reminded us.

"Can't you just teleport us up?" Onyx glared up the side of the steep stone pillar.

"I could," Qranyt replied, "or you could keep yourself in good physical shape and take this as a workout!"

Reaching the edge of the cliff, we began our ascent. The cliff face was rough, but the sharp stone edges actually made it easy to climb even for the most inexperienced rock-climbers. As if defying gravity, Hiinhia bounded up the stone with great speed, followed by Safaeir. I was able to follow close behind, but I almost slipped and slammed into Qranyt.

"Just as we hoped!" Hiinhia looked down at us. "The base is here, ready to use."

I came over the edge to see a bright white building with three large telescopes positioned around the center.

"Why did they make it so hard to get to?" I asked Avie.

"Good question, same as, 'Why couldn't we see it from above?'" they replied.

"Someone doesn't want this place to be found!" Hiinhia laughed, reaching to help pull me over the edge.

We grouped up at the top of the stone rise where the base lay and ate outside while Avie entered the base to see what it could do to help find the transmission.

"You think it's Akjaeir?" Ehnri looked at Qranyt.

"You're a funny one, Ehnri, but yes," he paused, "I think it is." Qranyt chuckled, biting off a bit of leftover dried fish.

"Where's Hiinhia?" Onyx looked about.

"Off on another adventure." Qranyt joked, taking a curious quick look himself. "He's fine! He managed to make it out of the depths of Noctaikiilakj alright, so he'll be fine here!"

"Oh, let's hope so," Ehnri said as he curled up.

Avie

Inside the base there wasn't much to be seen; just a few consoles. I sent Hiinhia off to find what he said had supposedly told him to come to the world just before I entered the complex, as I had a feeling that he might be linked to why we couldn't see the base earlier, but of course this could all be crazy suspicion!

I organized the switches to rotate the telescopes in the direction of the transmission. Although we have developed faster than light communication, we have not yet developed instantaneous transmission, so I knew that it would take a few minutes before the instruments would get a reading.

I watched as information slowly gathered on the screen. The scanners detected the transmission and displayed it as a scattered line, showing that it had in fact traveled several parsecs before reaching its current position. I was able to load the readings onto a datapad for later access before I was ready to leave the building, but just before I went through the door I saw Hiinhia in the lower level of the base.

Hiinhia

I felt a bit suspicious when Avie directed me to search for what had brought me here on my own, but I trusted them enough to take my chances. I quickly found a second entrance to the building that dropped below the ground and into the lower level. I looked above to see Avie through the grate at the door before continuing down the ramp into a large, bright, room.

At the opposing end of the room I saw what appeared to be the outer shell of a key, floating in the air. I started on my way across the room, soon to crash into some sort of invisible wall. After feeling and stumbling around a bit I realized that the walls were not only invisible but also made no sound on my hitting them. I continued to search the wall for any signs of passage through, but to no avail. I then heard a sharp click sound, and before I knew what it was, an invisible piece of the wall shot out and smacked me back towards the entrance.

Now I knew what to do! I swung out from behind the displaced wall and into the hole behind it. Great, now what...

I felt around for spaces, or even pieces that might come out and smack me. Nothing. As I increased the height at which I was feeling around, I noticed a hole in the wall that happened to be over the top of my head. I reached up and jumped through, only to reveal a new challenge. There on the other side I saw a pit that fell to great depths beneath me. I carefully lowered myself down from the hole.

"It must be a trick to make others keep back!" I thought, reaching my paws for the invisible floor. Sure enough, I made contact.

That was easy enough! I ran for the floating key case, and wham! I started to wonder how I hadn't learned the first time. I reached around the wall and found yet another invisible entrance.

I reached out for the key to discover that it was not in fact floating, but also on some sort of invisible object. The key seemingly materialized in my hand, the invisible center glowing like a star. I watched as the invisible objects around me re-appeared. After jumping about several times I found that all of my actions were muted while I commanded the key to activate through my head. I looked down at my body to see I was completely transparent.

"This is great!" I thought to myself, "Oh how fun this is gonna be

when I get back to the others; Ah, but now I gotta get back through this maze..."

Safaeir

We continued eating after Avie got back, still waiting for Hiinhia. Avie explained why they'd sent Hiinhia to go investigate.

"I hope he's alright," I commented, "he seems to be a nice guy."

"And I'm not?" Qranyt chuckled.

"Yeah, you're not!" Onyx mocked.

"WAHHH!" Ehnri exclaimed, seeming to have been flung backwards. He landed in the soft grass with a gentle "thud."

"Ohhhh—kay?" I said with alarm. A strange ripple went through the air and revealed Hiinhia, Ehnri quickly batted him on the nose.

"Oops not anymore!" Onyx laughed at me.

"That was awesome!" Sleepy told him.

"Sakjaicaratis," Avie said, "an old rumor about Reid having an artifact that causes things to become invisible."

Qranyt sighed, "I guess now we know why the base was invisible to the sensors."

"Thats so unfair!" Ehnri continued batting at the air in Hiinhia's direction, "Now he's gonna sneak up on us all the time!"

"And I'll be making extra sure to keep doors locked!" Onyx growled.

After our long snack was complete, we hiked back to the ship in search of the next scan location.

"Intafari?" Avie confirmed.

"Yeah, Intafari. Not somewhere you visit often is it?" Ziltri responded, *"You should."*

"Yeah, no place like it."

"Well be careful not to trip into any deep lakes, Ziltri out—"

"Well, sounds like we have our next location, you wanna fly, Qranyt?"

"Sure, I don't see why not, all I have to do is hit 'Map,' 'Intafari,' and 'Fly there please.'" Qranyt replied, climbing up into the cockpit seat.

"Keep yourselves occupied, it's gonna be a long flight!" Avie told us as Qranyt lifted the ship into the air. "Let's get ourselves a place to stay there too, let's enjoy our time on Intafari and have a chance to rest!"

I took a quick look out of the windows so I could see Reid pass by for the last time. What would my life be like without the protectors? I'd be stuck on Ealtae, perhaps I would never see the stars up close. Little did I know then, but after Akjaeir's transmission arrived, things would get a whole lot different.

Just before we exited the atmosphere, a shape caught my eye. It looked sort of like a dark snake-like cloud thing, wriggling in the air.

"Did anyone see that?" I shouted out.

"See what?" the others said.

"This dark, snake-like thing outside?"

"Go to sleep, Safaeir, there's no flying snakes on Reid." an exasperated Onyx assured me.

12. INTAFARI

[High orbit over Planet Intafari, Solia Maurazeal Star System]

Onyx

By the time I woke up the others were already at the windows looking out to the beautiful planet Intafari. The planet is about the size of Aviea and looks like a giant spider-web mesh of mountain ridges with their deep valleys filled with beautiful turquoise seas.

Qranyt flew the ship towards one of the flatter mountains, where a giant city shot high into the sky. I examined the city as we circled down to it. The buildings were tall, sharp, and skinny, wrapped up in a tall sparkling wall. Qranyt pointed the ship to the city side that appeared to have a set of several landing pads.

"I present to you the grand city Iatolin," Qranyt said.

"Noctael Sof-Transport ID. We have you on our radar, Ziltri informed us ahead of your arrival. The landing pads are open!"

After the ship landed, we all seemed ready to go explore, but we were surprised to hear Avie say they'd be going to the transmission scanning base thing on their own. The Intafari guards escorted us to a tall hotel building, where we got to choose wherever we wanted to hang out. Eventually we migrated to the center of the top floor, where an intricate glass dome lit the room for us to converse in our own private suite.

We all took the opportunity to freshen up in the giant showers and baths, Safaeir made sure to get there before the others made a mess of the place. We both took a liking to one of the conditioners scented with a local flower.

"Well, Avie is boring!" Ehnri exclaimed.

"We can find something to do without them," Safaeir suggested, "maybe do a bit of exploring on our own."

"You do whatever you want guys, I'm just gonna hang out in the city," I told the others.

"Sounds good. I'll go take whoever wants to actually do something interesting!" Qranyt mocked.

"Sorry Onyx, I'm gonna go with Qranyt," Sleepy declared when I looked at him.

"Okay, I'm just gonna slip away here, go to a, uh, bye see ya later!" I slipped out of the room not knowing where to go. Maybe on Intafari they have nice restaurants? Nah, maybe some sort of party? I got some things together out of my room and set out to explore the city.

Qranyt

"Well, that was awkward." Safaeir shrugged.

"Where to, Qranyt?" Sleepy asked.

"I say we check out the jungle, see what it has in store for us," I told them. "I bet we'll see some interesting creatures, the fauna on Intafari is like none you've ever seen!"

After gathering some things, including keys, weapons, and the usual gear like my heavy sword, we took a path down to the lower city levels and off to the City Gate. I can certainly say there were cats, humans, and other creatures alike that were very confused as to why there were Soliean Protectors roaming the streets, but they soon became settled as we approached the exit.

I turned to look back at the others, noticing another cloaked figure rushing towards me, seemingly a female human.

"Qranyt!" the human female whispered, reaching out and placing a hand on my shoulder. "We must go to the jungle, there's something there you need to see." My heart jumped as soon as I felt her hand, it made me uneasy. She was taller than me, slender but sturdy in form; her long red and orange hair flowed out of her hood into the sunlight.

The others looked about awkwardly, except Safaeir who seemed to be staring directly into her eyes.

"What is your name?" I asked.

"That uh, I can't tell you." She looked down, shrouding her face even more with the dark cloak.

"And how do you know my name?"

"You'll know mine in time, but we must get going."

"Okay, lead the way then, we'll see what we can do." I looked to the others and shrugged, "Another adventure!" I tried to pass it all off as just a nobody in distress and need of help to the rest of the group, but I don't know if I sold it. Safaeir especially seemed intent on keeping her eyes trained on the girl.

~　　　~　　　~

We followed the interesting human out of the city and across the mountain ridge. I began to wonder, why would telling us her name be bad? I studied her cloak as she walked in front of me. Using my super-bear sight I could see that it was not just any cloak, but a nanotech-cloak. My guess is as good as any, but the cloak looks like it can gather energy from almost anything it touches. This girl is carrying something that takes a ton of energy to run, and I'm sure it's not just a communicator.

"Miss?" Ehnri called. The cloaked human turned back to look at the small cat.

"Yes Ehnri?"

"What is this thing you are bringing us to?"

"I believe one of you has already seen it. A creature that should not exist yet in this universe."

"Wait," Hiinhia cut in just before Safaeir was about to say something. "You said you saw something out the window when we left Reid..."

"uhm— Yeah, some, snakelike thing flying outside. It looked like a black cloud ribbon thing." Safaeir explained, never taking her eyes off the human's face.

"On Reid?" The girl asked, "oh yes, of course. Don't worry about Reid. That dark cloud will pass soon enough. They are from Thraesa, now quiet, there is one here. We must take it out before it hurts this world or anyone else on it."

The female human led us through the vines, keeping us from the steep cliff faces on either side. I took a quick glance down the edge of the slope, estimating the drop to the water below. Perhaps 200 meters? Certainly no pleasant way to find out for sure.

Amongst the dips and squiggles in the cliff chain were several narrow rope bridges, none of them seeming secure enough for us to all cross at once. Fortunately, going one-by-one seemed safe enough.

"What is this?" Hiinhia whispered from a tree branch up above, pointing towards a dark mark on a tree.

"A sign we're getting close, take out your weapons," the female human commanded.

From her cloak she pulled out a longsword. The handle was black and the blade looked like it could be some kind of a matrix with the intricate noctium patterns and runes, with a bright orange glow from inside. The sword erupted into what looked like orange, yellow, and red flames, flames that licked and danced upon everything the sword touched.

"Let's go," she said.

Avie

I still felt bad about leaving the others behind, yet I didn't know what better to do. I didn't want them raising too many questions about the transmission and why we were going through all this, but they would certainly find things to keep busy with in the big city while I took care of transmission matters.

Inside the scanning facility I quickly discovered some bad news. The rotation of the planet was incorrect, out of alignment with the signal. There was no possible way to see the transmission for the next eight hours! I even attempted to link the signals with relay satellites, but it was still eight hours. Seemingly without any other option, I headed back outside to look around a bit, having not been on Intafari for several years.

The first thing I noticed was the water. It was only a bit after lunch time, our ship having landed just an hour or so earlier, so the sunlight shined directly into the deep, teal, abyss that was one of Intafari's many seas. However, the water seemed to be a bit darker, as if its depth was increased ten-times over.

I also found that the plants were a bit bitter tasting. Usually the wild Ckjirf plants are earthy and hearty, but when I ate one of the hard-green knobs off the tall stalk nearby I found it to have a more bitter and metallic taste. I then heard something, a sort of rustling of the leaves behind me. I turned to see another Ckjirf stalk sticking out of the ground. Its knobs were a bit different, as they were a more, deep black, flat, void kind of color,

unnatural.

I looked to the forest floor, where I then saw the grass around me growing darker and darker, as if being scorched by the very air around it. I pulled out my sword and leapt over the charred grass. Looking over my shoulder I spotted the culprit, a dark serpent-like creature weaving in and out of the trees directly towards me. That must have been what's causing this!

4##1+#

I was amazed by the team, they seemed to have such spirit and worth, I felt bad about bringing them into this mess. Sooner or later though, they would need to confront these dark creatures. Safaeir had already seen another on Reid, there's an infestation of them there. That's their trial world and they'll soon attack there if not for my plan to save the Aviean moon. There was something else, though, that interested me. The group took intrigue in me but nothing like how Safaeir looked at me, could she see into my true form? Her parents I knew were historians but through all their research there's no way they could learn something like that. It would need to be something in Saf's own soul that she could catch a glimpse of what's inside me.

I raised my flame sword and spun it around a few times, seemingly bringing delight to the small feline Ehnri. I looked ahead to see the serpent approaching, faster and faster, ready to overcome us.

"Whatever that thing is, I doubt what it wants is a hug!" Qranyt exclaimed, raising his noctium claymore with ease. "Safaeir, show that beastie what you've got!"

Safaeir pulled her matrix from her back, revealing its form as a bow-matrix, "Got it!" she replied.

I watched as she pulled the string back and let the invisible arrow fly. Upon impact, the serpent burst in two, taking a few moments to reconstruct into one again.

That bow is unique, I'd know it anywhere, and somehow it ended up in Safaeir's paws. Of course she was special. *I'm so sorry, sister...*

"It's gonna take more than that you guys!" I told the team.

"Got it!" Hiinhia said above me as he pulled his knives from his back, "Stealth mode acti—"

"Whoops I guess it mutes him too!" Qranyt said, "Hey, uh, no name female human?"

"Yes?" I asked.

"Why don't we take our approach too?"

Onyx

At first it seemed that the city wasn't very entertaining after all. Everyone spent their time reading old books and archives or shopping around in the high-quality malls. But then, out in the middle of who-knows-where, I finally found something of interest: an Experimental Technology Research Tower. The building was filled with intelligent creatures like me, all trying to build weird things.

In the tower lifts, something caught my eye, Archaic City Defenses Exhibit on the highest level. I quickly selected the top floor and waited. The doors opened to reveal a giant single-barrel laser turret, blocky in structure with a control deck on the back and several intricate designs in the paneling. If only I could get behind the controls of that? Or even take a look inside?! The whole room looked like it could open up and rotate to provide a line of fire in almost any direction using the turret, though they probably didn't use it much.

"Hello?" another cat said behind me, "Is there anything I can do to help you?"

"Ah yes, I was wondering if I could look through the scope of that giant laser?"

"That depends on your security level my dear," he explained, "of course you cannot fire it without a special key, but you may be able to take a look. Are you a leader of some kind?"

"Yes, I am Onyx Auqiin."

The cat held up his datapad, "Onyx of Aquat. Go take a look if you wish then."

I climbed up to The Chair Of Ultimate Destruction as I would then refer to it as, then started my telescope adventures.

It took a while for me to find something interesting, but there in the distance I saw the Transmission Scanny Base Thing with Avie outside. Even through the telescope they looked like a tiny bug. I rotated the scope slightly off to the right and discovered something moving through the trees;

"How curious? That looks like a flying dark snaky thing, maybe like the one Safaeir supposedly saw." I thought.

"Hey manager guy!"

"My name's Eta..."

"Yeah okay, I'm gonna need that special key thing."

"Uh, I can't do that, sorry."

"It's an emergency?"

"I think... I'm just gonna call the guards. GUARDS!"

"Oh my such a raucous," I sighed.

"Just give her the key thing Eta," the guards said, "she's a Soliean Protector."

"What!? Really!"

"Just give me the darn key!"

"Fine! Here, take it!"

Eta tossed the key through the air up to my seat. I quickly stuck the key into place and focused in on the shape that now was almost right on top of Avie.

"Bzzzzzzz!" I voiced as I held the aperture lever open. "There. Take that serpent thing."

"Wait, what serpent thing?" Eta shouted up to me.

"Oh I don't know, some black snake flying around in the air."

"Oh no, OH NO!"

"What? I just blew it into the, uh, water-void?"

"NO! It can't be dead!"

I looked back through the scope, and sure enough, the serpent was once again rushing towards Avie.

"Well, seems that this one's gonna take a while!"

Hiinhia

There was something entertaining about jumping around in the air without anyone noticing; I was the first to reach the beast, so I ended up needing to dodge a few invisible arrows from Safaeir since she couldn't see me. The serpent thing broke apart once more, re-forming only a moment later just like before. I then took my shot, dropping down on a vine to slash the creature's back. It gave a quick, loud, shriek before turning to look for me. The mysterious person and Qranyt took the opportunity and rushed the creature's back, slashing it down the side! The girl's sword seemed to, rather than part the creature like all the other weapons, cut and burn it deeply, causing it to writhe around in pain.

"Why do you need us if you can do that?" Qranyt shouted out to her.

The human once again slashed out at the creature. I took another few swings at it from my swinging vine above before I lost my momentum.

Avie

I nearly jumped out of my skin as a bright yellow laser shot from the city and straight through the serpent, but unfortunately the creature quickly re-assembled itself. Although it seemed to have little effect on the beast, the laser did cause the creature to back down a bit from the pain. I raised my sword up and leapt for its head, sliding down underneath to be sure I hit as much of the serpent as possible. To my surprise, this time it split right in two around my sword, as if made of cloud. Another laser burst came down on the beast, blasting it apart once more. I sheathed the sword across my back. Perhaps energy hurts it the most? A strange green spark brewed up inside the beast, then erupted into three green, glowing, rings. I stepped back in surprise and watched the creature and everything else in the rings disappear from existence.

Ehnri

I suddenly felt the urge to get involved with the assault on the beast and instinctively started shouting out attack strategies that came from thin air.

"Safaeir! You climb up into the trees. Flank the serpent around the right and shoot from there!"

"Ohh—kay Ehnri, whatever you say?" Safaeir accepted.

"Sleepy, have you figured out how to use your key yet?"

"No, Ehnri, but I can join up with my curved sword!" He said.

"Go for it!" I directed. "Head around the left side, and be careful not to fall off the side of the cliff!"

"Got it!"

I also rushed for the creature, pulling out a small laser-pistol Qranyt had made for Hiinhia but gave to me after Hiinhia took up his knives instead. The creature looked as if its energy was being drained quickly, as if our attacks were at least wearing it out.

"Safaeir!" I shouted as everyone backed down for a second to relax. "Bring a volley from above!"

Safaeir's arrows burst several holes in the beast, allowing for the girl to slice through each bit then stab through the center of its head. The creature shook violently, piecing itself back together again. The girl put the sword back in the shadow of her cloak and pulled out a laser blaster of some kind.

"Hold your attack!" she shouted, focusing the device's beam upon the center of the creature's body.

The beast continued to vibrate for several seconds before shattering into millions of dark shards. The girl put the laser in her cloak before reaching for what the beast had left behind: a dark, narrow crystal shard.

"Good work, all of you." She smiled, giving the crystal a small toss in the air before catching it again. "Just like old times..."

"What did we do?" Sleepy inquired, "Seems like you did most of the work!"

"Your teamwork and strategies wore the creature out enough for me to pull it back into the source of its own energy." She continued, "Besides, you're going to need all the practice you can get fighting these, I'm just here to give you a jumpstart."

Safaeir

The girl took us to a small clearing filled with wildflowers, where wide mossy trees with twisting limbs and floral carpets lined the forest edge. The air felt clearer after she defeated that mysterious beast. Who was she? I could almost see some strange sort of energy in her eyes, as if I could look through the dark center and see something on the other side. It looked like a flame in the darkness, almost like a star, but violent and wild. It almost seemed like fire's light shifted and combined into an ephemeral illustration, similar to the intricate patterns of light in the shadow of a crystal. Staring so long started to make me feel weak.

"Safaeir, can I have a moment with you?" she asked, I nodded and she motioned for the others to stay in the center of the clearing as we walked back to the forest. "You know something they don't, don't you?"

"What do you mean?" I replied;

"I saw you looking through my eyes as if you saw something there. You cannot tell the others what I am, not yet."

"I don't understand, I'm sorry, I won't tell them anything."

I felt something sharp in my mind, digging through my skull and burning down my spine with a power similar to a million lightning bolts, it was happening again...

"No!" I heard her shout to the others, "Stay back! I'll take care of this!" She fell to her knees in front of me as I slumped into the mossy floor.

EAL'AEHJ'ZHI ZHE VAUQOH'STZE ZAHU! EAL'AEHJ'ZHI ZHE VAUQOH'STZE ZAHU! EAL'AEHJ'ZHI ZHE VAUQOH'STZE ZAHU! eal'aehj'zhi zhe vauqoh'stze zahu! eal'aehj'zhi zhe vauqoh'stze zahu.... eal.....aehj....zhi......

The voice faded, I felt the palm of the girl's hand on my forehead, seeming to burn through the electricity with fire.

"There's someone in your mind, Safaeir..." she whispered, "I understand what you are now..."

"What I am?" I mewed softly;

"I've blocked the curse from hurting you, you won't hear her voice any longer until my protection fades."

"How long will it last?"

"Until I die," she smiled, "but by then you'll need to hear her voice again so you can find her!"

"I—"

"Saf, I'm sorry I can't tell you any more, I need to take care of something else, but take this..." She closed her eyes, I felt a soft warmth in my mind as a different voice emerged:

aahnraiitahhvaehj

A burning light sliced through my own eyes, it was the same pattern I saw in her's.

"What was that?" I shook my head free of the sensation.

"That's my name!" she ran back to the clearing, calling out, "Qranyt, your turn!"

"My turn for what?" He asked her.

"I'll need to see your key! The others will need to sit this out..."

Qranyt nodded to the others, "Why don't you catch up with Onyx or Avie while I'm gone."

"Don't worry, you do what you need to do, we'll find something else!" Hiinhia assured him.

"Just don't fall off any cliffs alright?" Qranyt laughed.

"Sure won't try to!"

For a moment, the girl turned back to me and I could hear her in my mind, her voice seemed even more soothing there. I could see a shining tear from her left eye.

"and if you can hear me, sister, please forgive me for that day. I love you, and our other sister loves you too. I'm sorry, Diiviide. Keep Safaeir safe when I'm gone."

She led Qranyt back to the clearing edge and motioned him to use the Key of Emerald. I watched as he shaped the rings in the air and slammed the key onto the ground, making them vanish into thin air.

Qranyt

Thraesa stood as quiet as usual, but this time it was only me and a stranger inside. The girl grabbed my paw and flew us through the void, dodging thousands of tiny filaments. It felt more and more like a new language to me now, a script written across the cosmos. I could see each filament and know exactly when and where it would go.

"Here," she said, stopping our movement, "Get your key ready, focus. You'll need to move the entire moon into Thraesa!"

She pulled the filament, bringing us to Reid. I looked up to see a giant space-rock hurtling towards the moon.

"NOW Qranyt!!!" She shouted, wrapping me in some sort of force-field.

I started shaping the rings, then shot my arms out to engulf the entire moon.

"This is gonna kill me isn't it?!" I asked her, holding the rings far out.

"I'll protect you, you'll be safe with my help! Think about my name!"

"I don't know your name!"

"CONCENTRATE!"

I closed my eyes and slammed my paws back together. I felt a hand against my back, burning like wildfire straight through my soul. It felt so familiar...

I opened my eyes to Thraesa, just as it usually was, except that this time it had a moon in the middle of it. I felt the energy almost completely gone from my body.

"You did well, but we're too late..." the girl shuddered.

I looked back at the moon to see that one side was fractured and glowing orange. I reached for the human to comfort her.

"It's not your fault, I should have set our arrival to an earlier time," she sighed. "The moon is mostly saved, but we'll just need to hope that you'll save everyone there in the future when this all comes to pass."

"Can't we go back?" I asked,

"No, it would break Thraesa."

"Very well, so what now?"

"Just before we left I sensed another dark creature going after Avie. It shouldn't be able to do much of any harm here, so I was thinking we could switch places with it."

"Okay, so how do I do that?"

"Think through the key, imagine the creature near Avie. Thraesa should do the rest for you."

As I pictured the forest of Intafari in my mind, Avie and the creature emerged. The rings shifted, and in a split second we were back out of Thraesa.

"Qranyt?" I heard Avie ask.

"Hey Avie, seems like you found a dark serpent too?"

"Yeah, we're gonna need to take a look into that. Who did you find, Qranyt?"

"I can't tell you my name." The girl sighed.

"Oh? Why's that?"

"Because I shouldn't be here, and I can't have you knowing who I am before we're officially supposed to meet."

"Wait—the others!" I said, reminding her we should meet up with them.

"Well I'll leave you to that, I still have a few hours before the transmission is in view."

I turned back to ask, "A few hours? Did you try the relay satellites?"

"Yep, tried that."

"Have fun waiting then!"

Avie

I waited until Qranyt and the mysterious person were off before I extracted Thraesa stone from one of my coat pockets. This stone I had taken from Ealtae in the future, I knew it would come in handy someday.

Qranyt

The girl and I started our run back to the others, but just before we got there, she stopped me.

"Qranyt," she said, "this is for you."

She pulled a small item from her cloak; it had the appearance similar to a key, except it had three radiating blade-like arms. The design over the core was similar to the one on her blade, and the inside also looked like a flame.

"For all that you did to help me."

"Thank you," I replied, allowing her to hand me the object. "Who are you, really though?"

"I am no one, I should not even exist yet, as I also come from Thraesa, but a different Thraesa. A future one."

"Were you the one that wrote the note?" I asked.

"What note?" she looked puzzled.

"The reason I was able to get this key in the first place."

"Ahhh... Noted," she winked.

"One more thing," I started, "what I felt when I moved Reid, the burning feeling through my soul, that was you?"

"I helped give you the energy you needed to move the moon into Thraesa, you wouldn't be able to move something that big without help."

"Was that real? On Ealtae in that cave?"

"You'll understand it all very soon, Qranyt."

Sleepy

For the next few moments after Qranyt and the other person disappeared we were left with few ideas about what to do.

"There!" Ehnri shouted.

We looked to see what he saw, and to our great surprise, it was Qranyt and the girl!

"Wait, how did you? You just left!" Safaeir stuttered;

"Thraesa—" Qranyt replied, trying to catch his breath.

"What to do now?" Hiinhia swung down from a vine.

"Perhaps we can go see what Onyx is up to?" I suggested.

"I best get going then," the human said, reaching out for Qranyt. "I assure you all that you'll be seeing me again very soon."

"Where do you want to go?" he asked her, removing the key from his belt and summoning the rings.

"Just Thraesa. I'll get where I need from there."

Onyx

Well there I was, having just witnessed some very strange events. A dark serpent thing, a dark serpent thing disappearing when a web portal appeared around it, a web portal appearing with Qranyt and some human inside, Avie themself disappearing into Thraesa, and the strange human giving a weird glowy thing to Qranyt. Wow. Telescopes are great! Especially when they double as a laser!

"Alright Eta have your key-thing back." I tossed the special access card down to the old cat.

"Did you make it go away?" Eta called back as I got ready to leap down.

"No, I don't think that I did, looks like my friends took care of it."

"Good!"

"Okay, enough of that! Is there any good place to build some tech?"

"Uhhh, any of the lower levels?" Eta shrugged.

"Got it!"

I soon found myself in a sort of tech shop, where I got right to work on trying to figure out my key. I found a microscope and some scanning devices that helped me analyze the structure, but...

"Hey Onyx where you at?" I heard Qranyt's voice over the communicator.

"Found a lab, doing science; what, the jungle too boring for you?"

"No, not at all, we did lots of interesting things!"

"Yep, I was watching you!"

"Uhh weird, okay Onyx, direct us to your lab, we got time to spare while Avie figures out the signal stuff!"

Avie

The instant I entered Thraesa I could tell something was different, was it that girl? Was it Qranyt? In a different plane through the Thraesa Void I could see a whole world had been placed within; It was a vibrant green and brown, a glowing orange slash straight through the whole world from side to side.

13. ZETRAFOR

[Iatolin City Community Lab, Intafari]

Hiinhia

It took a few hours before we heard anything from Avie, but we kept ourselves entertained in the technology lab Onyx found. The tower was filled with different devices that could scan objects and display their composition and internal structure without any need to cut them open or attach them to computers, making it the perfect place to learn more about our keys.

"It's quite curious," Qranyt started, looking at the Key of Emerald through some variety of microscope. "The key has an advanced crypto-structure seeming to consist of tiny channels etched in the crystal inside, all linked together in a way similar to that of a transistor."

"Yes," Onyx agreed, "and the tight spaces are kept from interfering with each other with the help of the insulation of the gemlike material. This seems to allow for nanotech so small that the processing power of these keys is immense."

"Look at Safaeir's matrix though!" Qranyt continued, "the structure of the matrix is much more advanced!"

"Yes, it is, if only we could figure out what each section does and how it all fits together?"

I decided to leave the technologists to their work and see what Sleepy was up to. I'll say, it wasn't much of an improvement.

"Hey Hiinhia! Whatchu up to?" He asked as I approached.

"Just walking around to see what everyone is finding. What are you doing?"

"Oh, you know, analyzing the seeds of the local biosphere. Botany has always amazed me, ever since birth!"

I didn't say it, but I knew it was because he grew up in a desert.

"I'm thinking that I might be able to remove the endosperm and cotyledon of each seed before gently freezing them for easier storage," He explained as he worked.

"Well you keep to that, Sleepy!" I told him in an attempt to sound enthusiastic, but like I said, not any more interesting than the others.

I continued on to where Ehnri and Safaeir were hanging out, building different weapon components and gear of sorts.

"Hiinhia!" Ehnri jumped up at my arrival.

"Hey Ehnri! I see you're working on something over here too?"

"Nothing special, just experimenting with my new knowledge is all. Safaeir over here is designing a few new things for our uniforms!"

"Yeah!" Safaeir jumped in, "Like this new tool here! It launches synthetic nanofibers at the target and sticks just like a grappling hook for us to swing on!"

"Sounds great!" I told her, "How do you know how to make all of these?"

"Well the database here seems to have a lot of useful blueprints we can use, I only figured out how to pick the best ones and modify them to our needs!"

I turned, taking a quick glance at Ehnri's weapons. "A staff of some kind?" I asked him.

"Oh yeah! I made one of those!"

I picked up the dark staff to take a closer look at the insane level of detail in the point. I found a stunning resemblance to the patterns on Ehnri's key.

"This is amazing! It would take days for most to even come up with a design for this, yet you've actually built it in an hour!"

"Thanks Hiinhia, that means a lot coming from you! I think the key wanted me to make something like this so it talked to the computers and showed me how!"

Ehnri, Safaeir, and I ended up tolerating each other long enough for a few interesting conversations about weapons and tools before Avie ruined the party.

"Alrighty everyone, I'm sure you've gotten enough of a break and you're ready to go to the next location?" Avie said as they came into the room. "We're going to Zetrafor, sleep on the way if you need!"

"Wait, Zetrafor?" Qranyt asked, gathering up his things. "Just what we need! The tools for nanotech here are very limited. Our research on the keys will double on Zetrafor!"

"Great, then gather your stuff and let's get on the ship!" Avie replied.

Safaeir

Zetrafor, a ringed world and the closest orbiting Solia Aqua. This planet was a stretch of the "habitable" category of worlds. The trip took long enough that a few of us, including myself, snuck in a good nap.

As Qranyt brought the ship down on Zetrafor, I couldn't help but imagine what could possibly make up the foul thick, green, atmosphere. The team quickly grabbed a selection of items from the stash while Avie set out for the scanner base on their own. From the landing platform, several worn old pathways winded away through the terrain. The pad itself was located in the smooth-bottomed valley between steep winding mountain ridges that reached far above into the noxious clouds. The valley was filled with chartreuse ferns and grasses, spotted with trees of white bark and red leaves. Farther down the valley were several ponds and swamp areas that seemed lush with unusual species of flora and fauna despite the looks of the world altogether.

"Sorry, Qranyt, but this does not look like a world where we'll find much nanotech!" Onyx mocked.

"Just follow me, everything will reveal itself eventually," Qranyt replied.

"Somewhere among the outposts and such, sure..."

"She does have a point," I agreed.

"Zetrafor was once a great nanotech factory before Tetratakj even became developed," Qranyt explained, leading us into the side of a mountain through a thick stone door. "The planet was shut down and returned to the wild after Tetratakj came into the picture."

The fluorescent lights flickered on when we entered, revealing what looked to be an ancient building.

"There's got to be tons of artifacts in here!" Sleepy exclaimed, running about to find things to examine.

"Check this out!" Hiinhia called, holding some sort of rock. "Green metal!"

"That, my friend Hiinhia, is Zetrite, a metal named after the planet." Qranyt continued, "Zetrite was an early material when forging weapons."

"Oh yeah I've read about that stuff!" Ehnri laughed and started digging up as much as he could find out of the collapsed rubble. "When mixed with noctium it makes a super-alloy!"

"Nice, and it looks like we already have a foundry and forge at the ready!" I told him.

"Well it looks like you've found something to keep yourselves occupied, so I'm gonna go to the next room over to see if they have anything I can use to construct a matrix..." Qranyt said, realizing nobody was actually paying any attention to him.

Avie

Zetrafor was quiet as usual with its red-leaved white trees and deep canyons filled with strange mysteries. The world didn't receive many visitors, so news of our arrival spread intrigue quickly.

"Avie?" a bear came up to me from the scanner base.

"Hello, I happen to need to use a scanner here to locate the origin of a passing transmission."

The bear was taken aback for a few seconds, but soon replied.

"Sure thing, I'm Ralu. I can show you around a bit if you'd like?"

"I think I got a handle on it, but thanks for the offer!" I told him, examining the three, large scanner dishes located around the facility. "It seems like putting the scanner dishes at the base of the canyon like this is a bit of a waste."

"Except that any on the top would be destroyed from the cyclones," Ralu informed me, "and acid rain."

"Right."

I walked up the steps and into the facility. Fortunately, each of the three sites were constructed so similarly it took only seconds to activate the scan. Once received and loaded on the data drive with the information downloaded at the other two sites, I could relay the information right back to Noctae for processing.

At this point I felt as if I was dragging the team around to each of the locations. Sure, they were following information about the keys, but it'd been a long time since any of them had seen their homes! Then again, it did seem as if they were enjoying their travels, learning about their universe, and hopefully slowly getting closer to understanding what Ket and I saw.

I loaded the last of the information in the datapad and readied for departure back to Noctae. This time, I thought it would be better for me to go on my own. The team could handle themselves and had no need to travel back to Noctae with me so soon.

"Ralu?"

"Yes Leader Avie?"

"Do you happen to have a shuttle that I could use, heading to Noctae or something?"

"Not at the moment, but I can get one ready for you..."

"Great!"

I decided to leave the others here with the ship we arrived on; I'd let them be responsible for their own adventures now.

"Qranyt?" I called over the communication system.

"Ya ready already Avie?"

"You know it, but I'm gonna take another ship back to Noctae."

"Let me guess, you're leaving me in charge and with the ship?"

"You know me well, Qranyt..." I told him, trying not to laugh.

"Well I guess we'll see you next time the universe brings us together!"

"Farewell my friend!"

The trip to Noctae was long and uneventful; unfortunately these communication devices cannot connect from even a few planets away, nevermind a star. It did give me time to rest, and wonder what the team would do next with Qranyt in charge. At any rate, I knew they would grow to do great things together, learn all the secrets I could no longer help them with. As I had arranged, my job was over for now. Time for them to lead their own path.

Qranyt

I wasn't surprised Avie handed me command of the Soliean Protectors. Secretly I do believe I am their favorite bear residing on Aviea. They had important work to do concerning what was up with that signal, whatever it was.

I stopped my mind-wandering and got back to the task at hand: constructing a new matrix from scrap materials.

"Now that is way too bulky to be a matrix!" Hiinhia said.

"Gotta start somewhere," I reminded him.

"Yeah I think I'm gonna start with food. Is there any of that on Zetrafor?"

"Yeah, out in the woods. I think you might find some, uh, tasty roots I think they call them?"

"I think I'm just gonna find someone else to ask," He replied.

"Good enough!"

After that brief encounter, I was able to get back on track. It took a bit to get the basic form laid out, but I eventually made a magnified example of some of the etch marks patterns and sections on a piece of ceramic for later reference. Looking deeper around the caverns within the mountain, I did find a particular room of interest filled with ancient equipment.

One such device looked like a tall triangular black pyramid with an upside-down pyramid connected underneath, labeled below on its shelf "Rift Detector." I gently stroked the surface, leaving a line through a thick layer of dust. Just a moment after my touch the device lit up, emitting a deep red glow between the two pyramid bits. Suddenly the surface as well was lighting up, flickering at first. I lifted the device and turned it around and around, watching the lights change so it looked as if the borders came together at an arrow-point. As I walked around, the arrow point adjusted only slightly each time I moved it. I ran back through the rooms, tracing the arrow's focus. In only a few minutes I was back outside and the detector was telling me to dig straight down.

"Right silly thing, so I don't have a shovel or drill or anything..."

No response from the device, as expected. Time to use my good ol' bear paws. I placed the Rift Detector on the ground and went to work, hoping not to fall into any rift of sorts. Then I had an idea...

I pulled out the Key of Emerald, perhaps the rings produced by the key would scuff everything up as usual, only this time, strong enough to rip apart the soil. I focused my energy into spinning the rings around faster and faster until, *CLINK!* I watched as a dark object was flung into the air. It fell into one of the odd Zetrafor trees where quickly I lost sight of it.

"Alright Rift Detector, is this what you wanted me to get?"

Sure enough, the Rift Detector had shifted its arrows to point towards the forest where the dark object had gone. I cautiously approached the object, tucking the detector into my belt.

The object was shaped like an eye in a way, a pointed oval; It seemed to be a crystal of some kind with defined, smooth faces. Inside I could see a deep indigo-violet glow vibrating around, twirling in whisps. I reached down and scooped the crystal up in my forepaw, where it glowed yet brighter. Upon returning to the doorway into the old lab site, I saw something was up with the rest of the group.

"Qranyt, you're back!" Safaeir shouted with relief.

"I was only gone for a minute!" I replied.

"We discovered something! It's a hole in the caves, it drops down very very far, and we're not sure about going down yet," Ehnri explained.

"Yeah let's go check it out!" I told everyone, "Get all your gear together and ready for immediate departure for the deep caverns of Zetrafor. It's completely safe!"

"Please don't put it that way, Qranyt..." Onyx said.

"Oh come on! It'll be fun!" Sleepy exclaimed, raising his key in the air. "Maybe there's another one of the keys down there?"

Our team stood, once again assembled for another adventure. One by one, we climbed onto the ladder to descend into darkness.

"Sleepy?" Hiinhia called down, Sleepy having gone first.

"Yep, got it!" Sleepy dropped a light orb, which drifted like a feather down the shaft.

The walls were built of worn brick, not something I felt good about trusting. This passage could have been built thousands of years prior and might not respond well to our presence. Fortunately I had just the device to get us out if I sensed a collapse.

"I've found the bottom Qranyt!" I heard Sleepy say deep below below me. "You are not going to believe what is down here!"

Eventually the last of us reached the bottom, and when I turned I saw that Sleepy had released a few more light orbs that were floating around. I looked out at what lay before us. There in the dim light was a giant dome in the deep mountain. In the center there were twelve grey stone pillars in a circle around some kind of protective field.

"I have a feeling we probably shouldn't touch those," Onyx commented.

"Definitely gonna touch those!" I told her.

"Should really not touch those, they're there for a reason."

I watched as a dark serpent rose up from the floor inside the field, leading me to notice the presence of strange shining pieces of metal underneath.

"Yeah we've already taken one of those down!" Sleepy added.

"Sooo gonna touch those!" I drew my sword, as well as the thing that girl gave me, then jumped down into the underground dome arena. "More light please, Sleepy?"

Hiinhia drew his knives and scampered up the wall before disappearing. Sleepy tossed the rest of his tiny light orbs into the air, adding just a bit more light in the dome.

"Ehnri, I'm counting on you to give the orders my friend!"

"Got it, Qranyt! Safaeir, you head to the other side of the dome! I'll stay near the entrance here! Hiinhia you do your sneaking, and Sleepy I'll need you on the left!"

Safaeir drew her matrix bow on the other side and aimed straight for the force field.

"Onyx, you head to the right, it seems that energy weapons do the most harm to these things, so get out your laser and plasma stuff."

"Nice key, Ehnri!" Onyx complemented.

"Thanks!"

"Alright you guys, here goes nothing!"

I ran from pillar to pillar flipping the switches, right down to the last one.

Safaeir

I readied my bow as Qranyt prepared to switch the last pillar off.

"Ready?" Qranyt paused, "Get'm!"

The tube of light disintegrated, releasing the long, dark serpent which immediately turned its gaze to Qranyt. I focused my energy into the bow and shot straight at the serpent's center. Onyx fired a plasma burst at each broken segment, circling around the wall of the chamber. Sleepy pulled out a small plasma weapon and joined the attack from the wall to my right. Qranyt began using the energy rings from his key in combination with his own plasma gun. Ehnri used his time to come up with a new tactic.

"Alright everyone!" Ehnri shouted, "Onyx get in close and keep your guns raised and I'll need Sleepy right beside you! Qranyt, keep using your plasma blasts and rings but use them to overwhelm the creature and make sure that you keep it from getting too close to anyone! Hiinhia and Safaeir, keep breaking up the pieces for Onyx and Sleepy!"

"Keep it up everyone!" Qranyt yelled over the sound of the upset beast.

In less time than I could comprehend, the serpent thrashed and its tail passed through Sleepy's chest. I watched in awe as a ring appeared below him with a blast coming through, taking Sleepy through the reverse direction where he fell to the floor next to me in sync with the blast hitting the back of the creature.

"Finish it! Quick!" I shouted.

Qranyt fired a plasma beam into the center of the creature and held up the device the mystery person gave him, and a blazing inferno blasted straight into the beast as well. Within seconds the serpent erupted a shower of ash, dropping a single dark shard of crystal in the center of the metal scraps on the floor.

"Sleepy, are you alright?" I quickly dropped to his side.

"I think so—" he replied. With my help he managed to lift himself up.

"I think he's okay, everyone, we'll need to keep an eye on him."

Hiinhia

From my perch up above I saw Qranyt approach the center, where he picked up the metal shards and the dark gem.

"These," Qranyt started, "are pieces of a matrix. I bet that with certain precision in detail, I could reconstruct it."

"So now what are we gonna do?" Onyx sighed.

"Head upstairs I guess, continue our research. Onyx you gather those light orbs up for Sleepy."

I dropped down in the middle of their circle.

"Hello all!" I said.

"You're one to spy on everyone!" Onyx laughed.

"Not spying if you already knew I was here!"

Qranyt

It took a bit of time to get the construction space set up. Once everything was in a logical location, I was ready to examine and construct a matrix with the help of the others.

"It looks as if the final product will be a sort of beveled cube," I told the team.

"This object you dug up, it is called a nebula shard," Safaeir told me, reading through one of her books from Ealtae.

"If I can combine the crystal with the dark shard, I could create a powerful hybrid crystal to power the matrix."

"I believe that may be what that girl had in mind. Remember her flame sword?" Onyx recalled, "Perhaps you can replicate that with the nebula shard?"

"That's the plan."

There on the stone desk was an instrument labeled "Shard Merge."

"This seems a bit obvious!" I showed the others.

After placing the shards in the device, I flipped a switch and watched the technology unfold. In an insane speed, the device sliced both gems into tiny pieces and rearranged each and every of the millions of grains, recombining them into a single, new gem so incredibly advanced that the crystal itself became a computer.

"That was, " Safaeir approached, "unexpected."

"Wow!" Sleepy exclaimed.

Ehnri jumped beside me, "This technology is so old, yet so advanced!"

"This metal," I explained to the team, "is iridium. It is very heavy, yet also a great conductor of electricity."

I carefully placed the gem in the center of the conglomerate of metal pieces and motors that made up the matrix's mechanical system. I placed the remaining metal conglomerates into position, just like a puzzle. The new iridium-noctium matrix was born, shifting and sealing itself until it became a perfect beveled cube.

"Give it a run Qranyt!" Ehnri said excitedly.

"Yeah, let's see what it does!" Sleepy agreed.

"Alright, you asked for it."

I took the matrix from the table and held it carefully in my hands. I heard it activate from the inside, I felt it reaching into my body and mind. It felt cold, sharp, nothing like controlling the Key of Emerald. This "matrix" somehow seemed dead and empty. Despite this, the matrix transformed one of its parts into a handle, which I then grabbed hold of. In my head I shaped the matrix into a blade. I opened my eyes and watched the matrix fold into a sharp longsword, the stone at the base of the blade. The others looked in amazement as the blade began to glow a dark violet-indigo, with currents of plasma flowing around the blade. The plasma erupted from the blade when it swung, heating the air around it.

"This is amazing!" Sleepy said in awe.

"Something seems strange about this," I began, a cold shiver running through me. I folded up the sword back into a cube. "I don't know what it means, but despite copying and working off what knowledge we have of matrix structure, this object I've created seems nothing like a matrix. Whatever this is, it feels cold and dead."

The team exchanged puzzled looks for a few moments, before the silence was broken by Sleepy.

"I don't know how to use my Key of Sleprah, but it's warm, and when I hold it I never feel alone!"

"Ahh," I sighed in disappointment, "If nothing else, it will serve as a good weapon against the dark creatures." I hooked the matrix onto my belts and motioned to the team, "Get your things and whatever else you might need!"

"Oh great! Where are we off to now?" Onyx asked.

"Aviea. I thought that maybe our team could take some time off on the beautiful world Aviea, maybe see my territory?"

"Sounds good to me!" Ehnri agreed.

"I happen to know there's a celebration happening quite soon there!"

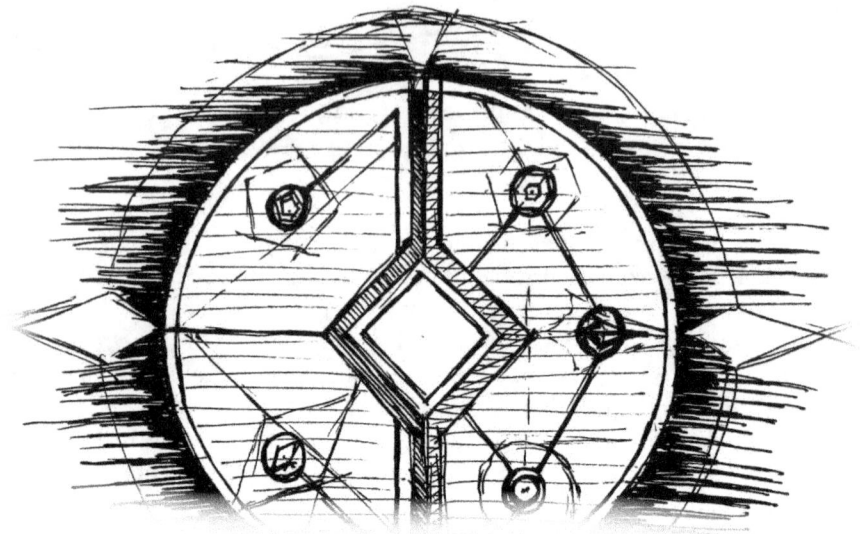

14. SEPARATION DAY

[Viikja City Spaceport, Maurakjnaun, Aviea]

Ehnri

Our small transport made its way to Aviea on the last of its fuel, landing in the Emerald Territory at night.

"This is your territory?" Safaeir asked.

"Well, hardly anymore since I'm rarely actually here!" Qranyt told her, shrugging.

"I still can't get over how amazing Maurakjnaun is!" Onyx reminded us.

"Oh c'mon guys, it's just a bit of land!" Hiinhia mocked.

Qranyt led us to the Leaders' Center, where he informed us was the place "where all the magic happens." He showed off the scanners and tools, fancy technology, etcetera. He also showed us how his territory equality, relations, yet also individuality from nearby territories was so important, because this date was Separation Day.

"So tonight is a party for what, exactly?" Onyx asked.

"Everything and anything, but it just so happens to be the same day West Filsa broke free from us and became its own territory."

"I remember that! Hiinhia commented. "That day you shoved a deuterium grenade in the face of the leader of Filsa!"

"Qranyt..." Onyx laughed, "was that really necessary?"

"About Filsa..." I started, "Any chance we can go there?"

"Perhaps, but why don't we celebrate, then get some rest, then go do that?" Qranyt replied.

"Gosh you guys!" Hiinhia remarked, "it's not even Separation Day yet! That's tomorrow!"

"So that's all you do here, party?" Safaeir asked, "Sounds great!!!"

Qranyt led us out on the balcony, where we could see a giant blazing fire in the city center, a big beacon tower lit, creatures joining up in circles! There were even boats in the channel, filled with candles and colorful exploding rockets!

"Confront your people Qranyt!" Onyx laughed.

"Maurakjnaun!" Qranyt began, catching the attention of the great, energetic, feasting, happy crowds below. "One cycle ago, we were having great conflicts with the territories of Filsa! In an attempt to repair our relations in a calm manner, my newly acquired apprentice Hiinhia and I set for the capital to make certain our territories would be able to repair and heal, then on to be separate lands, separate territories, each with the pride for their cultures and creatures and well being; on this day, the Eve of Separation Day!"

The crowd roared and cheered with enthusiasm for their leader.

"Today you see by my side a newly-built team; Avie themself organized this team of Soliean Protectors to help us learn about our universe. We were united to show other territories what we can do together, so I have brought with me these citizens of the Soliean Stars. Not all are leaders, some just like you, and every one of us is our own! Tonight we celebrate our differences, and how we can use them to bring us back together!"

More and more cats, bears, humans, and even the owls joined in the city, showing their support for Qranyt.

"Here you can see my great friends I have made, Hiinhia, the invisible assassin and Ehnri, the strategist, both from Ealtae! Sleepy, the new leader of our allies on Sleprah-Daecaser, Onyx, defender and new leader of Auqaut Territory! And of course, last but certainly not least, Safaeir, bow-master and historian of Ealtae!"

Qranyt pulled each of us forward to show us to his creatures, who cheered at every one of us.

"Wow, great speech Qranyt, now what?" Onyx inquired.

"I'm just gonna go down and see the people, you know, hang out."

"Nooo-way you're not!"

"Join me if you'd like!"

Qranyt slipped out of the room and, presumably, out the building too.

"Well then! Who's going too?" Hiinhia asked us.

"Absolutely not!" Onyx shouted.

Safaeir was rather confused and asked, "I'm sorry, what's going on?"

"The rest of you go to bed then, goodnight!"

"I'm not gonna miss out on Emerald delicacies!" I heard Sleepy say as he followed Hiinhia.

"That's my bear!"

"Weeelllll, I'm just gonna take some rest time then," I told the remaining two.

"Did they ever tell us where the beds are?" asked Safaeir.

"Oh great," continued Onyx, "so much for that."

Sleepy

The local farms of Maurakjnaun have an extensive selection of teas I discovered, teas that kept me very awake and energetic! Qranyt explained it was called kaf-een or something, oh well. We grouped up in a small fancy restaurant, where we ordered several frozen treats and swordfruit specialties, all of which Qranyt paid well for.

"You know, it really blows my mind," I started.

Hiinhia then said, "Yeah?"

"That there's a volcano here!"

The entire room erupted into laughter at hearing my joke.

"Where you learn to make jokes like that, Sleepy?" Qranyt chuckled.

"Despite being from Sleepy2c, there's many things I can't sand... but jokes in the desert are endless!"

After dozens more jokes, I got tired. Qranyt led us back to the tower where there were several soft guest beds and areas to sleep right underneath the clear sky. Unfortunately the stuff in the tea didn't let us sleep, even with our exhaustion, so it was mostly us three just staring at the surrounding Starhaven Nebula and bright stars beyond it all night.

Perhaps this really was the proper break we needed.

"Despite being close neighbors, Sleprah-Daecaser and Aviea have never really been allies..." Qranyt said softly, "I'm glad we could change that. Thank you, Sleepy."

"I should be thanking you! Without your support, my people would probably still be starving and I'd have never gotten a chance to travel with you!"

"With all that time apart, I imagine you have such different culture, ideas, maybe even different names for the stars... What do your people call that one?" He gestured into the heavens towards a bright violet-white point between the soft clouds.

"Oh, I suppose thats... Saefaun-de."

"We call it Veldessan Tule, but I think I like your name better."

~   ~   ~

Onyx

After the three idiots got back it was difficult for any of us to sleep. All their loud noises and comments on every tiny thing; it was easy to tell they were tired too, considering nothing they were saying made any sense!

In the morning I bullied the three all-nighters to get right to work preparing for our next adventure: I declared our trip to South Filsa, more natively known as Filsaera.

"Submarine at the ready everyone! All paws to work here!" I called out.

I ended up keeping everything in control on the Leader's Submarine, until of course the three decided to crash.

"Well look who actually got sleep last night!" I commented to the other two on deck.

"Gosh they look like they went through a lot!" Safaeir agreed.

"Emerald Territory, land of the parties!" laughed Ehnri.

"What a great example you're all setting!" I replied.

Then we were off, bringing the submarine down the Emerald Channel and out to open sea. With the help of the high speed engines on the sub (that apparently Qranyt didn't know about) I expected the trip to take only a few hours.

The peninsula of Filsaera is said to be one of the most amazing and beautiful places on Aviea. Nobody has ever been able to understand the structure there, so I thought perhaps in putting our heads together, we could learn more about it. Despite their lack of sleep, it seemed the whole team was eager to explore the area for any new information.

"So, crew," Qranyt started, leading us to towards the peninsula's center. "This place of interest, if I remember correctly, is a giant puzzle. I ask you now, what would this puzzle possibly be for?"

"A key?" I suggested.

"Maybe."

"Matrix of Aviea?" Hiinhia added.

"Perhaps..."

"Another mystery to follow?" Safaeir asked.

"Well, what evidence do we have?"

"Okay Qranyt drop this please," I told him, attempting to cut in front of him.

"Well, take a look there." Qranyt continued.

We looked into the distance, where there was a giant collection of arches made of stone, each one rose above the ground and bent to meet each other high in the air, splitting the clouds around into thin strips. Inside that stone cage was a smaller replica. At the top of the hill we then saw, far below, the cage was positioned over a giant lake, and the inside cage was over an island in the center.

Ehnri then asked, "Who built all this?"

"Filasans of long ago." Qranyt replied, "They supposedly built this place to contain directions to an ancient relic of their old beloved leader."

"So it is probably a matrix?"

"Well I guess we'll just have to go see to find out!"

We reached the edge of the lake, not knowing how to continue.

"I am not swimming out there!" I fiercely told the group.

"Well what else are we gonna do?" Qranyt asked.

"Maybe there's a boat around here somewhere?" Sleepy suggested.

"Nope, can't see any of those."

"A pack of Soliean Protectors, defeated by a bit of water!" Safaeir laughed, "What about these grappling things I made?"

"Qranyt, just use the key!" I reminded him.

"Oh right!"

Qranyt warped the rings of Thraesa, throwing one out to the island.

"That looks like a long drop out there," Ehnri noted.

"You're a cat, what do you care?" I told him.

Each one of us hopped into the ring, which transported us far out to the island in the center of the lake.

"Ouch!" Ehnri shouted as he bounced out of the ring and onto the hard, sandy stone.

"Well look what we have here!" Qranyt said, scanning the giant stone tablet embedded in the ground.

The others stepped back to join him in looking at the large stone, which appeared to be a map of some kind. Figuring that north was the top side of the map, it looked like there was a river running down the left side, which then had a canal breaking off to the right, then a giant box thing?

"A pyramid?" Ehnri pointed.

"Oh right, a pyramid of course," I growled.

"So everyone," Qranyt once again opened his mouth, "this seems pretty obvious..."

"Filnera, North Filsa" Hiinhia told us.

"Right you are Hiinhia, I guess we're gonna need a ship in the end anyways! Time to go back to Emerald!"

"Oh no you don't!" I held him back.

"Well where else could we go for a ship?"

"We are not going to your territory, that I can be sure of."

"Maybe we could get a ship from Aliira, the capital?" Ehnri suggested.

"Finally we've got someone with a little bit of sense."

"No need!" Qranyt shrugged, slightly leaning back towards the submarine which was beginning to rise out of the water. "It's an atmospheric craft too!" The craft settled at the shore, Qranyt motioned us to move along as the doors opened wide.

Hiinhia

It still took some time to fly to Filnera, but most of the time was spent baking Ealtaen food with whatever stuff was in the submarine's kitchen. Three members of the team from Ealtae? They sure knew how to cook their food, but I can't say it was what I'd look for in a meal.

"Check out some of these forest biscuits!" Hiinhia held up a tray of strange bits of food. It could be worse, I guess.

"Why didn't we just fly in the first place?" Sleepy asked.

"'Cuz submarines are cooler? Duh!" Ehnri replied.

"Look there! It's the mountains of Filsa!" I showed the others out the window.

"Looks like a cold spiky nightmare!" Sleepy commented, "I'm glad we are flying!"

Ehnri rushed beside me to look at the huge, snow-capped mountains. The air around the ship dropped several degrees in an instant as we entered the dark, grey clouds.

"Looks pretty nice," Onyx said, "except for, you know, the extremely dangerous gigantic storm clouds that could zap us out of the air."

"Look at the ice dunes!" Ehnri ignored Onyx's comments.

"Okay crew, just about there," Qranyt called back, "give 30 seconds or so and we'll be right over Filnera."

The team gathered by the windows, watching the aesthetic landscape flash by. The Filasan Territories are mostly snow, rock, and ice. The mountains work as climate boundaries, holding the freezing air in one area.

As we passed over the mountains on the other side, the clouds gave way to a thin mist, lit by the red light passing from the sunset.

"The pyramid!" Safaeir noted.

Out the window we saw the giant sandy pyramid sitting in the middle of the pale desert and thin wood. The faces of the pyramid were covered in engravings. It was hard to tell what the symbols depicted, but I suspected they were of importance.

Qranyt set the ship down on the wall of the canal we had seen on the map, giving us a bit of distance from the pyramid.

"We all geared up?" I asked the team outside our ship.

"Geared up and ready to explore Hiinhia!" Sleepy replied.

"All set!" Ehnri said.

"Ready as I'll ever be," Onyx returned.

The team grouped up with all the gear we thought we might need and started on our way to the pyramid.

Qranyt

The locals of Filnera were all up and about at the time we arrived, making it easy for us to ask where an entrance to the pyramid would be.

"Hello," Hiinhia called to a passing human.

"Yes?" the human paused.

"Do you happen to know where the pyramid's entrance is?"

"You mean the, uh... are you sure you want to go there?" He said nervously.

"Why?" I asked him.

"I should probably go..." The human ran off, giving us no hints.

"That was awkward," Onyx said, "next time let me handle this."

Within only a few seconds, another human walked by, and Onyx tried her skills.

"Hey!" she called out.

"Yes, fine feline?" the woman looked down.

"Oh, thank you! I was wondering if you could point our team in the direction of the pyramid's entrance? We're the Soliean Protectors. There's been some public concern in the area so we're checking it out."

"Ohh. I see." she replied, her tone significantly different than before, "Just over there."

The woman pointed to a cave entrance in a nearby rock outcropping that had lit torches on either side.

"Thanks for your help!" Onyx said.

"No problem..."

"You hear that? She called me a 'fine feline!'" Onyx snickered. "You're welcome team!"

"Yeah okay, now we know where to go," I paused, "that was weird..."

Solia Noctia had just passed beneath the horizon, giving the sky a hazy dark red glow. I led the team into the tunnel lit by torches despite their suspicions about the so-called "local concerns."

The tunnel soon came to an end, where we then entered the bottom of a deep, circular hole. Up above we could see the night sky, but ahead was a much less pleasant path. There in the side of the hole was a structure, as if a building had been covered in the stone above it. As I led the others inside the building, I'll admit that I had concerns myself.

The building seemed simple enough to navigate. We entered through the only visible way, where there was a stone spiral staircase. To both the left and right there were doorways, but the one on the right was open.

"This is intere—" I cut off Onyx the instant I heard voices that were clearly not ours.

"Over here!" I whispered, leading the team in through the door to the right.

In the other room there was a stone closet I was able to stuff the team in, leaving them for a moment to spy on the approachers and hear their muffled voices.

"...have you seen? Aliira's protectors are collecting the artifacts." the first human said.

"The people of the spirit are completely devoted to keeping his essence in the pyramid. We cannot allow the uninitiated into the tomb, we will stand guard, and we will be protected by him. His tomb will not allow them entry." a second one replied.

"I hear there is a dreamer among them, he holds her soul."

"interesting..."

The voices soon died off as the two people descended down the staircase.

"Alright team it looks like we're clear," I told the others and led them out of the empty room.

"Down there?" Onyx growled.

"Yeah, down there!" Hiinhia pushed.

"Keep quiet guys!" I told them.

"I wonder if my key will work on all of us?" Hiinhia whispered, activating his key and putting his paw on Sleepy. Sure enough, Sleepy disappeared.

"Maybe we will actually make it down there without being found..."

Onyx sighed, letting Sleepy hold her tail. All that was left was making sure nobody bumped into us!

The staircase continued for several long minutes before giving way to a large, rectangular room carved in the stone, decorated with black-scarlet banners and white-yellow candles. There were several chairs in the room, each occupied by one human. The humans sat unmoving, staring towards the front of the room.

Together we walked as a sort of blob, observing the humans carefully. A few of the humans wore masks which matched the grim color scheme of the banners. Ahead I saw a doorway that, from my gut instinct, seemed like a valid approach to the pyramid.

The doorway revealed a long hall, where on both walls was a consistent line of humans dressed in red cloaks with dark masks. I could feel the others tensing up as I dragged them down the hallway, as I truly hoped, in the direction of the pyramid center. At the end of the hallway things got much worse. We saw more human guards standing there, this time their backs were facing us. I saw no sign of masks on them, and from what I could tell from the back of their heads, I did not want to see the front!

I continued to drag the team toward the pyramid's center, up the ramp past the guards. Once we were perhaps ten seconds by the humans, I felt Ehnri claw at my uniform, presumably to get my attention. I turned to see that the guards were no longer stationary. Their dark, charred faces and black eyes seemed to see right past Hiinhia's key. I pulled twice on Ehnri, passing a signal the others may find to mean "run."

As soon as I thought enough time had passed, I brought the invisible Ehnri into a high-speed, or as high-speed as it could get, charge for whatever was at the end.

The passage slowly turned downward, cut off by what seemed a dead end. Onyx quickly broke the link on our invisibility to start her talk again.

"Well now we're screwed!"

"SHHH!" Hiinhia jumped, *"we don't know where any others may be!"*

We all stopped to look at the hallway's end as it began to shake about, the supposed dead end folding up just like the matrix I built, revealing a new tunnel for us to continue down.

"Quick! Let's go!" Hiinhia pushed us to continue.

"Oh great!" I heard Onyx say from ahead, "another maze!"

"Joy," Safaeir agreed.

The walls around us shifted around rapidly, creating only seconds of opening in different locations.

"Here!" I yelped, jumping through a hole in the wall and pulling the others through as fast as I could.

We fell into a sphere with shifting walls, something that would take a bit of time to get used to.

"We're gonna need to go fast!"

We then grouped up, keeping together as tight as possible. We jumped through several more spheres until we reached the last one, where one side was cut open to reveal the continuation of the hall.

"There it is," I told the others.

A giant circular door blocked the end of the tunnel, but inside the face of the stone door were five holes, each shaped differently. I stepped up to the door and took the Key of Emerald into my hand. There on the door was a hexagonal hole, just the right size for the key.

"I think we need only one more key," I explained, "we have Sleprah's Key, the Emerald Key, the Aquat Key, and the Reid Key, but there's— one more." I pointed to an unusual pentagonal shape carved out as the last hole, then I noticed Sleepy seemed fixed on another feature of the door, "What is it, Sleepy?"

"Writing of some sort, can we copy it down?"

"No need!" Safaeir exclaimed, "it's a name, Simisaurehj!"

"Simisaurehj," Sleepy repeated, "why does that sound familiar..."

"Simisaurehj was the spirit stone," Safaeir continued, "he created this world, didn't you read the book?"

"The book!"

"What book?" Onyx groaned.

The sound of heavy footsteps and shuffling could be heard from behind the chamber's walls, whoever those people were outside, they were drawing near.

"I think it's time to go," I told the others, opening a passage to Maurakjnaun with my key.

"Wait," Sleepy said, "Can't you open a loop right inside the door?"

I paused in thought; technically it was possible but the risks were great, we didn't know what was beyond the door, and the creator must have taken the Maurakjnaun key's ability into account when designing this place.

"We should go," I shook my head.

"Well there's gotta be something!" Onyx studied the door closer, "Come on! Maybe there's a clue about the final key!"

"It's too risky!" I cast the ring around her.

The passage opened up to the peaceful wilds of Viikja's highlands, the Eastern Valley Temple.

"Let's take a moment to rest here," I said, "I'll arrange transport to our next destination, but take as long as you need. In the meantime, Safaeir, I think we should hear some more about this Spirit Stone..."

Safaeir

"My parents often told me of the celestial spirits in stories, but I never really understood their meaning in full or if they were even real. While they taught me many things of Kiravaen, it always seemed like they were sharing stories of the past, because none of my family had ever truly witnessed the evidence of our spirit lamp...

...They told to me of the stars, and how all whisper to one another like echoes in the eternal dark. They told to me of the spine, which connects every existence back to the spirit lamp. They told to me of the creatures that protected us all, the spirit ealtaurate themselves, but they never told to me the truth...

...Only when I saw Sleepy's key did I begin to understand."

"So those people in the cave, they were talking about Sleepy?" Onyx inquired,

"*I hear there is a dreamer among them, he holds her soul.*" I repeated, nodding. "The story says Sleepy's key is not a lost technology, but something far more powerful. It is the soul of a celestial spirit."

"So, Sleepy's key is a ghost?" Onyx winced, "We got a ghost following us everywhere?"

"I—I don't think that's what we should be worried about... As far as the stories say, Sleprah was a benevolent entity, besides, I don't think any of us have seen evidence of her having any supernatural influence over anything?"

Qranyt held out his own key, "Are all of the keys containing some sort

of— celestial spirit as you say?"

"I'm sorry, Qranyt, I really don't know."

It was true, everything I said was based on stories from my parents and speculation on my own part considering what we had seen so far. There was one detail I decided to leave out, however. My own matrix had already communicated with me...

Sleepy held the key to his chest, closing his eyes, "I understand the meaning of this now, I must vow to protect her for all eternity, just as she had protected us."

15. CALL FOR POWER

[Eastern Valley Temple, Viikja, Maurakjnaun, Aviea]

Safaeir

"Transport is arranged!" Qranyt announced, "I have something to show you that I think you'll all be happy to see!"

Qranyt gathered some fancy data drives and called upon one of his fancier Emerald Cruisers for our trip to Solia Aqua's outermost planet, Zekj. The ship picked us up from a nearby landing pad hidden within the dense rainforest slopes, and just like that we were on our way.

Qranyt dragged us all into the ship's map room and started messing with the display, "Okay! Check this out!" He jammed one of his fancy data drives into the device and pressed some more buttons. I jumped up on the side of the display and crouched down to take a look at what seemed like a giant blueprint.

"This is amazing!" said Sleepy.

"What is it?" Onyx asked.

"It's a ship, designed by Avie and I to serve as a moving base of operations for the Soliean Protectors and leaders. Unfortunately with a project this expensive, we need to get the vote for from the majority territories of Solia."

"Wow, way to ruin the excitement!"

"This is a really big ship just for us?" asked Ehnri.

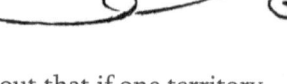

"Yes, sort of, but we didn't get the vote. Turns out that if one territory leader is crazy enough to pay for the entire ship, then that leader can gift the ship to the Soliean Protectors."

"Oh? So you paid?" Onyx continued, making a funny face.

"Sure did! That's why we're going to Zekj, their facilities of course being one of the primary construction sites of the Soliean Fleet."

"And how are you going to pay for all of this exactly? I'm not chipping in..."

"Well," he shrugged, "we will be sharing the ship for some time, inviting researchers on board and even offering education as part of my new mobile university program! It'll be easier to cover costs with the grants from the Soliean Education Fund and all that!"

"So much for peace and quiet..." she groaned.

"Oh please, Onyx, you'll hardly notice! Maybe I'll even share some of the funds raised with you!"

"Okay, I'm beginning to like this plan..."

The ship slowly descended down into the grassy plains of Zekj, but just ahead we could see the giant towers and ship parts.

"Hey, uh, Qranyt?" Onyx started, "your device is making some noise—"

"Device?" he asked, "which device?"

"That one from Zetrafore?"

"Err?"

"This one!" Onyx tossed the device to him, revealing the rapid short bursts of sounds that signified some sort of something.

"Ah yes, the rift detector."

"Yes, of course, the rift detector," she rolled her eyes, "I knew that."

"Well, I'll leave that to, uh, Safaeir, sure!"

Qranyt tossed me the unusual device.

"You take care of that, and I will get to building a ship!" he said, setting for the exit.

"Okay then everyone, I guess I'm in command here!" I told the team.

"Rift detector?" Hiinhia pointed, trying to get an idea of our next move.

"Yep, sure, let's check it out. This time we'll bring a shovel," Onyx stated.

Hiinhia

Safaeir had us out on a chase to find some sort of crystal using the rift detector, but so far, no such luck.

"I thought it was pointing this way!" Safaeir said.

"Just like you thought it was pointing the other way a few minutes ago?" Onyx asked.

"Wait! I think I've been reading this wrong. I think it's supposed to go, ah!"

Her short burst of excitement jerked me back to reality, "You got it?"

"Just about, yeah!"

Safaeir encircled the rift detector's focal point, closing in on the supposed location of one of those strange gems.

"It's here!"

She took the shovel, and just below the surface found a red gem. The team gathered around to see the treasure, a narrow red crystal. In the heart of the crystal was what looked like a powerful blue electric bolt.

"Hm," Onyx sniffed, "Maybe it's some kind of power source crystal, reminds me of some index entry in Auqaut about a 'rift crystal.'"

"I wonder if there are any more here?" I thought out loud.

"Well team," said Sleepy, "let's get our gear and start exploring!"

We made Onyx carry everything to the next location, despite all her complaining. Sleepy spent most of his time studying the local flora while the rest of us sat back enjoying the scenery while Safaeir bounced around in the meadow holding the rift detector in her jaws.

"Ugh! All this stuff is sooo heavy!" Onyx groaned deeply. "It feels like there's three Aviea gravities here!"

"Sorry Onyx, only 2.4 Aviea gravity," I told her.

"I wonder how long it will take to construct the new ship?"

"Considering the priority of the ship, the amount of resources, and the speed at which Zekj usually produces ships with such a huge scale and amount of power, not very long," I shrugged.

"Power? What power?" Safaeir asked, looking every which way.

"No Safaeir," I walked up to her side. "Not down here, up there."

I pointed her to the sky, where the Zennial Orbital Platform was but a pale line cutting through the sky.

"What is that!!" She asked, "it is sooo huge!"

"The Ring of Zekj, a mechanical weight that is filled with reactors. The reactors produce energy and force byproduct in one direction around the ring, turning it. The cables attached around the ring connect to the poles of the world, turning a giant motor which fuels the production shipyards down below."

"That's terrifying!" Onyx laughed, staring at the mechanical wonder.

"So only a day or so of building? We can find stuff to do in a day!" Safaeir said.

"Well, one Zekj day is not the same as one Aviea day, but I don't remember exactly how long it is."

"Alright, let's get to work then!" She exclaimed energetically.

Qranyt

The Zekj engineer team was quite pleased with my order, and just for efficiency I decided to include a little bonus of a few million extra Noctia.

"Leader Qranyt, your ship will be ready before noon tomorrow!"

"Thank you! It's about time the Soliean Protectors have a ship of their own!"

"Sure thing, Qranyt!"

Just to make sure that we had the best deals, I even told them they could take the Emerald ship outside for extra payment!

I was then led into an observatory pod, where I would be given a full view of the ship's construction. The pod was outstretched on a robotic arm so it could spin around the ship, get in close, drop below, or rise above the ship at my command. I decided to put the pod on its default orbit and listen to the ship's statistics over the instrument panel while I waited.

"Hello Customer Qranyt,

Your order, a custom designed A-Class Aviea-Zekj Soletria Capital Ship

Length: 1.37 km

Width: 0.55 km

Height: 0.29 km

Maximum Sequencer Speed: 5 vaer/ovim

Shuttle Crafts Carried: 78 medium-range transports"

This ship is designed to be effective in every way. It has almost impenetrable defenses, overcharged weapon systems, concealed long-range communications, and advanced electric propulsion systems that never needs refueling. The ship has a 12-bay cargo hold designed for storing any materials necessary.

"Thanks computer, it sounds impressive, but I'm gonna take a rest," I told the panel, and yes, the pod even had a bed in it just for me! "Warm up the cabin a bit for me, would ya?"

"Cabin temperature increased."

Hiinhia

The team was showing little success in learning about the land, so we returned to the ship.

"Qranyt?" I called over our communication device.

"Oh c'mon Hiinhia, you had to wake me up?"

"Stop being a lazybone!" Onyx shouted to make sure he could hear.

"What's up?"

"We've decided that our findings here are running thinner than we had hoped, so we're considering taking the ship to Tetratakj to continue research on the matrices, keys, nebula shards, and this 'rift crystal' your weird gadget led us to."

"Oooh, a rift crystal? I tell you what, take the ship, just bring it back in good condition. I'm trading that thing in for extra credit!"

"Sounds like a plan Q, just make sure you send us a signal when construction is complete!"

"A deal forms here... More like I'll pick you up!"

"That's not entirely necessary, even communications will work, Tetratakj is right next to Zekj right now! Even for our ship it will take minutes to get there."

"Okay, whatever you say, kid, go do your thing!"

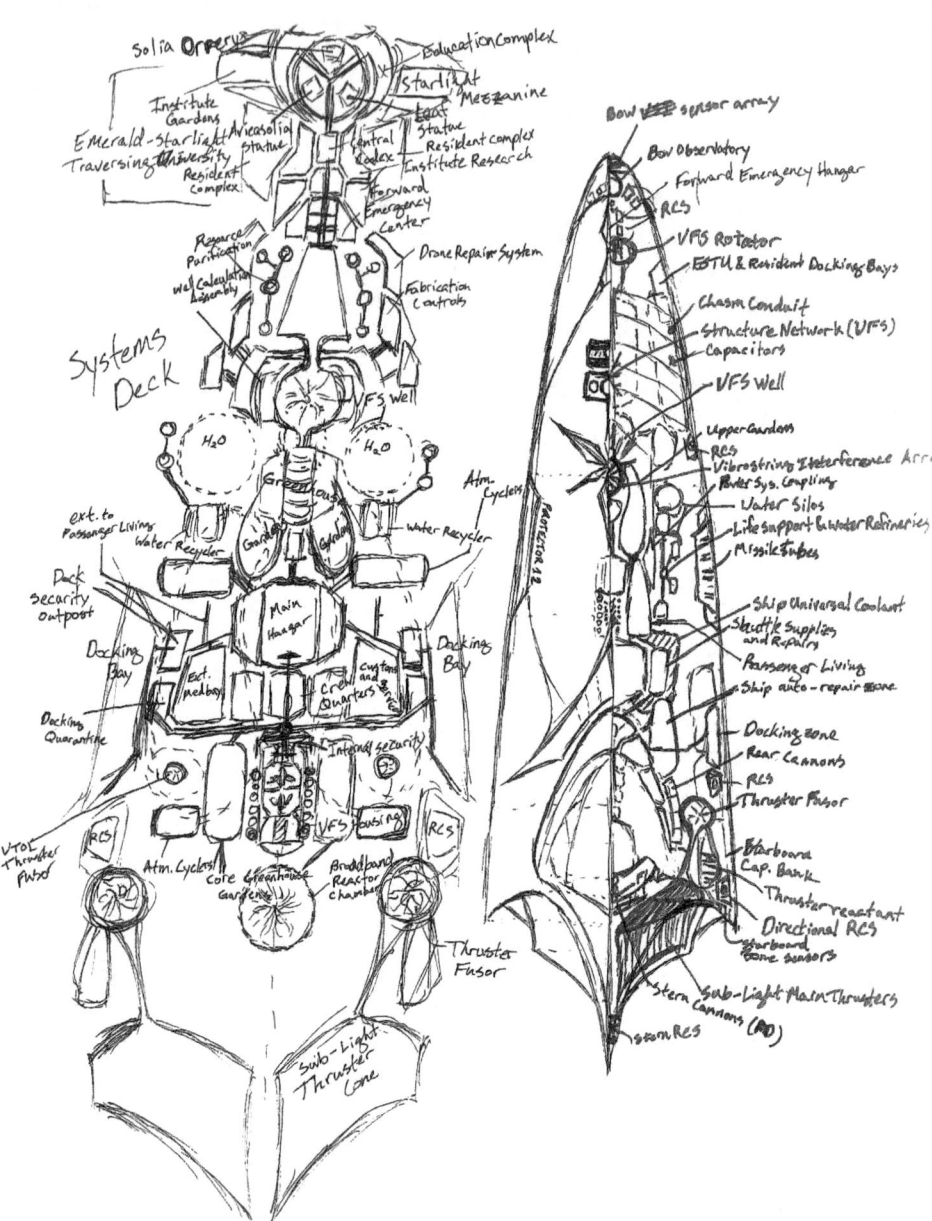

Early design of Savuk the Protector 12

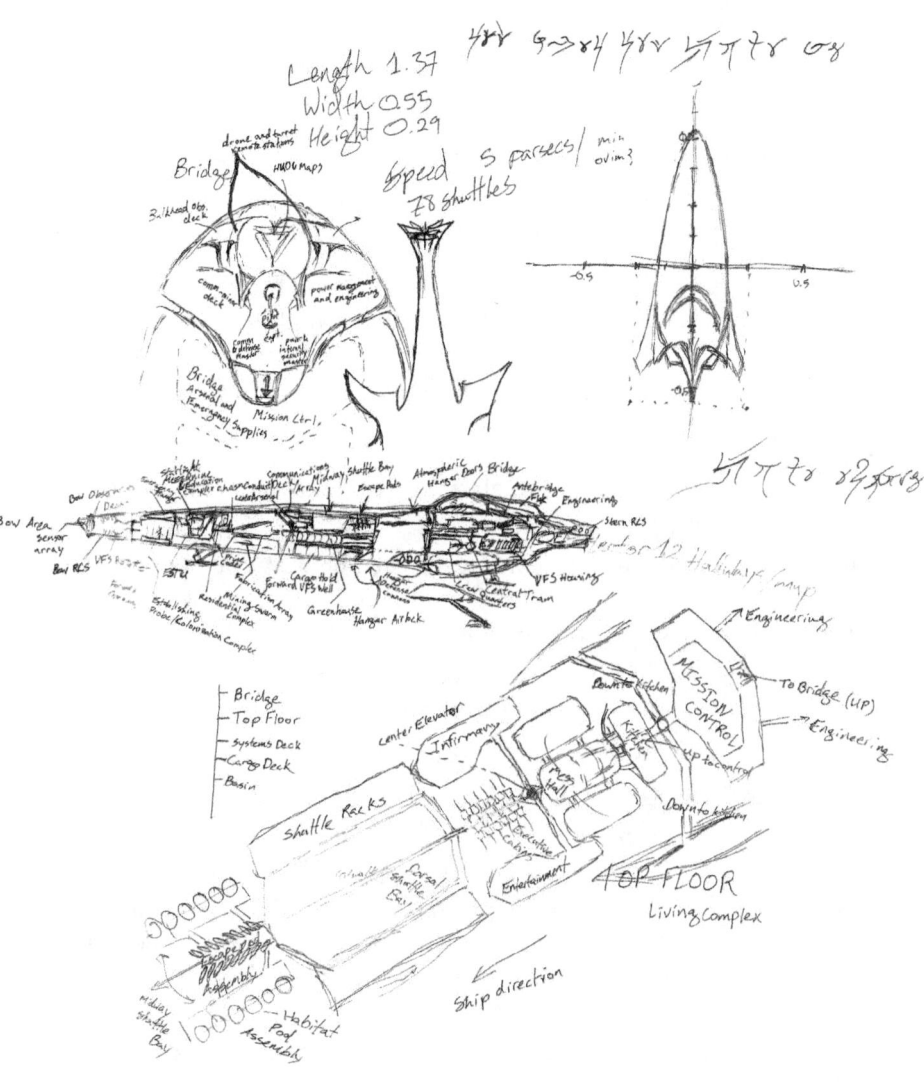

Just like I expected, minutes. We reached Tetratakj in no time. The planet Tetratakj is a curious one. Like Zekj, the whole planet is a factory. According to the books of Ealtae, every world has its own matrix, yet where could it be on the strange cityscape worlds around Solia Aqua?

"Here we back 'gain!" Onyx laughed.

"Flashbacks?" Sleepy chimed in.

"This time, we've visited a more populated sector, maybe we can actually learn more?" I said as I took the front of the team out of the hangar.

"Greetings, visitors!" a tall, female bear guide approached.

"Hello, we are a section of the Soliean Protectors under command of Qranyt," I explained.

"Ah, yes, the Soliean Protectors. What may we do for you?"

"Hiinhia of Ealtae."

"Ah, Doctor Aekjtra of Intafari, nice to meet you!"

"You too!" I replied, "We've got research to do on some ancient artifacts of legend that were once researched here. We've tried to follow the sparse information trails, but it seems our leads are growing thin," I held out my key for her to examine.

"This is amazing! This technology is certainly ancient, but I think I might be able to find something of worth."

"Oh," Safaeir ran up beside us, "and this, a rift crystal."

"Wow! This is not the usual stuff! Usually we get complaints about broken microprocessors and other boring things."

Aekjtra led us down a series of hallways past thousands of engineers working on the usual technological advancements that would end up being split to locations all over. Some would go to Kjitafor, many to Zekj, and even more to more populated worlds of Solia Noctia.

"Here we are!" She said, "This is our ancient database recovery section. Believe it or not, our teams here have also been doing research on old artifacts that may prove useful to your own."

"Thanks for the help, Aekjtra!" I told her before heading into the other room.

"I thought that the research teams on Keys and Matrices had been dissolved a while ago?" Onyx asked.

"It was, but I guess some sort of event brought it back to the attention of the Alliance, and we got a huge grant to work with government contracts from the Arion system to re-open the labs."

"Outsourced research from the Capital?" Onyx looked caught off guard from the response, "that's very unusual, isn't it?"

"We don't often work with the Soliean Alliance's labs, but something caught their attention, and our researchers here found the prospect exciting."

In the recovery section there were thousands of data drives lining the walls, as well as several researchers.

"Hello Protectors, I am Fretaal," a large grey cat introduced, "I am the lead researcher in this sector."

"Nice to meet you! I'm Hiinhia, and we've got Onyx, Sleepy, Ehnri, and Safaeir here!"

"Nice to meet you!" he replied. "I hear you're wanting to learn more about the ancient artifacts of this universe?"

"Yes! Is there anything you have, perhaps on the rift crystal?"

"Ah, yes, the rift crystal. It took us a long time to find that name for it, it was eventually uncovered in some old Zekj literature and cross-referenced in some data entries in Aviea's Sanctuary. Zekj is the planet where the rift crystals are most commonly found, but I assure you that they did not naturally appear there. The rift crystals of this universe were constructed with extreme detail and care to serve as tiny computers and power generators. Inside the core of the crystals lies the blue streak. This streak is a strip of what we call 'passagers,' tiny mechanisms that open holes between planes to access free-flowing energy. Something did at some point place them on Zekj, we're just not sure why or how they ended up there."

"Other planes being where?" Sleepy jumped in.

"We can't figure that out, but some of the theories are very stretched and even disturbing. It is thought that the rift crystals may open passages to dark areas in the universe that are teeming with unknown subatomic particles that can be tamed for great amounts of energy able to power any known device if hooked up correctly."

"This tiny crystal can do all of that?"

"It seems so. Now the nebula shards are another similar type of crystal. These crystals use energy, as well as rift-born xenon, to generate powerful arcs of plasma that can be warped into different forms."

"Like Qranyt's sword!" Safaeir reminded us.

"Yes, Qranyt's sword," I agreed. "Our team leader, who is currently on Zekj, found several pieces of a matrix. He combined a nebula shard with some sort of dark fragment to make a powerful matrix!"

"A dark fragment?" Fretaal was clearly amazed. "You found one of those?"

"Well, not really," Onyx said, "we kinda killed a dark serpent of some kind, and in its brain matter was this dark fragment thing—Wait, there was something Qranyt said after he put that thing together..."

"I have a feeling I already know," Fretaal began, "there was something different about the one he made from other matrices?"

"Yes, that's it..."

"When research on keys and matrices was initially active here, they attempted to create a replica of a functioning matrix." Fretaal explained, "It ended up being a powerful object, but nothing to compare to the original. We still don't know what went wrong, but hopefully by opening the lab once more we can get closer to the truth."

"Paging all team-members on Zekj! Is the ship from Emerald empty of your belongings?"

I took a brief look around the team for an answer.

"Nevermind don't answer that I already checked. The ship is on its way back to Zekj."

"Wait, is the construction done early?"

"Earlier than ever! Look out the window!"

The team turned to look out the tower's large glass windows where a giant parabolic-nosed ship descended between the towers.

"Holy—" Onyx cut off.

"I think I'm gonna call it Protector 12, Savuk for short!"

"Err, why 12?" I called back.

I watched as a bit of green light appeared in the room, which of course burst into a web ring.

"I don't know, alright, it sounded cool!" Qranyt replied after he came through.

"Nice entrance, Qranyt!" Fretaal complemented.

"Qranyt, this is Fretaal, he's been telling us stuff." Onyx introduced dramatically.

"Well then! You guys ready to check out the new ship any time soon?"

I couldn't help but laugh at that, "You're gonna bail out of information this quick!?"

"Aw but it's just so exciting!"

"Chill Qranyt, leave your spaceship parked out there for a bit," Onyx patted him with her tail.

"Hey Qranyt, show Fretaal your matrix!"

"Okay fine, I guess we can stay for a bit."

Qranyt pulled out the matrix, and in a flash it turned into a plasma-whirling dark blade.

"I've certainly seen some amazing things today," said Fretaal, "but this is the best! Can you turn it into other weapons? You can test it on the wall there, it's reinforced with everything we can manage!" Fretaal pointed to a far wall that was covered in scorch marks.

"Let me see what I can do..." Qranyt paused to close his eyes. When he opened them, the sword transformed into a compact plasma blaster.

"Wow! Give it a whirl!"

"That would be the last mode, more like, 'give it a—' boom." The plasma bolt flew from the barrel and smashed into the wall, bursting a wave of violet energy on impact. The matrix collapsed back into a cube in less time than the blink of an eye. "Yeah, it can't really keep it up for long though." Qranyt winced in pain.

"You good, Qranyt?" Onyx nudged.

"I don't know, there's just something weird about it."

Fretaal sighed, "Looks like even the Protectors can't fix our issues..."

"It just feels cold and dead inside, I don't know any other way to explain it."

"And Safaeir," I called, "you're ready too?"

"You betcha!"

Fretaal watched in awe as the bow fired an invisible arrow to the wall. As soon as it hit, the wall cracked from the amount of force, but did not breach.

"Can your's transform into anything else?"

"Uh—" Safaeir began, "I'm not sure, I've tried before but it almost feels like it resisted the thought of transforming?"

"Ouch!" Fretaal jumped, turning to see what had plucked his tail fur. Without him noticing I had snuck behind him, "You can become invisible?"

"Completely undetectable!" I answered.

"And Qranyt, that energy ring thing, it uses the web?"

"Sure does, my friend!"

For hours we kept ourselves busy exchanging thoughts on the ancient devices. Fretaal made us promise that we would visit again soon, bringing more keys for them to record data on. Unfortunately their team had only limited information to share, and only on the more technological trial side. Soon it was time for us to check out how the Zennial Shipyards could possibly build such a huge ship in so little time, and what sort of new accommodations we had!

Qranyt provided a quick teleport to the ship for us all, explaining how we need not worry about the Emerald ship because the autopilot flew it to Zekj already.

"I'd love a tour of this monstrosity, but I'm afraid that my bed is calling to me, wherever that might be." Onyx yawned loudly. "Qranyt, you can tell us where the rooms are, right?"

"If you insist!"

Qranyt led us to our individual rooms, then gave us a bit of a first greeting over the ship intercom.

"This is captain Qranyt of Savuk *the* Protector-12*, we are in space, so technically there is no nighttime. Oh well! I'll let the crew rest anyways, but be sure to be up by the time I next yell at you or you'll be skipping breakfast!"*

I find it funny Qranyt plays the cold act sometimes. Everyone knows who he really is, how sweet he can be, yet effective when his strength is needed. I would even say that if the 35 years did pass and a new Leader of Solia would need to join Avie, the Sanctuary and the powers that hold control over Solia's leadership would choose Qranyt of Emerald in an instant. Even so, I had a feeling it would be no end for our beloved Akjaeir.

Sleepy

The new personal cabins were a welcome change from being thrown

from one small ship to another multiple times per trip. Even so, it was likely we wouldn't be staying on this ship all the time. Perhaps we would finally get a chance to settle down, though, maybe I would even do some decorating if it was okay with Qranyt!

I took a moment to look through all that I'd brought with me this far. Most of my portable belongings were in the form of digital information on my data pad, but I did happen across some sealed seed storage tubes from Noctaikiilakj which I found a small place for in a drawer by the bed.

"Sleepy?" I heard a gruff yet somehow sorrowful voice near the hallway door.

"Qranyt?" I slid the door open, faced with the familiar figure. "Come in! I haven't gone to sleep yet, In fact I've been wondering if we'd get an opportunity to personalize our new spaces!"

"That sounds like a good idea, Sleepy." Qranyt came in, leaning himself against the frame of the closet doors.

"You seem, tired? Aren't you going to bed soon?"

He gave his head a quick shake, then replied "Yeah, I just wanted to talk things out a bit first I guess."

"Okay? What's going on?" I sat back down on the bed after closing the hall door again. Somehow, something was different about Qranyt.

"It's nothing, I just feel like we've been rushing through all of this so fast, maybe we don't know what it is we're getting into. Something could sneak up on us and—boom!"

I nodded, "We've got these powerful keys, and the backing of Avie and all but, yeah, we're still fragile creatures. I think I understand."

"I'm sorry, Sleepy, thanks for your kind words. I should go."

"It's no problem, Qranyt! We should talk like this more, all of us!"

"It's not that..." he opened a portal with his key, stepped through and turned back. "Goodbye, Setai."

Always full of surprises, that one, but he wasn't wrong. We were thrown from an everyday life to exploring powerful objects scattered throughout the cosmos. Something was sure to come up and catch us by surprise if we weren't careful.

I fell to the sheets in exhaustion, that was enough deep thought for the night.

"Alright you lazies get out of your pods and smell the fresh breakfast cookin' it's time to rise and dine!"

Oh joy, why did we ever let that bear get ahold of an intercom? Oh well, I'd rather not miss breakfast.

Upon Qranyt's suddon awakening I discovered the extensive new wardrobe behind those closed doors. Someone was looking at Safaeir's research and designs for new suits, and mass produced them for the team! Qranyt's been planning this for a while now... I was quickly greeted outside the personal rooms by the other ol' pals, all ready for the adventure awaiting: food!

"Mornin' you guys!" Onyx greeted us, more cheerful than her usual grumpy self.

"Did Qranyt let us sleep in?" I pondered. "Seems like we're all a bit more energetic than usual!"

"Hmm, maybe?" Hiinhia shrugged.

We entered the room that our noses led us to, a large "mess hall" just for us.

"Well there's the chefs, they are very confused!" Qranyt ran up to us.

"You hired a crew, but did their work for them?" I asked.

"Oh Sleepy, I just wanted to give them a bit of a surprise for their first official day on duty!" So much for him getting rest after our chat the night before!

"I'm guessing you didn't get any sleep then, Qranyt?" Onyx smirked.

"Nope!" Qranyt smiled, grabbing a bit of bread.

"Well thanks for all this food!" I told him, stuffing my face with what food was nearby.

"You guys take some extra time to chill," Qranyt said, "and eat food, and when you're done I'll show you around! After that we're gonna plan for our first trip with this giant ship!"

"Sounds like a plan, Qranyt, we'll eat 'till we're stuffed," Onyx replied.

It didn't take long for us to finish up with breakfast. Despite how much delicious food there was, our stomachs only have a certain maximum capacity.

"Ready for the tour I think," Hiinhia said as he wiped his short muzzle with a cloth.

"We'll see to it," Onyx agreed.

"So you are?" Qranyt came up behind us at the table.

"So ready!" Ehnri exclaimed.

"Sounds like a plan then, you'll get a bit of a tour, but first you need medical examinations," Qranyt laughed.

"Oh—really?" Onyx sighed, "I'd rather not."

"Just think about all the nifty things you'll get to see after it's over!"

Medical Examinations were just as boring as expected. The others went before me, so they were all outside the room talking restlessly when it was my turn to head into the infirmary.

"Hello Sleepy, I am Aqua, head nurse on this ship," the female owl said.

Well, that was about the only interesting thing that happened.

"So everyone, that was the infirmary." Qranyt told us.

Onyx growled a faint "No kidding."

"You've already seen your rooms and the mess hall. From your rooms you can go left to the infirmary, straight for the mess hall, or right to the entertainment areas." Qranyt led us about, giving us a simple idea of the ship's layout. "These rooms are on the top floor. Here behind your rooms is the Main Hangar."

The area ended at a wide window, which dropped several meters to the bottom of the hangar. Inside there were several of the shuttles we were used to, except these ones were a bit fancier. Qranyt led us across the "catwalk" hallway that stretched from the front of the hangar to the back. The hangar ended at another hallway, where several cylindrical capsules were sticking out of the walls at an angle.

"This is the escape and habitat pod hallway. Make sure you know the difference! The escape pods are designed for use if you have another ship nearby you can escape to. The habitat pods are for if you might need to go days without reaching another ship. Right, now one last room for now!"

Qranyt led us all the way back up by the mess hall again.

"And if you head straight through here, you will reach the Mission Control Room, where we plan stuff and stuff stuff."

"Right, so descriptive," Onyx said. "Now what are we planning?"

"Our first destination for the ship!"

"Well, with our failure on Aviea I think it would be nice if we did something to greatly help the Soliean Stars and earn more of the peoples' respect" Onyx replied thoughtfully.

"I say we sort things out on Kjitafor, we can get supplies in the process," Hiinhia suggested. "There's always something that needs to be fixed on Kjitafor!"

"True..." Qranyt agreed. "Any other ideas?"

"Wherever it is," I thought back to last night, "We should be extra careful! Let's look after each other, we don't know what kinds of danger might be waiting for us!"

Qranyt looked back at me, puzzled, "Where's all this caution coming from? Us Soliean Protectors got nothing to worry about!"

16. DARK TRADE

[Savuk, Auqua Interval Space]

Safaeir

"Kjitafor it is then!" Ehnri exclaimed.

"I guess I will now show off another room," Qranyt laughed, "the bridge!"

He led us to an elevator, which brought us up to another whole floor filled with entirely new rooms. The bridge was at the end of the hallway, giving us plenty of space to spread out. Across the spread were several consoles of different sorts: orbital, scanning, command, and navigation systems, as well as everything you could possibly imagine about the ship displayed on an array of screens.

"Here we are then!" Qranyt got right to work at the controls.

Through the window we could see the top of the ship's expanse far out in front of us. I could see the lasers, the plasma burst cannons, the shielding, center hangar entrance, the backdrop of space. The ship was black, silver, and green in color, the itraseletia in dark metal in the center of the ship's topside. At the bow in the distance was Tetratakj, but Qranyt turned the ship around and pointed it for our new destination.

"This is captain Qranyt speaking to his crew..."

"Here we go again!" Onyx laughed with us.

"We've decided to set course for main and have some lunch, but before we do that, we're going to Kjitafor to sort out the issues my team is sure have arisen there."

"We just had breakfast, Qranyt!" Ehnri squealed.

"So I beg you, HOLD ON!"

Without giving much of a chance for anyone to grab something to keep hold of, Qranyt flipped a lever and sent the ship accelerating in Kjitafor's direction.

"Uhh Qranyt, how fast does this thing go?" I tried to say while squished against the back wall of the bridge.

"Don't you worry, we're almost there!" He assured us. "Just, you know: 5, 4, 3, 2, 1, there!" The spiked planet Kjitafor appeared in the window and the ship came to a halt, causing everyone who was stuck to the back wall to slam into the window.

"Owww!" Onyx shouted.

"Should've taken my warning!"

"Maybe if you gave it to us a little sooner!"

"Okay team, now that you have a basic understanding of the ship, get your gear and meet me in the hangar in 15!"

"Right boss!" I teased, running out of the bridge to follow the groaning others. Then of course Qranyt had to get on the intercom again.

"I hope you all took my warning seriously, cuz now we're in orbit around the planet Kjitafor. You guys have six hours to come up with a list of everything you need for supplies, and then to also go get those supplies from the planet. So yeah! Qranyt out!" ...We really needed to take that thing from him.

I somehow managed to find my way back to my room, but I can't take all the credit as I was mainly just following the others. I laughed at Qranyt's business with the new suit thing, taking the design from me. I got my suit operational and got the gear together for what I hoped would be an action-filled Kjitafor adventure; Off to the hangar!

"There are a lot of shuttles in here!" Sleepy said in awe.

"I think today we'll take this one." Qranyt walked up to one of the transport vehicles, slapping the side with his paw before leading us all inside.

"Do you have control of the hangar doors in here, Qranyt?" asked Onyx.

"You bet I do," replied Qranyt pressing a few buttons. "We'll take the lower hangar door."

Qranyt lifted the shuttle and flew under where our rooms were. He lowered the ship through one door and closed it behind the ship, allowing for the air to empty back inside the ship's reserves so the pressure would match that of space. The second door opened below us, allowing Qranyt to tilt the shuttle down and give us a beautiful view of the amazing, yet somewhat sickening, Kjitafor.

Qranyt shot the transport towards the planet, where several large ships were hanging out like our own, only smaller.

"This world is the Soliean trade center, where products enter and leave the three stars," Hiinhia told us.

"What kinds of things enter? Isn't Solia self-sufficient?" I asked.

"Well we can't be selling and not buying anything!" Qranyt replied before Hiinhia got a chance. "The other systems make sure of it! Sure, the Soliean Stars are still making tons of money for its projects, but what we do tend to buy is a bunch mineral materials, which we can later process and make new things to sell back!"

"Sounds like a great system!" Sleepy said.

"What sorts of minerals?" Ehnri asked out of curiosity.

"Ores of iridium, gold, silver, iron, copper, etc." Qranyt listed while he slowed the ship down to land on a giant parking pad. "We're here everyone! Time to see what we can do!"

"Where did you park us?" Onyx asked outside the shuttle.

"Right by the planet's Protective Center for Civilian and Trade Defense."

"Look!" I pointed, "I can just barely see our ship."

"Good," Qranyt said, "I like it that way. If we have some conflict, we keep the shiny new toy back so we can use it from a distance."

"I get that!" Ehnri agreed.

"Of course you do, Ehnri, you're the battlemind here!" Onyx patted him with her tail.

For a moment my head became clouded, there was a sort of growing pain from within my heart as I felt a familiar voice from within me.

"why are we here"

"..."

"please, you should leave this world, nothing good will come of staying in His domain."

"Diiviide?"

"Safaeir?" my attention was drawn back by Onyx waving her big paw in my face. "You good?"

"I—is it safe here?"

"I think that's what we're here to find out!" Onyx purred, "Don't worry, we'll keep you safe!"

"Let's get to work then," Qranyt pressed. "I bet the guards here have something they can give us that will keep us busy and entertained!"

"So apparently there's air here?" Onyx asked.

"Yes, Onyx, that is why we aren't currently choking to death..." Hiinhia attempted to explain.

"Seems like I'm rubbing off on you!"

"Well I guess not everyone got a good night's sleep last night," Sleepy sighed.

Qranyt led us up to the fancy defense building, where he hoped we would get a job, or maybe even a lead on another matrix. There was a human at the front desk who took much interest in the approaching team with swords and sophisticated weapons.

"Hello sir!" Qranyt approached.

"Hello, err, is there anything I might be able to, help you with?"

"Maybe. You need some help around here? We're the Soliean Protectors, and we've been doing some work around this star lately so we thought we might stop by and see what we could do to help. Anything weird or interesting going on around here?"

"Very thoughtful of you. What is your name, sir?"

"Qranyt. Qranyt of Aviea. Selected by leader Avie to lead this team of Soliean Protectors through the systems in search of knowledge and understanding the universe as a hole. Get it? Cuz we haven't found anything?" He took a glance back to see if any of us got his pun.

"Ugh, you guys are cold." Qranyt looked away.

I heard Onyx snicker at that statement more than the 'hole' pun.

"I guess I might be able to give you something to help with, maybe with the gangs?"

"Gangs!" Qranyt jumped to attention. "Great! Gangs are grea— wait, not great! Okay team, split up and look for gangs!"

"Qranyt!" the person at the desk attempted to call as we walked back out of the building.

Qranyt stopped us to quickly pass out some information before we set off on our ways.

"So team, I see you are all wearing your new uniforms? Time to learn a bit about them. Off to Safaeir then!"

"Right. So these suits have some new features, like Qranyt told you. To activate the communicator, slide the switch on the left side of your neck. To transmit, toggle the button next to it. On the right side of your neck is another sliding switch. This switch controls the light in the front of your neck, just in case Sleepy forgets to bring his orbs!"

I watched as the team instinctively started messing with the new stuff.

"Those white pads on the left side of your suit are actually sample bags you can use to store items. The suit also has a connection to your account for Soliean Noctia, which you can use anywhere with its powerful security system. I even heard Qranyt sent you a little bonus to your personal accounts! Your front legs have a thread-firing device you can use to latch on to objects, swing, whatever... Then of course there's your belt, as well as a multitool. I think you can probably figure the rest out on your own."

"Uhh, about that bonus—" Qranyt started, cut short by a wink from me, "Ahem...Thank you, Safaeir. Now go, all of you! Let's sort out this gang activity!"

I ran to the edge of the platform and looked down at the towers far below, thinking of which one may have some suspicious activities going on. There—a building painted a dark red! That looked the most promising! The building was just below us, so one would think its proximity to the guard building would make it irrelevant for gang activity, but I decided to take a look anyway. I switched on the communications device before jumping into the abyss.

The grappling device made a satisfying click as it shot out and grabbed onto the building's side. The cord stretched to slow my fall, then held in place to allow me a chance to find a way in.

There inside the building I already saw some unfortunate evidence of illegal activity, but it seemed strange in the back of my head... I could just barely make out a group of bears inside that appeared to be creating some sort of material and sticking fuses in it.

"Great sign!" I laughed to myself.

I drew my bow and launched myself from the face of the building before firing an arrow into the side, which shattered into hundreds of tiny glass window fragments. Managing to pull myself up before entering, I ended up hitting the side of the building again. The bears were then rushing for the now open window, and to give them a bit of a surprise, I kicked out once more to fire a low-strength arrow to push all the glass out of the way for my landing.

Three bears clad in brown suits pulled out their plasma-burst weapons and began firing at me, but I shot an arrow right at them, attempting to give a wider range on the impact. The three bears flew back a few meters, one of them dropping his gun. I ran up to them and quickly noticed a pile of boxes that I could dump on top of them, so I did just that.

"*Qranyt!*" I heard Hiinhia's voice call over. "*The Guards have explosives right on their doorstep!*"

Another two bears were waiting after the boxes fell for me to pass. I remembered seeing more, but the others apparently disappeared to another part of the building.

"*Yes Hiinhia, we've found the same. I've sent Onyx and Sleepy back to the Guard Center to make their faults known. I sure hope it makes a difference.*"

"*Right. I'll keep to it here Qranyt.*" Sounded like the others were encountering a similar situation.

The two bears rushed at me with guns as well, and I knew that the first three would probably be finding their way soon and getting back up. I decided to take a bit of a stretch, backing to the table and grabbing a bit of the clay stuff and throwing it towards the bears.

"WAIT WAIT WAIT!" one of them yelled as I fired the arrow straight at it. In a split second the clay passed between them and exploded outwards in a burst of flame, knocking the bears down to the floor. Wait? What did they mean? Was it a distraction tactic?

"You're telling me to wait? Why are you making explosives down here!"

"Please, stop fighting us! We'll explain!" a voice cried behind a pile of debris.

"We won't attack you, we're just trying to support our families," another said, "you're different from them, you're a protector of Solia, isn't that right?"

"Yeah, yeah." I said, "I'll hear you guys out, something about this isn't adding up."

The bears got up, beginning to tend to each others' wounds.

"We work for the trade company that interlaces Solia's production and export here, we do it to support our families and we are forced to live in these lower levels of the city."

"We make barely any money to survive, and they force us to work the whole day, we're barely sleeping or eating."

"Meanwhile, they're taking extra cuts of the sales, what was meant to go to us,"

I stopped and thought, they remained silent. I tapped the communicator button to broadcast to the team, "This is Safaeir, maybe we should hold off on the PCCTD orders, something else is going on here."

"You believe us?" One asked;

"I do, but what of the explosives? What are these all about?"

"You see, the Protection Center and upper trade management knows they can make an extra payout with weapons dealing, something the Soliean Alliance swore to outlaw. We make these explosives to sell to them discreetly so we can feed ourselves and then they use whatever they can't sell to keep us from revolting!"

"What do you have, Safaeir?" I heard Qranyt's voice.

"I'm calling off our mission! Meet me below the platform where we landed, you'll see the hole I made."

Hiinhia

I left the platform right after Safaeir did, except in a completely different direction. Rather than jumping right off the side of the platform I took a safer approach. The path seemed pretty clear towards the taller tower to the east, so I hitchhiked a ride on one of the shuttles heading that same way.

Dropping through the air, I quickly used my key to make my landing on the shuttle unnoticeable. Right before the destination tower, the shuttle made a quick left turn, kicking me off. I quickly found the way to activate the suit's grappling hook, which shot onto the side of the building. I swung towards the tower, and through personal experience was able to reduce the surface area of my impact to prevent the glass from shattering. Releasing the hook, I flattened myself against the tower side and scampered along to find an entrance.

Around the corner was a landing pad that would work as an entrance for me. I kept the key activated as I walked into the building to avoid detection, but I could hear something going happening on the floor below and quickly looked for a way down. I looked around the room to find several containers that one like me would easily recognize as explosives. I switched on my communicator, deactivated the key, and got in a corner to message Qranyt.

"Qranyt!" I called over. "The Guards have explosives right on their doorstep!"

"Yes Hiinhia, we've found the same. I've sent Onyx and Sleepy back to the Guard Center to make their faults known. I sure hope it makes a difference."

"Right. I'll keep to it here Qranyt."

I turned the volume down on the communication device in the suit and continued on my way to the elevator. I was able to bring the elevator down one floor, and when the doors opened, the humans on that floor turned to look, but didn't see anything. Little did they know, I slipped out of the elevator to walk about with them to see what was going on. There I saw several more explosives lined up in the halls, and I heard a faint voice over the communicator:

"This —Saf—ir, maybe we— hold off on the ... orders, something else —going on!" What did she mean something else going on? There were people here getting ready to explode the building!

It didn't take long for me to notice that the people were being sent to the next floor up, and I could only guess they were leaving the building. The last of the people there were typing something into one of the explosives before they also ran to the elevator. There at the end of the hallway I saw a window open, which I quickly ran for, pulling the explosive with me after the elevator doors closed. The explosive was heavy, but I managed to bring it to the window ledge. Above, the ships from the landing pad were departing, signaling the approaching threat.

I looked to the bomb and saw the counter at five seconds, so I gave it a good shove out of the window— The bomb exploded, shaking the entire building. These people meant to have it up here to set off the other explosives! The building's top would have fallen, crashing into the whole city on the way down!

"What do you have, Safaeir?" Qranyt called over the communicator.

"I'm calling off our mission! Meet me below the platform where we landed, you'll see the hole I made."

Onyx

Sleepy and I successfully reached the Guard Center of Kjitafor, where Qranyt wanted us to try to get the people moving to keep the world free from harm. Unfortunately, this planet is Solia's most vulnerable world, one that could harm the rest of the Soliean Stars if those in charge here let their guard down. It's not the first time, and certainly won't be the last time if we don't get involved.

"You're back?" the person at the front desk asked.

Qranyt called over the comms in the suit, *"What do you have, Safaeir?"*

"I'm calling off our mission! Meet me below the platform where we landed, you'll see the hole I made."

Suddenly, we heard a large explosion behind us, shaking one of the nearby towers. Here? Meet here? Safaeir had dropped below us, meaning she probably was near where the explosion hit!

"Sleepy! We gotta find Safaeir!" I yelped;

"What do you need us to do?" inquired another cat, perhaps the Guard Leader.

"Just stay out of it!" I replied, grabbing Sleepy and bringing him to the shuttle pad edge,

"Was she down there!?" He cried back,

"Yeah, she said she's calling off the mission, something must have happened!

"Guys get down here, I need your help!" Safaeir called.

Sleepy and I used our grapples to swing down below the Guard Center where Safaeir had gone, sure enough, the side of the tower was heavily damaged from the explosion. Through a hole in the building we could see Safaeir and a group of bears; we landed inside the open wreckage, weapons ready.

"Onyx, Sleepy, these creatures are the living and working citizens of Kjitafor," She started, as Qranyt landed behind us, Ehnri on his shoulders, followed by Hiinhia. "They're making these weapons to sell to the Protective Center for Civilian and Trade Defense, for them to sell out-of-system; They don't protect their citizens, they use them!"

A bear joined in behind Safaeir, "If you don't believe us, just take a look at how we're living. This is what we're given to live off of. That explosion wasn't supposed to fall down here, it was supposed to fall on our families in the city, to show us what happens when we revolt!"

I looked back at Qranyt, he looked defeated at these words;

"Is all this true?" Qranyt asked, "They must not be giving you the pay from the exports, they should be making plenty enough off the production and trade routes here to give you more than enough to live here!"

"What you see here is what we have," another bear said, gesturing at the dark, cold space in the tower.

"I will address this immediately," Qranyt declared, deploying a long range transmitter.

"Wait," an older bear called out, "there's something else you should know. The guards are using their resources and money they get from the trade and weapon dealing for a secret project, but some of our braver family members have been able to find out what they are doing."

"What are they doing?"

"Deep in the core, according to old records of the founding of Kjitafor, there was a piece of technology like no other, able to influence the very mechanisms of a living creature to do your work for you. They should never get that technology in their hands."

"It's just a tall-tale," another bear scoffed, "leave his ramblings, we need to make sure our people are fed!"

"Tall tale or not," said Qranyt, "I don't like the sound of something like that getting into the hands of someone as corrupt as you say these Kjitafor Trade Operators are. Onyx, Sleepy, Ehnri, you take a look into this technology and see that it's out of anyone's reach if it really exists. As for the rest of us, let's send a message to the real traitors of Kjitafor!"

Sleepy

"I say you start by going down-down-down the elevator," the old bear wheezed, "the record says it's deep in Kjitafor's heart."

"Eeelevator!" I said, scanning the room.

"That way, young one," he turned and pointed me into the dark.

"That way!"

"Here we go..." Onyx sighed.

Sure enough, the elevator had a lot of buttons. We pressed the bottom one in hopes of getting as close to the core as possible. It took aaages to get down that far, and when we stepped out to take a look out the glass of the tower, it still looked so high!

"We've made it like, a hair of the way down?" Onyx scoffed, "Maybe we should just, I don't know, jump out the window?"

"Looks like there's another elevator! Ehnri chimed, nosing towards the other side of the elevator tube we came down in. "There's probably lots more elevators to get to the bottom!"

"Oh yes, greeeaaat."

This elevator seemed a little faster, kinda bumpy though. At the bottom of this elevator we came out to see we were much lower!

"Just a bit further everyone!!" I exclaimed, hoping to keep their spirits up.

"Man I really wish Qranyt waited on the whole diplomacy thing and came down here with us," Onyx whined, looking up towards the sky out the window, now tinted orange with the haze filling the lower levels, "Maybe he'll think to use his key to get us out of here once he remembers."

"Looks like another elevator!" Ehnri announced, "come on everyone!"

"Am I the only one that's had enough of this?"

This elevator seemed to be the last; We stepped outside to no expansive scene of skyscrapers, only a radiating set of hallways.

"Sleepy, what's your key say?" Onyx asked, "doesn't it, like, tell us where to go or something?"

I looked down to my belt, "Maybe if I hold it and?" I held the key out in front of me and squeezed my eyes, "Anything? Anything?"

"No, no Sleepy it's doing nothing..." Onyx sighed, "Let's look for a way deeper into the planet."

"It looks like a maze!" Ehnri commented as we came to an intersection, "I can definitely get us through this!"

The left went up a flight of stairs, the right went down, to which we

chose right, of course. The stairs stopped at a level and went back the other direction around a bend, continued down. The walls were dim, faintly lit by a pale orange light that the dark cold walls sucked any warmth out of. It was stair after stair and several switch-backs before anything of interest happened, by now all trace of sunlight and life was completely gone.

"Smells like grease," Onyx noted, her voice echoing down the empty tunnels.

What first broke the dead silence of the depths of Kjitafor was the sharp *ca-chunk ca-chunk, ca-chunk ca-chunk* of metal at the end of the tunnel. Slowly and slowly growing nearer as we progressed through intersection after intersection was our feeling of unease and nausea, and rising temperature.

"It's getting—hard to think," Ehnri huffed, slowing his pace.

The end of the tunnel glowed like a blazing inferno, twisting left and right as our eyes tried to focus. Hotter than the sands of Sleprah-Daecaser, hotter than the fires of Noctia. We all knew we were getting close—

The space opened up to a gigantic spherical chamber, five other tunnels entered the same chamber with their end at the same ledge as our own. At the center was another sphere, a rotating cage around it with only small holes for openings we could barely see through as it spun. Between us and that sphere were several axles, cogs, and flywheels churning away, occasionally letting out an ear-splitting shriek.

"I don't like this!" Onyx yelled out at the edge, her body waving around in the heat.

"It's so loud in here!" Ehnri cried out; I tried to cover his ears with my paws and shrink into the tunnel wall from the blasting furnace of the sphere.

"It's gonna be me, isn't it, Sleepy..." Onyx twisted hey face in anguish, "ooof course..."

We heard another deep *ca-chunk*, only to notice that a new wall had appeared in the tunnel we came through, slowly pressing towards our direction.

"Uh oh!" I exclaimed, rolling out onto the ledge in the spherical room.

"Ugh of course! Alright Sleepy, I'll do it, but you gotta protect Ehnri while I do this!" I nodded, pulling Ehnri close and huddling to the only slightly cooler wall.

Onyx

Sleepy and Ehnri were safe, for now, but I had a feeling that wouldn't last. I set my sights on the center of the large chamber. Between me and the core, a thousand jumps and turns, twisting and dodging. I leapt to the first gear, it was turning slowly but gaining speed; There! An axle just ahead! I landed hard on the metal and crouched down as a flywheel passed over my spine. A spinning beam under my axle, I landed, but almost lost my balance. Timing it carefully, I planned a path along a trail of three horizontally positioned gears— I accelerated along the beam and launched, passing just over a flat beam, landing on the first gear. The gears were close enough to each other to bounce from one to the next, but I hadn't planned on where to go next.

I saw in that moment a wheel, several times wider than my length head-to-tail, each spoke ended with a large metal ball. What I hadn't seen was the beam coming up behind me;

SMACK!

The beam hit my back, but I clawed into its top to hold on.

CLAANGGGGG!!

The beam came to a sudden halt, sending me flying off the front of the beam, right into—

THWUMP!!!

"ONYX!" I heard Ehnri yell over the shrieking metal.

I was caught by a ball on the giant wheel, hurdled up to the ceiling, and back—

PWHUD!

Onto the top of a vertical gear.

I clawed around the rim of the gear just in time as it turned; I found myself hanging at the bottom of the gear, near to the center of the sphere but much too low to reach it. I was pulled back onto the top of the gear just in time to see that the wall had finally reached the end of the tunnel.

Holding Ehnri tight, Sleepy leapt onto a moving beam, wrapping around it while still managing to keep Ehnri safe. I needed to move quicker.

Another beam, this one moving upward— I leapt, landing squarely on top of the beam. Like the other, it came to a quick halt, launching me up. A strangely shaped pendulum swung into reach, I grabbed as it passed above me.

"EEIIIAK" I howled; the force had overextended my forearms, causing me to let go. I landed on my back on a slow-moving worm gear. The core was just below me.

The shell around the core was spinning faster than anything else in the chamber, and it was the final challenge. If I messed this up, there would be no getting out of here. The force of the sphere instantly snapping my spine was the best outcome, throwing me at high speed back into the machine where I'd be torn apart slowly was the worst outcome. I was tired, there was no other way out.

I took one last look to Sleepy, he was holding up at least, Ehnri had found a slower gear to hang out on, but Sleepy wasn't as agile. He probably threw Ehnri up there, knowing it'd be safer than staying in his arms. I had to do this for them.

Closing my eyes, I thought back to everything that had led up to this point. Why was I even here? I wasn't some hero destined to save the universe? I was at most just second to the leadership of a small territory on Aviea, destined to fill out paperwork and do government work while occasionally getting a chance to play with electronics! But now, I had the lives of two creatures I was responsible. With this artifact, perhaps a whole planet's fate stood before me.

"There is nothing else. I do this for them."

My heart stopped dead in my chest

one glance over my shoulder

Gravity.

Eyes Closed

Gravity works the rest...

Nothing.

THUD.

Was I alive?

I opened my eyes, the world was spinning; Right beside me was an ornate mechanical pedestal, claw-like hand wrapped gingerly around a black-brass outlined sphere of clouded violet glow. This was it, the Matrix of Kjitafor, it must be! I reached out, looking beyond the spinning sphere to Sleepy, I touched the sphere, He was balanced atop the end of an axle, nowhere to jump from there. A glistening pendulum come from behind him—

"NO!" I cried— my heart exploded with pain, my claws dug into the matrix, "SLEEPY!!!"

Sleepy

"EEIIIAK" Onyx's scream ricocheted back and forth through the chamber, but I had to stay focused. The wall forced Ehnri and I to leave the tunnel and ledge and start navigating through the machinery like Onyx had; I needed to keep Ehnri safe!

"Is she gonna make it?!" Ehnri asked from my arms,

"A big strong cat like her! I know she can do it!"

"What about me!? I'm scared, Sleepy!"

There! Above us, a firmly-planted, much slower gear was seemingly safe from other moving parts, but I wouldn't be able to get up there. Our sliding gear moved into position;

"Ehnri! You'll be safe up there, ready?" He nodded, and I launched him towards the upper gear. He safely scrambled up, but I still had myself to worry about. I spotted a potential path, a big gear I could hitch a ride on to get up to Ehnri's level, just needed to hop across the top of an axle, then to jump and grab the gear!

I hesitated, then composed myself, readied my jump and leapt the gap. The landing was a bit tipsy, the intense heat made me feel dizzy. This was it, I had to jump and grab on the big gear now... but it was farther than it looked before I landed! I panicked, the axle was now shifting to the side, I'd cornered myself!

"NO!!" I heard Onyx cry out, I tried to see if she was alright, "SLEEPY!!!" I turned to look behind me, but it was too late.

My blood boiled, I felt my limbs turn to stone, tingling, on fire, it felt like they weren't mine. My legs jerked to push me out of the way from a direct hit, but the giant pendulum still hit my side hard— I didn't tell them to move...

My chest felt cold, frozen, like everything in my body was trying to make me breathe, but it wasn't my body;

My arms were held out in front of me as I fell, I tried to catch my fall on a beam, but they didn't budge. Everything burned in my body, I was suffocating. Everything went dark.

Onyx

In an instant his arms fell in front of him, he rolled off the axle but too slow, the pendulum knocked him out of the way, his legs held out stiff and arms reached outward, unmoving. Metal scraped as the pendulum dug through the top of the axle. Sleepy fell, landing atop a platform still unmoving, arms still outreached in front of him. My heart was pounding as if to leap completely out of my body. Gradually the whole room slowed its motion, the air began to cool, light began to fade to pale blue.

"SLEEPY!" I yelled, panting, trying to catch my breath, still holding the ball out in front of me, digging my claws into its patterns of machine and bramble. In a moment of terror, I realized what I'd done. "NO! SLEEPY!" I ran to the edge, shoving the orb into my toolbelt. Ehnri had already begun on a path towards where Sleepy fell, I was soon to follow. "Sleepy I'm so sorry, I'm so sorry!" He gasped for breath, I skidded to a halt beside him just as Ehnri arrived.

"Is he gonna be okay!?" Ehnri whimpered,

"I— I think so, he didn't take a direct hit but it still hit hard, I—" I stopped, still trying to comprehend what had happened, "It's m-mmy fault Ehnri! I used it on him!" He looked down to my toolbelt.

"That's it then, you moved him out of the pendulum's path!"

"I think? But— I was so freaked out I caused him to lose control of his limbs, he couldn't catch his fall, I, I stopped him from breathing!" Ehnri came to my side,

"He's breathing now, though! He'll be okay! He's alright isn't he!?" I fell to the hard surface of the platform,

"I don't want this, Ehnri, nobody should have it, not even me!"

"We should still bring it back— maybe Qranyt will know how to destroy it, or lock it away forever—or..."

"Itts.,, okayy— Onyx" Sleepy wheezed, "You savv—ed me."

This matrix, it wasn't like the keys or Safaeir's matrix we'd found before. This one was different, vile, corrupt, immoral, it needed to be destroyed. I never wanted to use it, I never wanted to see it again.

Safaeir

The pain returned to my chest once more on Kjitafor, and in that moment I could feel something very, very wrong.

"you feel it, don't you. It's because of what he did to me."

"..."

"what the 'Soliean Protectors' found today should have never been discovered."

Qranyt

Hiinhia and Safaeir worked together to help the wounded Kjitaforians as I stepped out to contact Aliira;

"Avie and the entire leadership of Aviea, this is Qranyt Avinta, on Kjitafor. The Protectors agreed to visit here to check on trade systems and the status of the workers and we discovered a grave danger to Solia. The upper management of trade and civilian protection offices are corrupted. Civilians are under strict control and not receiving the pay they need to survive, much less than they were originally promised. There's reports of officials forcing the locals into weapons manufacturing for a black market arms dealing ring. I request immediate backup and arrangement of the Soliean Fleet from Zekj, including a team of anti-explosive specialists to arrive on Kjitafor to get the situation under control. Kjitafor must be given back to its people."

"Copy, Qranyt, This is Qorshia Zorae. Your orders have been recorded and the defensive fleet of Zekj has been dispatched to your location. Avie and the laersana of planets and of Aviea will be discussing the situation and begin investigations."

"Diavii, Qorshia, give your partner my regards."

"ta'lum ta Qranyt."

The Zekj fleet notified, things were going to get tense, best we get the citizens out of the way.

"Safaeir, Hiinhia! I've notified the capital, we need to get everyone as far away from here as possible!"

"Qranyt, there were humans loading up explosives in the tower I visited, I believe they're planning to drop the tower on the city!"

"You two, get them out of here and I'll try to buy us some time by talking to the Civilian Guards themselves, I'll try to get them to stall on blowing the explosives."

"Understood!" Safaeir shouted.

Using the grapple, I climbed the wall back up to the shuttle pad. They were bound to be suspicious, as much time had passed since the explosion with nothing to show. If what Hiinhia said was true, they were probably re-rigging those explosives as I climbed.

"Qranyt!" A human guard called from above, "Seems you must have encountered those gangs, haven't you?"

"Ah of course!" I laughed, "How'd you let this place get so full of these pests then?"

"It's been relentless, last few ovitrae years, didn't you see that explosion hurtled right towards the guard tower!?" I stepped onto the platform beside the guard.

"I sure did, but," I paused, "Why not ask the capital for help? All this time dealing with this vermin, violent and hateful gang activity and not once considering to request backup? Brave, I'll grant you, but we could have come to help sooner!"

"Hey, you didn't happen to let them know, back on Aviea, did you?" the guard growled, I stepped away from the edge towards the doors into the guard complex.

"Ha! Don't worry about it, us protectors got it all under control!" I smiled, "I'd go so far as to say they're having... fun!" I gave the guard a wink, just as the first Zekj Battlecruiser warped into the atmosphere. Three more human guards came running out of the building;

"What's the meaning of this!" one yelled, looking up to the sky in awe.

"Bye-byes, Kjitafor!" I waved tauntingly. The guards pulled out their guns, but I was too quick. I opened a loop just behind me that exited inside our brand new shuttle, then launched off the pad.

"*Zekj Termina Uk to Savuk registered shuttle, we need a status update. What are your orders?*" a voice called over the shuttle broadcast.

"Qranyt of the starship Savuk, Protector of Solia, we're in need of immediate civilian evacuation from the city nearest to the Kjitafor Civilian Guard Tower. There's a bomb threat on civilian lives and we must work to clear out any potential explosives before allowing civilians to return. After evacuation, discussions with the Guard Tower occupants may begin."

"*Understood. Dispatching transport craft around the city.*"

"Qranyt to Protectors," I called over the suit communicator, "The fleet has arrived, they'll be sending in transports in just a few moments to evacuate the citizens of Kjitafor. Stay on high alert for guards, as well as any potential rigged explosives."

Safaeir spoke through, *"Copy that Qranyt, our group has flagged down a transport."*

Now for the other three, where were they? The old bear had sent them to find this piece of technology deep within the planet, I wondered if they'd made it down that far.

"Qranyt to Onyx, Sleepy, Ehnri, we're evacuating the city, do you copy?" I called as I flew the shuttle into the depths of Kjitafor. "I repeat, Onyx, Sleepy, and Ehnri, where are you guys?!" Nothing came back. The deeper I flew, the hazier and darker it got, pressure was pushing in on the shuttle from all sides.

"Wwe — adly-jured—nee- immedi— med-al atte-tion"

It was Ehnri's voice; What in the name of the stars had they found down there? I had to get them out.

"This is Qranyt, report! Can you get to the tower's windows? I can get you out from there!" In one of the windows I could see a faint flashing light through the haze, Safaeir's suit lights! I dropped the ship low and steady, sure enough, all three were there. Ehnri looked okay, but Onyx and Sleepy looked like they were on the floor, motionless. I opened a loop in the tower to the shuttle interior,

"Come on, come on!" I called, Ehnri hopped through while I jumped into the tower to get the others. "Ehnri, get us back to the Savuk, I'll start taking a look at their wounds!" Ehnri nodded, jumping up to the controls. "What happened down there?!"

"Onyx found the technology that bear was talking about, she got injured badly navigating the challenges that protected this matrix. Sleepy got hurt protecting me," he whimpered;

"We'll get them all patched up Ehnri, It'll be okay!"

"Qranyt, I just heard your report," Avie called through the ship, *"This is an unforgivable turn of events! We're organizing a meeting on a diplomatic vessel from Aliira to Kjitafor right this moment. We're all regretting not keeping a closer eye on Kjitafor. My team will handle this from here, know that as a territory leader you are of course invited to this meeting if you so choose, under no obligation."*

"Avie, I'm glad to hear you're on your way. I am honored by your

offer but I'd like the citizens of Kjitafor themselves to speak in my place. I am needed with my team right now."

"I'd expect no less, laersana Qranyt. I will let you know of the outcome here on Kjitafor when it is decided."

As the shuttle settled and locked-in on its pad in the Savuk, Onyx and Sleepy began to stir,

"Captain Qranyt to Savuk medical team, emergency assistance needed in the main shuttle bay!"

"Qran—yt," Onyx rasped, "see that this is locked away, where nobody can ever find it," A violet ball wrapped in ornate brass and black metal accents fell from her tool belt, it was not much smaller than my paw, and heavier than it looked. "I never want to see it or think about it again."

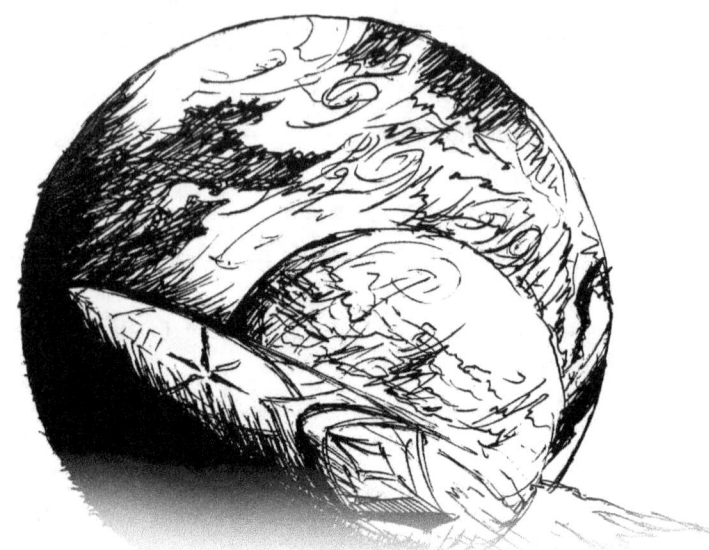

17. A NEW HOME

[Solia Interval Space, Starhaven]

Ehnri

Qranyt made sure that he had it set that the people of Kjitafor would be protected, once again sacrificing his territory's funds for now another whole world. At least this time it seemed like Avie was going to take over the situation from there.

"So, Captain Qranyt," Hiinhia said while the team was on the bridge. "What's the plan for us now?"

"Oh, you know, dinner?" he replied, doing some sort of tweaking on some control panel.

"No specific time for lunch when we're hopping from one world to another and hanging out in space in between," Sleepy said, "but I can agree that food would've been nice."

Qranyt got us back to the Mess Hall of the ship safely, where we continued the discussions over some big tasty salads.

Sleepy dug into the food quick, but Onyx mostly poked at it uncomfortably.

"So about where we're going..." Safaeir started, "I think we should make some sort of base on a planet too!"

"We've done lots of work in the past months. It would be a nice break, you know, adding bits to the ship and, like Safaeir suggested, making an official base," Hiinhia agreed.

"They've got a point," said Onyx.

"I'd like to pick up some things to personalize my room here and on a new base!" Sleepy added.

"Sounds like a nice idea," Qranyt said, taking a bit of kja pasta from one of the food counters. "Someone else is gonna need to pay though!"

"Yeah Qranyt, you're pretty much run dry on Noctia now!" I laughed.

"I wonder where we could put a base?" Safaeir pondered, looking around the table for suggestions.

"Intafari is a pretty nice world!" Hiinhia suggested.

"Nah," Onyx disagreed. "We should try to keep the base close to the capital, yet far enough away from it to make sure Avie doesn't get involved."

"So, Reid?" Safaeir asked.

"Sleepy2c!" I exclaimed, then regretted after seeing some of the team's disappointed looks.

Sleepy certainly agreed, "Yeah! My people would love to have company there!"

"It's certainly a possibility to consider," Qranyt told the team.

"And a tactically advantageous location!" I added.

After several more moments of discussion, we finally came to an final decision: we would have a vote on the best place to put a new base for the Soliean Protectors. Sleepy brought out a piece of paper and a pen for us to cast our votes.

"Here we are," Qranyt started, tearing the paper into pieces and passing out the slips. "Today we will decide the location of the new Soliean Protector Ground Base of Operations. Pass the pen around everyone!" Qranyt collected all six of the slips of paper and began to read through them.

"Intafari got one vote," he read, "Noctae got two, and—"

"Sleepy2c?" I jumped to listen,

"Sleepy2c got four!" Qranyt finished, looking to see the team's reaction.

"Welcome to the desert everyone!" Sleepy smiled. "The sunsets will amaze you!"

Qranyt

Despite the opposition to living life in a desert, it really didn't take much to get the team excited about what ideas they had for building a base on Sleepy2c. I decided to once again send them off on their own, leaving them the ship and me to my own thoughts and ideas.

Fortunately the team was occupied with their construction ideas rather than exploring the ship, and I was able to visit the communications deck to keep my eyes on communication channels throughout the Soliean Stars. I got a bit nosy and rotated the scanners to the nebula wall, and what I found seemed quite interesting.

"Welcome to the Communications Deck, ID Qranyt recognized," the systems said. *"An unidentifiable transmission detected from unknown coordinates. By the system's calculations the transmission will hit the planet Noctae at: +5.43 system hours. We cannot scan the transmission, as it is both broken and encrypted."*

Clearly the transmission Avie was chasing was soon to arrive on Noctae, something I found myself extremely interested in.

"Communications Computer, set an alarm for my suit to go off on receiving any transmissions from Noctae."

"Yes Emerald Leader Qranyt."

Sleepy

The villages of my moon were very happy to hear word of the Soliean Protectors building a new base in Sulentuun City. They knew that with their new fame, the world would change from a dry desert to an action-packed soup of life.

Many of the villagers assembled to work in the sandstone quarries with Onyx and I, making our workload much easier. Meanwhile, the other three were putting the sandstone bricks into place for the basic building, as well as designing furniture to construct from the leftover scraps of materials. We made quite the crafty crew together!

"I hope that we can get some paint to make the sandstone a bit more interesting!" Onyx exclaimed as she chopped at the stone.

"Yeah! That's a great idea! I bet that we could make a dye sink for the Ealtaens of the team to make some paint from their planet's plants!"

"Oh and, maybe we can make some sort of a greenhouse here too, if we can get the water over from one of the nearby aqueducts!"

"You're one to plan Onyx! Get some power here from the sun, as well as fusion!"

Hiinhia

"Hey rest of the team!"

"Onyx?" I asked.

"Yeah! Who'd you think? We just got the great idea of making paint from your home's fruit and plants. Does that sound like something you can do?"

"Sure! It sounds great! The transports on the Savuk are able to travel from planet to planet if needed, so I can take one of the three we landed here."

"Alright Hiinhia, see you in a bit then!"

"Sounds like I've got my own adventure to see to!" I told Safaeir and Ehnri.

"Good luck, Hiinhia!" Safaeir called out.

"Say 'hi' to Ealtae for me!" Ehnri said.

We parked the three transport shuttles just outside the village. I took the first of the three shuttles off world and started on the trip to Ealtae. Though my memories were faint, I knew the plants of my tribe well. Many of them would be used for decoration of stone and fabric and even clay.

Safaeir

Ehnri and I were in charge of building the actual base, and fortunately I could sit back and relax while building! A big robotic crane arm did all the heavy lifting for me; I had the control over the robotic arm while Ehnri spread the super-strong brick mud glue all over the wall to stick the new sandstone bricks in place.

"Ehnri! We've got a turn to the right here!"

"Alrighty Safaeir!"

"Hey builders!" I heard Onyx.

"More bricks?" I asked, lowering the current block down on the wet glue.

"Sure thing! Got those hard-cut bricks on the ready!" Onyx pushed another large cart up to the building. "It's looking good!"

"Woahh Onyx, you're so strong!"

Qranyt

I woke up suddenly to the alarm on my suit going off.

"Qranyt, as you requested. Noctae Command has sent you a message."

I looked at the panel to see that the transmission had in fact arrived.

"The message is as follows:"

"This is Admiral Ziltri requesting Qranyt. We have received the transmission, decoded, and recompiled it. Avie has visited and seen the transmission, but before leaving, they told us to call to you."

I immediately jumped up and got ready to go.

"Computer, send a message back to Noctae Command. Tell them that I have received their message and will be on my way immediately."

"Yes Protector Qranyt, as you wish."

I ran to the hangar as fast as I could and hopped into one of the shuttles. The trip to Noctae would be much longer than I hoped for, but another rest would cut the time down.

Safaeir

"So we're turning in then?" I asked.

"Yeah, unfortunately my territory calls priority, and Qranyt letting us run about like this is a rare opportunity. I need to return to Aquat to help them repair there," Onyx explained.

"Well, can I come with you?" I inquired.

"Of course! Some extra paws wouldn't hurt!"

"Good luck girls!" Ehnri mocked, waving his paw about.

"See you later!" Sleepy called.

Onyx and I took our own shuttle back to Aviea, landing in Auqaut just as the sun set over the ocean in the east.

"This way," Onyx motioned to a small two-section cabin on the outskirts of the city, "I know it's been annoying spending the night in a different room literally every time we get a break, but I hope this will do well, for now."

"It's okay, Onyx, I suppose it's what we're signed up for now."

"Yeah, sure is." She slumped against a post out on the cabin porch, "You know, this last mission really changed how I feel about it though."

"Something happened out there, with you..."

"Yeah. You see, all your matrices and junk make you some kind of hero, but you know what I found down there?"

"Onyx, I think I should tell you something..."

"Huh? I'm kinda in the middle of something, kid—"

"I already know what you found, she warned me." I motioned to the heavy triangular matrix strapped on my side.

"The hell are you talking about?"

"I'm not sure, but the celestial spirit that occupies my matrix somehow told me we should leave the moment we set foot on Kjitafor."

Onyx scoffed, "That would've been good, huh, though I suppose Qranyt'd say something like 'it's good we got that matrix out before they got it,' or 'it was our duty to save the citizens from corruption on Kjitafor.' Safaeir, you're young, you're just a little cat from a village in the middle of nowhere. This is some real scary shit out here and, I'm not used to having lives depend on me like this!"

"Onyx, I agree, but I think there's more to it, I don't think we have a choice anymore. Do you believe me? Whoever's soul is in that matrix you found, he did something unforgivable. It's bound to you now, though, and we can keep it locked away forever. You all are my ownly family now, and I will protect you all with all that I have. I understand the pressure, Onyx, but all of us will stand behind you no matter what. Sleepy will be okay, we'll take care of each other!"

"I'm letting some kid give me a speech," she sighed, looking off to the horizon, "I'm sorry, get some rest Safaeir. I'm gonna go find Ket."

The inside of the cabin was a bit more homey than the new starship, but I had plans of how I'd decorate that space to feel more like my own. A giant sliding glass door framed perfectly the last moments of sunlight on the water.

Onyx was right, there was something different about this last mission that changed our perspective about, well, everything.

"hey." I whispered to myself, burrowing into the pillows on the big fluffy bed. "you there?"

"..."

"hellooo," I concentrated, trying to focus on the ghostly blue glow from the Matrix of Ealtar. "I guess she doesn't want to talk..."

"she doesn't want to use his soul?"

"huh?"

"your friend, she locked away the soul of Qosaumora? you can't just lock an ealtaurate away...it's a part of her now."

"can we destroy it?"

"..."

"ugh, why talk to me at all if you just stop randomly all the time?"

"my sisters tried to destroy it, over and over again. It's impossible."

"can all creatures bound to a matrix speak with the soul within?"

"you're not——no, you're not like the others."

Sleepy

"Well take a look at that, Ehnri! We've got ourselves a new place of living!" I smiled, returning to our "base" after a short walk around the city.

Many vendors were selling local foods as well as imports from Maurakjnaun, and we would need some fresh food for our new base anyways! I set down the food baskets at the door, sizing up our current shack to how I hoped it'd look when we were done.

"It's a bit rough around the edges, but it'll do!" Ehnri laughed, looking around the first small room of our future base.

"Hey Ehnri," I walked over and kneeled to give him a tight squeeze. "I'm so glad we're in a team together."

"Me too, Sleepy. It wouldn't be the same without you."

"Let's see how much we can build in the next few days while they're all gone! I wanna surprise them!"

"Woo! Woo!" Ehnri cheered, rolling over into his makeshift bed of blankets.

"Sleep well, Ehnri."

As I lay down to rest that evening I had to take a moment to think through all the past experiences I had had with the team: all the adventure, the helping those in need, the making new friends and family. These experiences were life-changing to me, inspiring me of a new way to build my moon, even an entirely new way to exist. For this I thank Qranyt, for he has shown me a better way to live. No need to stay home all the time with your people when they are already happy! Once my people are happy I can leave this world, I can explore with those I love. My father died, but my family lives,

It lives in the bond we share as Soliean Protectors.

Akjaeir's Transmission to Noctae Command

Transponder Code: Kqaet-Avai

I call to those hearts of Solia in this dark hour. I will tell all who read this message what I found in the unknown. The unknown is darkness, emptiness, yet I feel there is more. I see not what is, because there is nothing here that can be heard, seen, tasted, smelled, touched. There is only what can be felt. I feel the darkness seeping from all around me. This far out is something we were never meant to see. I am afraid this is the end of my study, my investigation. There is nothing more that can be revealed from here, but perhaps it can be found back home in my Solia, the Soliean Stars.

I believe in the life that Solia still holds, a life that must continue in Avie. The republic will believe in them when the darkness draws near. Qranyt will stand too, a beacon of hope, a bringer of light. It will not last forever.

What I have found here is darkness, there is no more. I am afraid it is the end, it is time for me to go back to a familiar heart, where I will wait for the end, the end of Solia, when all will be revealed of what has been found here. It is the end that will show us the truth.

the story of solia continues in:
light of fire

GUIDE TO OUR UNIVERSE

NOCTIA

Aviea

Moons: Sleprah Daecaser, Reid
Notable Territories: Aliira, Maurakjnaun, Auqaut, Filsa, etc...

Main world of the Noctia system and core of the Three Stars of Solia, Aviea is home to billions of creatures of hundreds of different specie.

Yikjtae

Moons: Yikjtar

A world covered in ice due to an unknown phenomenon. Only a few outposts exist on Yikjtae for research purposes, otherwise, all that exists is ancient and deserted.

Noctae

Moons: Noctaikiilakj

Central hub of the Three Stars' navy. All operations here are under heavy protection and secrecy.

Ealtae

Moons: Ealtar
Notable Territories: Faelk-kja, "The Rivers," "The Forests"

Cultural origin of Solia, home of the "sieqte" or "those who hear the stars"

Nytyl

An inhospitable wasteland of a planet, the surface is covered with reactive gemstones and relentless electrical storms. Somehow, the world is detected to have structures on the surface anyways.

Azilli

Populated by only the most persistent and hardened of creatures. Azilli is known as the "cold desert," where sand whips across the world with a touch of ice all day and night.

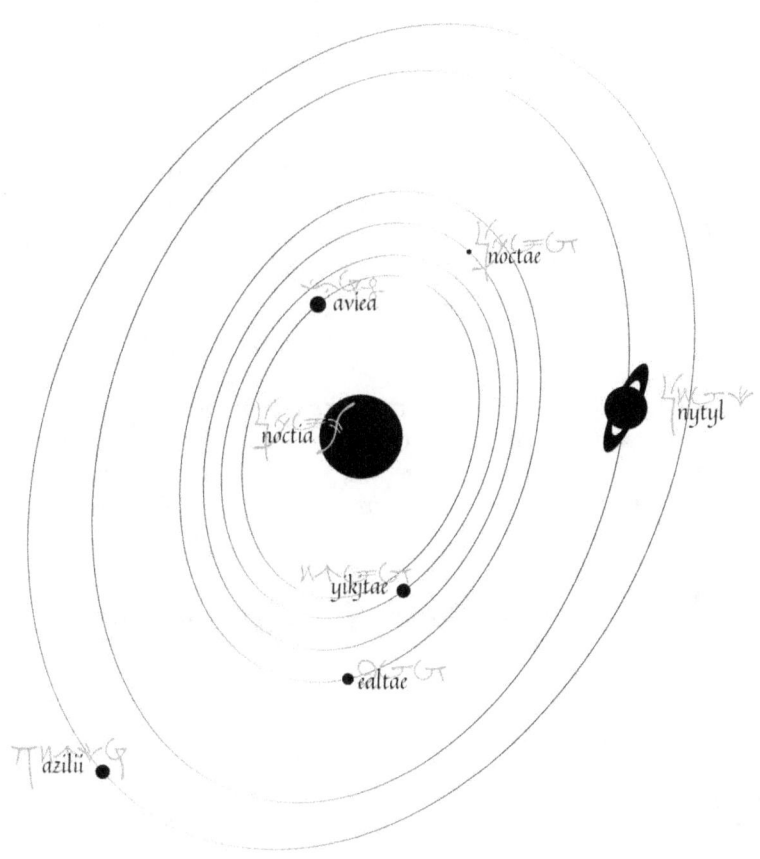

Solia Noctia, Starhaven Nebula

Soletria

MARAZEAL

Intafari

> *Much like Noctia's first world Aviea, Intafari is a beautiful world with gleaming cities millions of creatures call home. The world is easily recognized by its high mountain ranges where the cities rest, contrasted by the low flooded seas in between. This vibrant green world is teeming with life everywhere you look.*

Kjitarat
Moons: Kjitar

> *Often looked upon as a barren and inhospitable wasteland, Kjitarat is far from it. Despite being harsh on many intelligent lifeforms, this planet is extremely biodiverse. Researchers here have even discovered some specie constructing giant hives in some locations in the endless red desert.*

Faeaiinhia

> *An unusual world which seems quite hospitable, yet nobody has dared venture close enough to explore. Countless expeditions have set their sights on this world, and those who ventured too close have never been seen again.*

Thvetia

> *Th███ no entries on ██s worl█ in T█ Sanctuary. It d██ not exist.*

> *Stop looking for it.*

T?███a
> *???*

Kir█e█

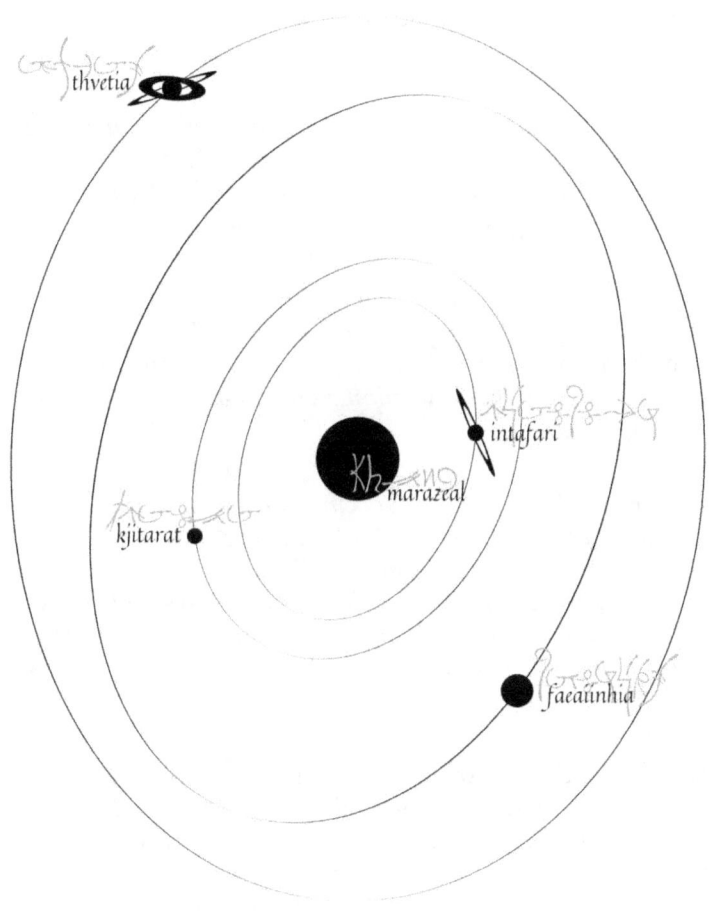

Solia Marazeal, Starhaven Nebula

thvetia

intafari

marazeal

kjitarat

faeaiinhia

Soletria

AQUA

Zetrafore

Once known for being the largest hub world for technological innovation, Zetrafore has now fallen into post-apocalyptic desolation. The sky is forever stained green, and poisonous storms rip across the high mountain-tops.

Kjitafor

Central trading hub of the Three Stars with systems outside of the Starhaven Nebula. Trade with the Soliean Alliance is the only trade that can bypass this world. Kjitafor has been known for conflict in the past due to the world's importance in Solia's trade.

Iilazaur

A mostly remote-operated world and center for mineral refinement from large-scale mining operations.

Tetratakj

After irreversible damage had occured on Zetrafore, technology research and development in the Three Stars moved entirely to Tetratakj. Like Kjitafor and Iilazaur, Tetratakj is a mostly metal and stone construct of a world, though some have said to have seen natural "growths" and strange plants taking root in the lower levels of the world.

Zekj

The hub world for most starship production in the Three Stars, Zekj is a largly terrestrial world which has been modified to suit large-scale fleet production. On the surface of the world, however, life exists much the same as you'd see on any other world with giant grassy fields and flowering meadows. However when you look up, the giant orbital ring, where most of the production happens, crosses the entire sky.

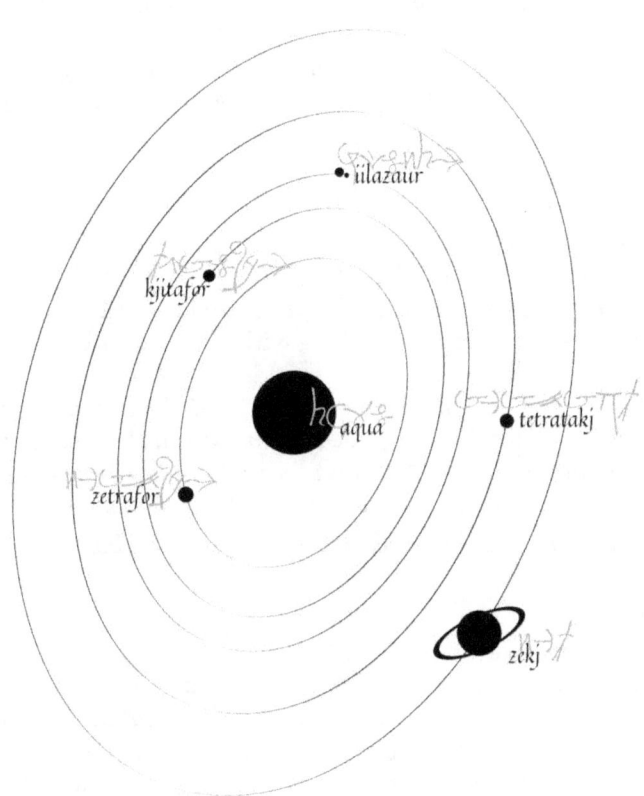

Solia Aqua, Starhaven Nebula

iilazaur

kjitafor

aqua

tetratakj

zetrafor

zekj

Soletria

PROTECTORS

Avie Avinta Kiravaen

Title: Leader of Solia

Species: Aviean Human

Appearance: Tall androgenous human with dark, short hair and dark eyes. Often seen wearing a long coat.

Leader of the Three Stars, founder of the "Soliean Protectors." Avie is held accountable for leaving Solia with only one leader in charge, and hopes to set things right by continuing their investigation into what happened to Akjaeir, this time closer to home.

Qranyt Avinta

Title: Leader of Maurakjnaun

Species: Aviean Forest Bear

Appearance: Sturdy muddled black-grey furred teddy-bear just over a meter in height. Often wears bulky clothing with a dark sword at his side. Pitch-black eyes.

Avie's go-to second in command since the disappearance of Akjaeir. Qranyt is commended for his part in the recovery of Aviea after the mysterious disaster within Mt. Emerald. Qranyt is often considered the true Leader of Solia due to his more frontline position in issues within Starhaven Nebula.

Hiinhia Ealta-Siina

Species: Ealtaen Forest Bear

Appearance: Small mossy-furred bear with dark eyes.

An Ealtaen tribe-leader family member brought back from the future. Despite his origin being in Solia's future, his knowledge of future events is limited for unknown reasons. Due to his shortfalls and guilt in lack of ability to help his family, Hiinhia took Qranyt as his master in combat arts in hopes it would one day make up for leaving his tribe.

Ehnri Ealvhren

Species: Ealtaen Siaka, Cat
Appearance: Small cream-coated feline with brown legs, muzzle, ears and tail. Very large whiskers and blue eyes.

Child of the Ealtae Faelk-kja Plains, orphaned in the war against the "Marsh." He was raised in part by a snake named "Pond," who told him stories of the sieqte and the secrets of the stars.

Setai Sedecaur, "Sleepy"

Title: Leader of Sulentuun
Species: Sleprah Bear
Appearance: Tall, short-furred teddy looking bear around half a meter in height. His eyes, nose, and mouth are pitch-dark black.

Successor to the leader's position on Aviea's first moon Sleprah-Daecaser, Setai pledged to take up the name of his world, "Sleepy," and forge a new future as allies of Aviea and Protectors of Solia.

Onyx Auqeta

Title: Leader of Auqaut
Species: Auqaut Cat
Appearance: Sturdy large feline about 1.5 meters in length, nose to tailtip. Her fur is black, her ears small and eyes a crisp ice blue.

Daughter of Ket and successor to the leader's position in Aviea's Auqaut territory. Onyx's free time mostly consists of taking apart and repairing electronics, modding plasma weaponry, and helping out citizens of her hometown.

Safaeir Inteal

Species: Ealtaen River Cat
Appearance: Slender, silver-blue furred feline with silver eyes. Only slightly larger than Ehnri.

Daughter of two Ealtae historians, locally called "sieqte." After she was left an orphan because of Ealtae's war with the "Marsh," Safaeir joined the Protectors hoping to finish her parents' work and learn the true history of Solia and the celestial "ealtaurate." Perhaps she will also learn the meaning of the voice in her mind?

OTHER CHARACTERS

Akjaeir Inteal Kiravaen

Title: Leader of Solia
Species: Ealtaen Sieqte, Human
Appearance: Tall, tan-skinned woman with dark, shoulder length hair and dark eyes. Wears a blood-red triangular pendant around her neck.

Leader of the Three Stars, missing since the disappearance of the starship Kqaet-Avai. Her final mission was to seek answers from the Spirit Lamp "Kiraveal," or at least to find out if it exists. Akjaeir was known to appear emotionless or empty to many upon first meeting her, yet she was known to be very kind to all of her friends and everyone she was tasked to take care of.

Selevenera Zorae

Title: Leader of "Soliiae" Territory Alliance
Species: Feline
Appearance: Small blackish brown-furred cream-spotted cat with yellow eyes.

High-security operative within the Sanctuary of Aviea. Not much is known about her other than her sassy attitude and her ability to lead her territory while also executing top-secret missions with expert efficiency with her partner Qorshia. Due to her high ranking position within the Sanctuary, some say she has more political power over Solia than even Avie or Akjaeir.

Qorshia Zorae

Title: Operation Specialist
Species: Feline
Appearance: Small black-furred white speckled cat with orange eyes.

Director of all high-speed secret operations within Solia's navy working alongside her partner Sele'. Qorshia is cold and stern, able to solve problems in an instant and a formidable strategist when faced with complex diplomatic issues.

Sleprahj, *the Dreamer*

Species: ???

Appearance: ???

> Celestial spirit of the world Sleprah-Daecaser according to the
> sieqte of Ealtae. Sacrificed her body to create this world to save
> those who prayed to her. When she fell, her soul crystalized into
> an object the bears of Sleprah-Daecaser hold sacred.

Simisaurehj, *the Builder*

Species: ???

Appearance: ???

> Celestial spirit of the world Aviea according to the sieqte of
> Ealtae. Sacrificed his body to create the world of his imagination,
> lying in wait for the return of his sister Sleprahj.

Diiviide, *the Silent*

Species: ???

Appearance: ???

> Celestial spirit of the world Ealtar according to the sieqte of
> Ealtae. Sister of Ahnraitahvaehj and ???. Killed by ???.

Ahnraitahvaehj, *the ???*

Species: ???

Appearance: Tall human woman with long flame-colored hair.

> Sister of Diiviide and ???, fought ??? to avenge the brutal
> annihilation of her sister Diiviide. Amplified Qranyt's abilities in
> attempts to save the moon Reid, yet failed.

ORGANIZATIONS

Saertian Rift

Often used to refer to all "known" civilizations, while technically referring to the entire universe. In the first case, it is usually interchangable with the "Kjianoaa Galaxy," as few known civilizations exist beyond said galaxy.

The Three Stars, Starhaven Nebula

An alliance of the star systems Noctia, Aqua, and Maurazeal as the "Core" systems of Solia, located within a nebula near the center of the Kjianoaa galaxy.

Soliean Protectors

Task force of specialized creatures in the Three Stars assigned to investigate the mysterious Keys and Matrices, all while attempting to prevent a war seen to occur in the near future.

Soliean Alliance

A larger conglomerate of star systems flying the Soliean flag, centered around the capital star system Arion. The Soliean Alliance acts as an outer shell for the core "Three Stars," but they often do not have dealings with one another unless situations are truly dire.

"Sieqte"

Often used to refer to those who learn and teach the stories of Kiraveal and the Celestial Spirits, but in truth this term has a far older meaning. A "true" sieqte has the ability to listen to the voices of the worlds and the stars, which is often cited as the origin of the Soletria language.

"The Marsh"

A warring race of creatures with an unusual and daring interest in the Three Stars, specifically the world Ealtae. Not much is known about "The Marsh," other than the fact that they provoked the Three Stars with no warning and set down on Ealtae with some unknown intent.

The Sanctuary

The Sanctuary is the core foundation of the Soliean Government, even more powerful than the "leaders." In truth, the "Leaders'" position is mostly symbolic; while Akjaeir and Avie do have a large amount of control over laws and organization of the territories, and often act as the lead decision-makers when it comes to pressing matters, The Sanctuary is always there to listen in and guide their decisions. The power to overthrow any leader immediately is held within The Sanctuary.

They are also a location, the largest building in the Akjo Ventrael district. The Sanctuary houses the largest database in all of Solia, recording every event recorded, fact or fiction, every star, every world, everything. Some say that even information unknown to anyone currently alive exists within, yet with the size of the database it's unlikely anyone could find such information unless they were specifically looking for it.

Teccan Conglomerate

An ally faction of the Soliean Alliance located farther out in Kjianoaa. Solia often works with the Conglomerate on research, ship development, and even intelligence operations.

AVIEA'S TERRITORIES

Aliira, "Agate"

Leader: Akjaeir and Avie

Capital: Akjo Ventrael District

Capital territory of Aviea and the Starhaven Nebula's Three Stars. Location of the Leaders' Center, Aliira City and the Sanctuary. The Aliira archipelago is often cited as Aviea's most unusual geological feature, considering its shape. Perhaps this is why it stands as the world's capital today.

Maurakjnaun, "Emerald"

Leader: Qranyt Avinta

Capital: Viikja City

Leading production territory of agriculture, known for lush rainforests in the west, high mountain ranges in the center highlands, and arid plains in the east.

Fiilsa, "Snow"

An unusual region in perpetual frost, at the center of which lies a giant mountain-carved bowl where the territory's center lies.

Kaefiilsa, "West Fiilsa"

A region disputed between Fiilsa and Maurakjnaun, who's dispute originated initially when the Mt. Emerald disaster occurred.

Auqaut, "Quartz"

Leader: Ket Auqeta, Onyx Auqeta

A desolate landscape of smooth, grey stone by the sea, known for its eerie red desert lighting when the sun is low in the sky.

Acurkjna, "Aquamarine"

The coastal region is often cited as Aviea's most beautiful territory, featuring high mountains and steep fjords.

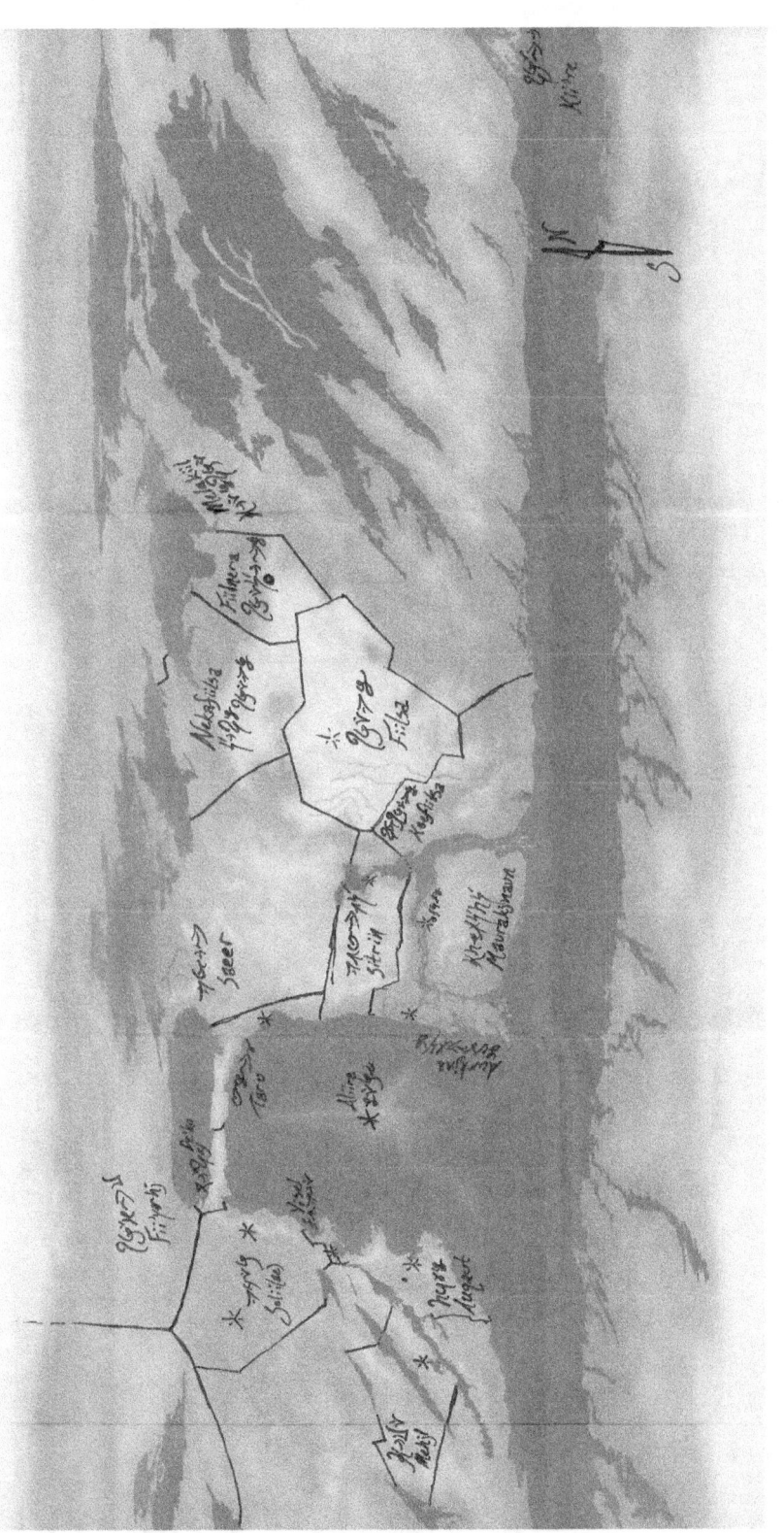

SAVUK

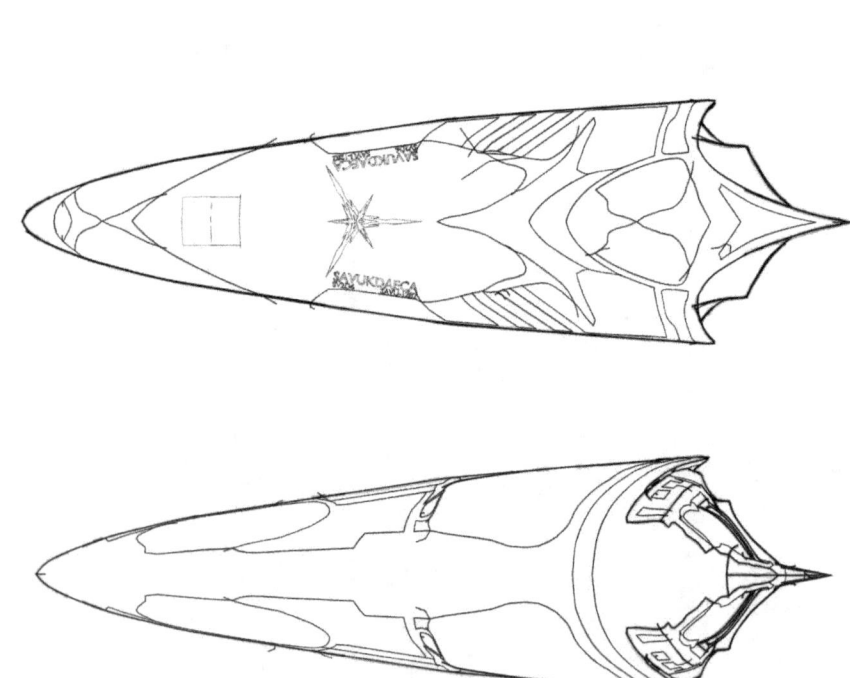

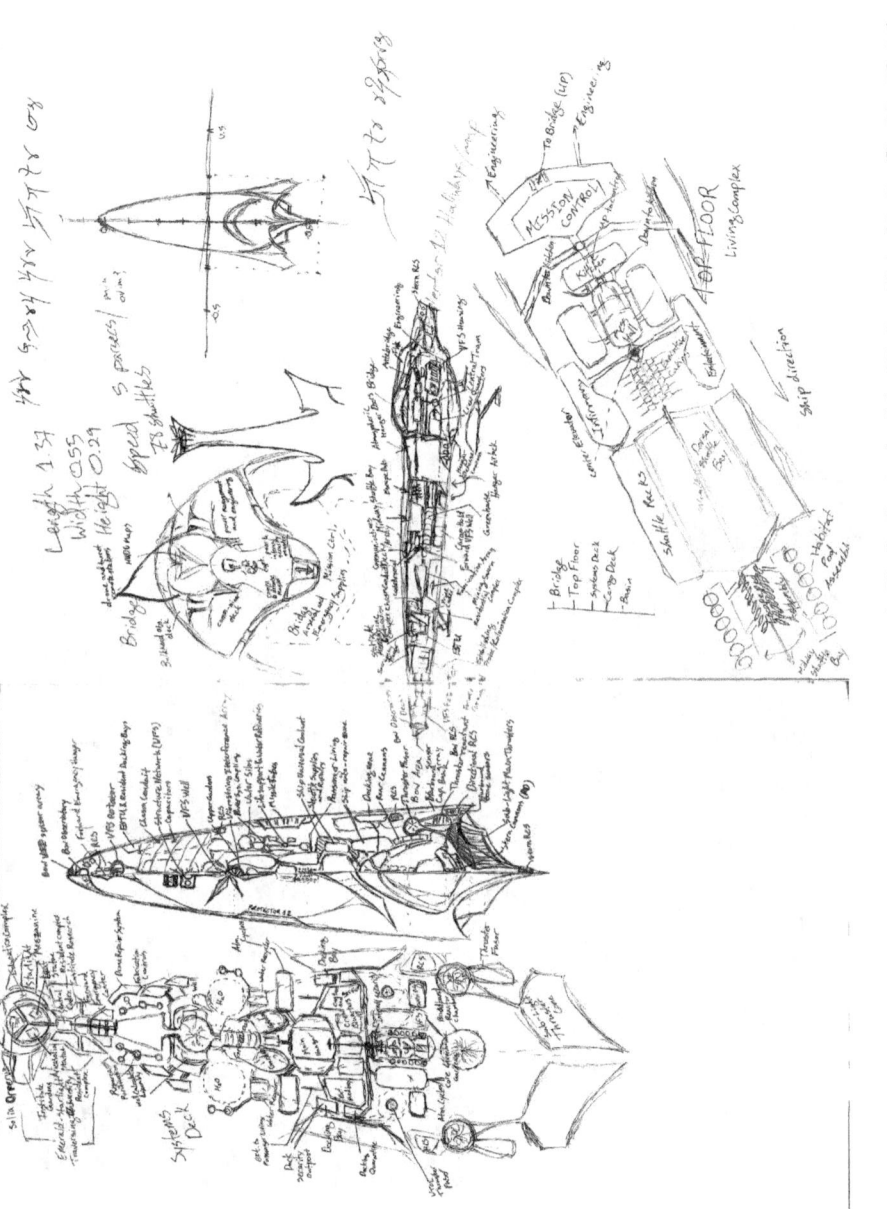

"Abandoned outpost on Fenesol"

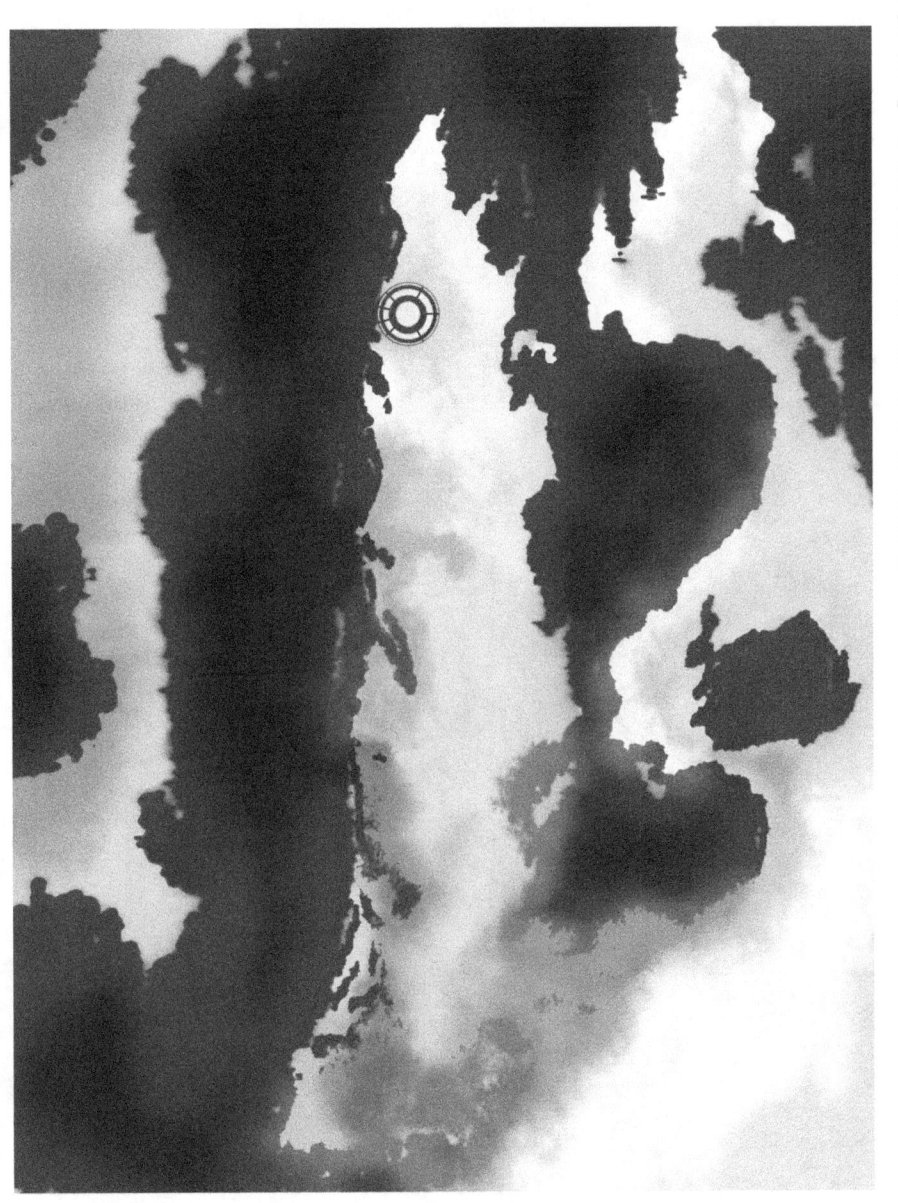

Akjo Ventrael, Aliira, Aviea

"Stone pillars of Reid"

SOLETRIA LANGUAGE

Within the Story of Solia, you will encounter many uses or references to the native "Soliean" language, or "soletria." The language itself was, in universe, created on the world Ealtae by the "sieqte" in ancient times, based loosely off the telepathic "words" the sieqte heard during their meditation.

Despite its uses in passing throughout the novel, Soletria is a fully functioning language with gramatical structure and somewhere around 500 words.

Soletria has 42 "letter" glyphs, each representing their own unique sound. Throughout most of the language, all uses of a character represent one and only one pronunciation. Due to the nature of the language being directed off sound, dialectal differences lead to changes in spelling, not the other way around.

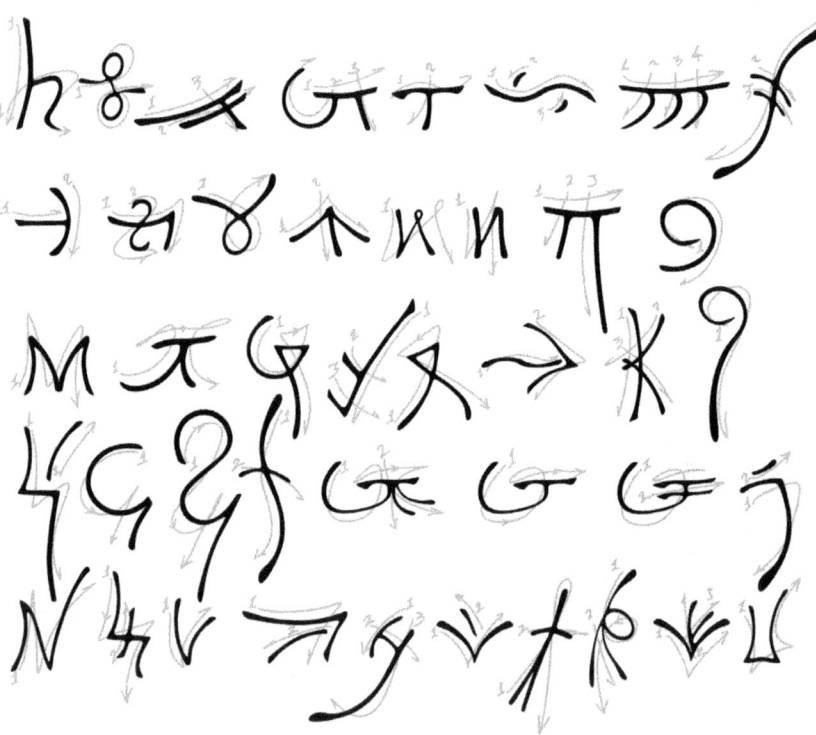

^ Stroke order of the 42 Soletria letters

Pehaps to an English-speaker, the best place to start when learning Soliean is the groups of sounds they may be most familiar with. We will use Latin script to better help differentiate Soliean characters and their pronunciations.

"au"	"aa"	"ra"	"ae"	"hzsrae"	"av"	"ai"		"ia"

Characters with combined sounds are Always in the same syllable, even if it is difficult to pronounce. Here's the hardest part of the language, understanding the relation to the sounds you already know. Let's start with the "A" group.

"au"	ɑ	s<u>aw</u>, p<u>aw</u>, p<u>o</u>d
"aa, ā"	ʌ	c<u>u</u>t, "<u>uh</u>", l<u>u</u>ck
"ra"	rʌ/rɐ	<u>r</u>ough, <u>r</u>ust
"ae"	e	s<u>ay</u>, b<u>ay</u>, g<u>ay</u>
"hzsrae"	ʑzrɐ	no English equivalent
"av"	ʌv	<u>o</u>f, ab<u>ove</u>, l<u>ove</u>
"ai"	ai	<u>I</u>, s<u>igh</u>, b<u>ye</u>
"ia"	iʌ	<u>yu</u>ck, "see <u>ya</u>", ch<u>ia</u>

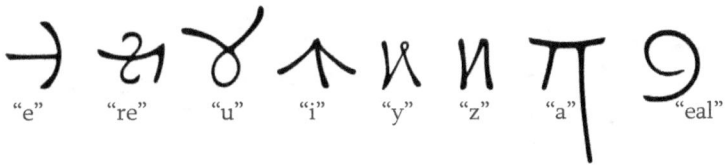

"e"	"re"	"u"	"i"	"y"	"z"	"a"	"eal"

"E" Group

"e"	ɛ	cr<u>e</u>dit, "<u>eh</u>", "b<u>et</u>"
"re"	re	<u>ray</u>, cr<u>ay</u>on
"u"	re	s<u>oo</u>t, "p<u>u</u>t," t<u>oo</u>k
"i"	ẹ	<u>i</u>t, s<u>i</u>t, <u>i</u>ck
"y"	ʎ	<u>y</u>es, <u>y</u>our, <u>y</u>et
"z"	z	bu<u>s</u>y, da<u>zz</u>le, ja<u>zz</u>
"a"	a	<u>a</u>t, c<u>a</u>t, cr<u>a</u>ss
"eal"	el	<u>ale</u>, p<u>ale</u>, t<u>ail</u>

"I" Group

"di, dī"	di	detail, deep, demon
"tr"	tr	train, "r" is rolled
"ii, ī"	i	eat, sheep, beat
"kjii, kjī"	qi	key
"d"	d	pronounce the same as in English
"r"	r	a rolled "r"
"m"	m	pronounce the same as in English
"f"	f	pronounce the same as in English

"N" Group

"n"	n	pronounce the same as in English
"q"	q	low pitched "q" sound
"k"	ʒ/z	"zh," does not occur in English
"v"	v	pronounce the same as in English
"th"	ð	this, that
"t"	t	pronounce the same as in English
"ct"	qt	connect, sect
"p"	p	pronounce the same as in English

"uu"	"so"	"c"	"s"	"o"	"l"	"kj"	"h"	"yl"	"hj"

"O" Group

"uu, ū"	u	boot, crude, vacuum
"so"	sǫ	sew, so, sow
"c"	i	eat, sheep, beat
"s"	s	pronounce the same as in English
"o"	ǫ	code, bone, crow
"l"	l	pronounce the same as in English
"kj"	q	higher pitched "k" sound
"h"	h	pronounce the same as in English
"yl"	ʎl	"yil" without the "i," does not occur in English
"hj"	x/ħ	like a hiss, back of the mouth; does not occur in English

WORD STRUCTURE

diauvii: thanks,
thank you

some words are often shortened,
noted by the soliean apostrophe:

seleo: hello,
sel': hi
common greeting for friends
or friendly strangers

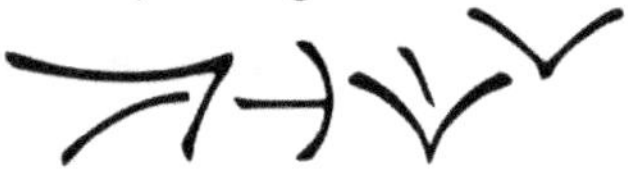

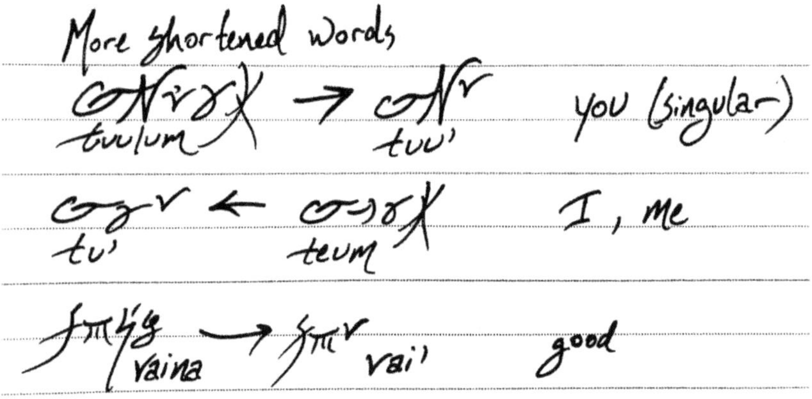

More shortened words

tuulum → tuu'   you (singular)

tu' ← teum   I, me

vaina → vai'   good

Prefixes and how they're used:

Gᴿ, "ae" : in, as, or "to." GrḱʋᴉᴐᴄG(ɣ)
    ae'soletria - in soliean

    Grᴉɟɟᴇᴀ vᴏᴠᴀ - to see

Gᴇ-, "ae-" : become. Grᴉɟgᴄᴐhɟ aefeaᴉtaun - become warm

ᴐᴉɟ-, "un-": negative GᴏᴢNᴉ iiruun /iᴛᴏn - know
                                    ↓
            ᴐᴉɟɣᴏNᴉ uniᴛᴏn - don't know/unknᴏ

ɣᴿ-, "e-" : ownership prefix. ᴉᴉᴏNᴿ e'tᴜ' - your

            crᴉɣᴏʀᴉx ᴉᴏᴏᴢᴠ
            tᾱqᴜnd e'tᴜ' - my name

fᴍ, "vai-" : good. fᴍᴢᴉᴉᴉᴍᴍ
                        vaisenzai - good morning
            fᴍ9 vaieal - happy
            fᴍᴨNᴉᴉɣ vaisᴜᴛnᾱ - good sleep!

ɟᴢᴉᴇ, "pers-": new, ɟᴢᴇœᴉɟ perstren - tomorrow "new day"

nhᴿᴉ "zau": "that which" nhᴿᴉɣᴉᴉk zau'minau - teacher
                                    "that which teaches"

Many Soliean words are built from other words split into parts and put back together as "prefixes." Learning these prefixes is a helpful way to interpret meaning without understanding the entire word.

More Common Words

МНᚠG **díavī** — thanks, thank you

МЦGᚱgg **dīhjí'dǎ** — expression of thanks when accepting food (zoven, ЦᶜԒᶠᴥ)

uh⇗Gᚱ **zausio** — 'please,' or a request

oᚠ **tā** — is, are, am

oᚠᏎᴑᚱᴑᚢ **tāgund** — 'name,' 2 identifying trait/ "nickname"

ᚢᴑᚢᚢᴑᚢ, ᚢᴑᚢᶠ — hello, hi **Seleo, sel'**

↳ ᚢᴑᚢᚢᴑᚢᵧ oᚠᏎᴑᚱᴑᚢ ᴥᴑNᶠ

"**Seleo, tāgund e'tū?**" Hello, your name is?

œᴑᶠ — **tren**, — day
ᚵᴥᴑᏕᴑᴑᴑᶠ **metatren** — midday

4ᴥᶠ **solia** — spirit star
ᚢᴑᚢᴑᚢᴑᶠ **seletia** — star

ᴑᶠ **e'ia** — of

goᴑᚱ **ealtā** — peace

goᴑᴑᴑᴑᴑᚱ **esttaurate** — celestial spirit

ᴥGᴑᴑᚱᏎᏎ, ᴥGᴑᴑᴑᶠ — leader (of soliean territory)
laersāhā, laer'

œᴑᏎᚱᴑᚱ **thresā/thraesa** the web connecting all space & time
all contain in a celestial constru

Characters of Solia

〜ᵴᵍ , Avie / avī　　　≈　　≈ or ᴏᴄᵴᵍ　in other dialect

〜ᵴᵍ　　　　　　　↑
　　　　　　opposing variant

ᴄᵴⱼᵉᴄᵒ , Qranyt

ᴇᵍᵴᵴᵉᵹ , Hīnhia　or　ᴊᵍᵴᵴᵉᵹ , Hjīnhia

ᵴⱼᵍ , enrī　or　ehnrī　ᵴᵴᵍ

ᴛⱼᵍᴛᵗ , Setai

ᴴᵴᵍᵗ , aunykjs , Onyx

ᵗᵧᵍᵍᵍ , safaeīr

ᴴᶜᵍᵍ , auqaeīr , Aljaeir

the soletria trilogy

the spirit stars

light of fire

planet of peace

light of fire

"Eal-ta, rehia ze noct, sie-rel kelon ze alith irqe. Dauqae ta ehmsqava srulke ta faeth, sie-rel aesohraene akjaeir kjer."

The woods and plants almost seemed to settle with the song, following its soft tone as we worked our way deeper and deeper below the canopy. By now, every plant seemed to glow and pulse with energy. It provided us with some light, but no security, knowing that any one of them, or in any of the darker spaces, there were sure to be creatures ready to have *us* for supper.

"That song, I've heard it before, I know it." Ehnri whispered.

"I'm sure Safaeir would know it, maybe even your parents."

"It's about rain, right? Rain tapping on roof-stones."

"Mmmm" I hummed in affirmation.

"Eal-ta, rehia ze noct, sie-rel kelon ze alith irqe. Dauqae ta ehmsqava srulke ta faeth, sie-rel aesohraene akjaeir kjer."

The bark of the trees was rigid and sturdy for navigating along the limbs of the trees, however the occasional patch of moss and coverweeds kept us aware of our situation, high above the ground.

The occasional rustling of leaves was following us as we continued in the shadows, perhaps the creatures were at peace with us here.

"They say you lose all sense of direction in these trees," Hiinhia said, stroking a large leaf covered in water droplets. *"Wander too far from the group and you'll be sure to never find a way out."*

"Those are just tall tales!" Ehnri laughed, then looked around cautiously. *"You don't think we'll get lost out here do you?"*

"We'll be okay, Ehnri, I promise."

The Magic
Necklace
of Al-Andalus

A Novel

Robert H. Boyer
Author of *Sundays in Manila*

The Magic Necklace of Al-Andalus
A Novel

© Robert H. Boyer, 2017. ALL RIGHTS RESERVED

Authored by Robert H. Boyer
Edited by E. L. Risden
Prepared for Publication by Travis J. Vanden Heuvel

Published by Peregrino Press, LLC
2284 Glen Meadows Circle
De Pere, WI 54115
www.peregrino.press

Cover design by Travis J. Vanden Heuvel
Typeset by Euan Monaghan
Cover photo © Peregrino Press. ALL RIGHTS RESERVED

ISBN (paperback): 978-0-9969426-7-6
This title is also available in electronic and audiobook formats

Printed in the United States of America